Filigree Rings and

SKY-BLUE WINGS

R.M.SELG

Book Two of the Filigree and Fire Series

Cover photography courtesy of Richard Dennis Daugherty.

Cover illustrations, design and book design copyright © 2018 R.M.Selg

Kalmus Publishing, PO Box 459, Mitchell ACT 2911, Australia

ISBN: 978-0-9876374-1-3

www.rmselg.com

For my family

ACKNOWLEDGMENTS

I would like to thank my family and friends for their ongoing encouragement and support during the writing of this novel, in particular my husband and children for their patience and unerring faith. For their proof reading abilities, Linda Reid and Kim de Gruchy deserve a special mention.

I would also like to thank Lainie from AJC Publishing, Writing and Editing Services for her Beta Reading services. Her thoughtful suggestions were greatly appreciated.
Also, a bug hug goes to my advanced reader team at Booksprout for their honest appraisals.

Thanks also to Richard Dennis Daugherty who has graciously allowed me to use parts of his beautiful fig tree photo for the cover art of this novel.

And last, but definitely not least, thanks to you – my dear readers – for giving me the enthusiasm to continue my writing journey.

Fire

Sydney, Australia twenty-two years ago

It is the middle of the night. The young boy wakes suddenly, unsure of what has woken him. He squeezes his teddy hard.

His lips feel dry and his bedroom is hot. Really hot.

He sits up and the orange night light plugged into the socket near the floor reveals smoke curling up from under the door and drifting to the ceiling. He watches it transfixed, not quite comprehending what he is seeing.

A flickering light on the other side of the room captures his attention; flames are rising from the heating grate in the floor. A moment later, the wall of his room erupts into orange flame and he cries in alarm. The intense heat makes the skin of his face feel taut. Suddenly, the ceiling is on fire and so is his bed.

He opens his mouth and screams for his mother but the heat is burning his throat. The roaring of the flames drowns his voice.

Smoke is swirling around the ceiling and starting to fill the room.

Holding his teddy close, he slips out of the bed and onto the floor. Get down low and go, go, go! as he has been taught in school. He scrambles to the door but when he touches it, it is hot and smoke is still seeping into the room from underneath it.

There is no other way out. The window has a security screen. He screams for his parents, tears streaming down his face. There is no reply.

He has no choice.

He crouches low and pulls the door open quickly, feeling the hot metal of the handle searing into his palm.

A blast of fire engulfs him, racing in to suck the oxygen from the room.

He is on fire; his pyjamas, his hair, his skin, his teddy. He screams and screams and screams.

Detective Inspector Tom Hayes woke in a sweat; his whole body shaking.

A Faerie Obsession

Detective Inspector Tom Hayes and the two uniforms assigned to him were wading through the files from Jeff Layton's computer. They had been at it for weeks. Jeff Layton had been the brains of a group of three who worked out of an old garage dealing drugs, re-birthing cars and any other rackets that would turn a dollar. In the months before their fiery demise, they had branched out into kidnapping, murder and acquiring babies to sell on the black market.

The murderous group had been overseen by Bill Leonard Doyle. A disgusting individual who spent his days tending to the needs of the patients at a posh nursing home and his nights forcing runaways into a life of sexual slavery. He was in gaol now, and Tom and his team were hoping to find enough evidence to keep him there for good. They were also hoping to find evidence that Bill was the Stonefish; a dark underworld figure spoken of in whispers on the streets. Only a few members of the police force knew of the Stonefish's existence, but those that did wanted him brought to justice.

Layton's computer was proving to be a goldmine of information. He had documented all the kidnappings. Places, dates and times, names, physical descriptions and a brutal assessment of their sexual attractiveness or otherwise.

Tom rubbed his hands across his eyes. There were so many. The lives of young men, women and children reduced to an entry in a stock register of human flesh for sale.

Constable Leia Gardiner was compiling data to send over to the missing persons branch. Whether these kids would ever be found was another matter. So far, the documents had not revealed where they were taken after they were handed over to Bill Doyle.

Tom's informant, Andy Roswald, had told him that the local prostitutes believed there was a den somewhere; that Bill and his cronies were providing services to rich paedophiles and also breeding babies to sell. Well, the files from Layton's computer seemed to confirm that. The question was where were they being held?

Constable Ivan Peale entered the room and broke his train of thought.

'You need to see this, boss,' he said handing Tom a document.

Tom started reading but stopped about halfway down the page.

'So, Bill Doyle is not Mr Big. He's not the Stonefish.'

'No.'

'Shit. I don't suppose Mr Layton has done the big reveal in here anywhere and given us a name?' Tom asked, scanning the rest of the page.

'No, sir. Whenever he does mention him, he always calls him 'The Big Boss' or 'Stonefish'.'

'You know, for such a blabby little shit, you'd think he would have spilt his guts on the boss at some point wouldn't you.'

'Too scared?'

'Yeah, I'd say so. Or he simply didn't know his real name. Everything I've read so far has been about his dealings with Bill. No mention at all about anyone higher up. How many files are left to go through?'

'About another hundred.'

'Well, we might hit pay dirt yet. Keep looking.'

Peale nodded and headed back to his desk.

Tom was heartily sick of reading these shitty files. From the mundane bank statements and phone records to the cold, horrific catalogues of their crimes; it was a job of alternating tedium and disgust. He needed a change of scene.

Time to talk to Bill again.

The room was dim; up-lights positioned on the wall between each bed cast a subdued glow onto the ceiling. Machines on wheeled stands beeped and flashed in a syncopated rhythm.

There was a chair beside the bed. In it was a woman, her upper body slumped forward onto the bed, her exhausted face resting on her arms as she slept. Beside her, a small pale face lay on a mountain of crisp white pillows.

Renee watched from the shadows in fairy form. She was the size of a Christmas beetle and had dimmed her fairy glow to a very pale green. Someone would have to look right at her to notice her. The other beds were empty tonight. The nurses had done their nightly rounds and retreated to the nurse's station, leaving the exhausted pair to sleep. As soon as Renee was sure that she would not be seen she fluttered down onto the bed.

This was the third time this week that Renee had come to the girl. On the first night, the little girl had been hooked up to numerous machines; her breathing, her blood and her heart monitored constantly with doctors and nurses coming and going around the clock. It had been extremely difficult to get close to her.

That had been Renee's first trip to an Intensive Care Unit. Andy had made her practice on the children in the recovery ward first, where the children were in less immediate danger. As it was, she had found it difficult to limit the amount of healing power she gave them. Her maternal instincts were hard to fight; she would have drained herself to exhaustion if she had given in to them.

On the first night with the girl, Andy had accompanied Renee to Intensive Care to help Renee assess the girl and monitor her self-control. He had helped her to limit the amount of fairy power she expended. The trick, Andy told her, was to give just enough fairy magic for the scales to tip. Just enough for the child's own powers of healing to get the upper hand. That first night he had shown her how to heal the damage in the child's crushed chest. By repairing some of the damage to the girl's diaphragm, heart and lungs the girl had the power to oxygenate and pump her own blood. It had stopped the damage from spreading.

The second night, Renee had come alone and had found it harder to pull back; the desire to take the child back to full health was incredibly strong, but she knew the danger. If she drained herself too far she would be too feeble to escape or, worse, she could be weakened to the point of death. She had almost reached this point once before when she had healed the policeman, Tom Hayes. It had taken several days to recover from that episode and it caused her a measure of guilt that she had never told Andy about it.

Tonight, the little girl was sleeping peacefully. Her breathing was no longer laboured. Her mother was deep in the exhausted sleep of two lost nights; an unexpected change for the better allowing her to pause her vigil.

Renee had given the little body enough magic to continue the healing itself, but there was some damage that the child would not be able to recover from without her help. The massive chest of drawers that had pinned the child to the floor had sent the little body into survival mode. The reduced blood flow had been directed to the control and command centres of her body; the brain and the heart. The girl's injured legs had been deprived of vital blood flow and oxygen.

There was no human medicine that could repair that damage now. The doctors were concentrating on saving her life and, though they might suspect severe nerve and tissue damage, they would not know for sure for some time. Tonight, Renee would repair that damage before the doctors were aware of its existence.

She walked along the undulating blanket mountain until she reached the girl's legs. A frame had been positioned under the blankets to keep the weight off them. A fold in the blanket created a tunnel large enough for her to slip into the cavern. She increased her glow to give her light and walked up to the heavily bandaged legs. Renee knelt down between the little girl's feet and searched for exposed skin. She placed a hand on each foot and as soon as she touched the bare skin she felt the damage radiating out from the wounds. The broken bones would heal themselves in time, once the vessels and nerves were healed, and a kick-start would help to speed things up.

Renee concentrated on the injuries and passed her healing energy through her hands and into the girl's legs. She reached into the bones with her mind and began to repair the worst of the breaks. After a while, even though there was more damage, she pulled back, forcing herself to stop. She breathed deeply and then focused her concentration on the nerves and blood vessels. Once these were working correctly again, the bones would be able to finish healing without her help. Again, she plunged her mind and her powers into the child; meshing and patching, healing and rebuilding. The complex web of veins and nerves writhed and rippled as they re-joined. At last, she was finished and she pulled her hands away and sat back on her heels. For a moment she rested and assessed her own strength; had she overdone it again? No. She was a little tired, but she was still fully functioning. Good. She was comfortable that she could fully control this power now.

She placed her hand on the child again and assessed the girl's health. She was not fully healed, but she was much better. In time, she would make a full recovery; Renee was sure of that.

Renee stood and stretched her limbs and her wings. It was time to go. She slipped out from under the blankets and turned to see a nurse checking the little girl's pulse. Renee froze. The nurse caught sight of her through the corner of his eye and was already turning to look at Renee when she increased her glow to hide her features.

The nurse's fob watch slipped from his fingers and dangled on its chain, bumping against his chest as he looked at her in surprise. She flew up into a ceiling vent to escape his view. She peeked down through the grill to see him looking up at the vent in confusion. Another nurse entered the room and looked at him quizzically.

'Something wrong?' she asked him, talking quietly so as not to wake the patient or her mother.

'Bright light just went up into the vent,' he whispered.

'Really? Oh, that's wonderful! What colour was it? Is she doing better?' the nurse asked, struggling to keep her voice down, and slipped the patient notes from the end of the bed.

'What?' he asked, confused.

The nurse looked at him querulously and then she smiled in understanding, 'You haven't been here long, have you?'

'Two weeks.'

'So, you don't know the legend of the healing sprites?'

'The whaaa?'

'Healing sprites; little lights that float about in here sometimes. People have been seeing them in the children's ward for about forty years. The kids always get better after a visitation, so try not to scare them away, OK?'

'Sure,' he said looking up at the vent again, puzzled. 'Sorry, up there,' he whispered gently waving a conciliatory hand.

Renee waited until she had caught her breath and then she turned and flew along the air duct and out into the night.

Detective Inspector Tom Hayes and Constable Leia Gardiner were guided through the gaol to an interview room. The guard opened the door and ushered them inside.

'Take a seat and I'll go and get him,' the guard told them.

Tom sat down and looked the room over. It was bare and white with cameras mounted in the ceiling. A single table and four chairs were placed in the middle of the room.

Gardiner pulled out a voice recorder and placed it on the table. She did a quick voice check and played it back. The device was working correctly.

'All set,' she said to Tom.

'Good.' He said leaning back in his seat. 'If our witness holds up, we will be able to get Bill on Babayaga's murder. I don't see the point in pushing for a confession at the moment, we have enough to have him put away for a long time already. My top priority is finding his den and getting the rest of his prisoners to safety.'

The door opened and the guard led Bill into the room and pushed him down into a chair opposite them. Bill sat down awkwardly, unable to steady himself as his hands were cuffed in front of him.

'Put your arms out,' the guard said. Bill placed his arms on the table, palms up, so the guard could remove his cuffs.

'No funny business,' said the guard, 'or they'll be back on so fast it'll make your head swim.'

Tom noticed a strange scar on the inside of Bill's left wrist. It looked like a brand; the pink skin was puckered into a strange twisting pattern. Gang mark? Tom wondered.

As soon as the handcuffs were off, Bill folded his arms and the scar was hidden again.

The guard took up position in front of the closed door.

Bill scowled at them, 'Back again. You just can't help wasting all our time, can you?'

Gardiner started the recorder and listed the attendees and the time.

'For the record,' Tom said, 'I note that you haven't requested your lawyer, Mr Hewson, be present for this interview.' Tom glanced at the papers in front of him.

'He is no longer my lawyer.'

'Smart man.'

Bill glared at Tom.

'Do you wish to call another lawyer, or have the court appoint a lawyer?' Tom continued.

'No. I've got nothing to say to you.'

'Well, Mr Doyle, we have lots to say to you. For starters, we have a witness who saw you murder Babayaga, the old homeless woman.'

'I don't know what you're talking about.'

'And we also have DNA evidence that places Rebecca Cole's baby in the garage that *you* own. In addition, every day we are finding more gems of information from the archives of the late Jeff Layton. I must say, his record keeping abilities are, beyond a shadow of a doubt, the work of an anal retentive of the highest order.'

'Bull shit.'

'What I am telling you, Mr Doyle, is that *you are screwed.*'

Bill watched him with contempt.

'You have one glimmer of hope left Mr Doyle. You see, Mr Layton has told us from the grave that you are *not* the kingpin in this murderous shit fight; that you are just the second fiddle.' Tom leaned forward, 'so here is your chance. Tell us what you know. Give us the location of the other girls. Give us the name of the Stonefish and I will make sure the police prosecutor goes easy on you.'

'No deal.'

'It is only a matter of time before we add the murders of Rebecca Cole and Babayaga to your charge sheet. Talk to us now and we might be able to cut a deal, wait too long and there won't be anything I can do.'

'You've got nothing. Fuck off,' Bill sneered at him.

'Your loss,' Tom said, 'Oh and Bill, how did you get the scar?' Tom asked pointing to Bill's wrist.

Bill tucked his arm closer to his body.

'None of your fucking business.'

'Right. Well, this is going nowhere,' Tom said and gathered his papers. He nodded to Gardiner.

'Interview terminated at 1:17 pm,' said Gardiner and turned off the recorder.

Bill placed his hands on the table, palms down this time as he glared at Tom. The guard moved forward and cuffed him. Tom would have liked the opportunity to take another look at the scar again, but Bill was having none of that. The guard marched him out of the room.

'Well, that went as well as I expected,' said Tom.

'You already knew he wouldn't talk?'

'Well, there is always this irrational hope that things might be different this time, but no, I did not expect to get anything out of him. Now that he knows that we know about the Stonefish, I will be interested to see if he tries to contact anyone.'

They were escorted back to the main entrance to sign out.

'Has Bill Doyle received any visitors or had any calls since he was locked up?' Tom asked the guard at the desk.

'None today.'

'What about since he was incarcerated?'

'Dunno. You'd have to talk to the super about that, but he is on lunch at the moment.'

'We are supposed to be receiving reports about all his calls and visitors.'

'Can't help I'm afraid, that's above my pay grade.'

'Can you get your supervisor to call me as soon as he is back from lunch,' Tom said passing him his business card.

'Sure,' said the guard, dumping the card to one side of his desk. 'Next!'

They walked out through the security barriers to the car park.

'Do you seriously think you are going to get a call-back?'

'Nope. I'm guessing my card has already been filed in the bin. I want you to call them after lunch and get them to send over the visitor log, the call records, and I want a photo of that scar on Bill's wrist too.'

'What do you think it is?'

'Don't know. It could be a gang mark. I want a closer look at it anyway.'

Bill was escorted back to his cell and locked in. His cellmate wasn't there. Probably on kitchen duty. He sat down on the grey-blanketed bunk and stared at the ground, listening to the receding footsteps of the guard until they became part of the background noise.

All the other cells were empty, the occupants out on exercise break. It was oddly quiet. Bill felt unnerved. Johnny had people in here, he knew that. People who could help him get out. But Johnny had abandoned him; it was more likely that one of Johnny's associates would come and finish him off. It wouldn't be the first time Johnny had silenced someone in gaol. He found himself straining to hear, waiting for approaching footsteps. Would they attack during the day? Or would they wait until night time? Would they make it look like suicide or would they torture him first?

Had Babayaga put a hex on him? He had never been locked up for anything before. In all his years of pimping, drug running and murder, he had never come close to being caught. And then he had cornered Babayaga, and she had reminded him of the choice he made twenty years before:

'You have sealed your own fate,' she had said. 'The end is nigh. The door will open soon!'

And in a silent rage he had killed her; as slowly and as painfully as possible.

He rubbed the scar on his arm. Had he sealed his own fate? Everything had gone to shit after he had killed her.

He could not believe that Johnny had abandoned him. Him of all people! He shook his head.

His lawyer, Mr Hewson, was refusing to take his calls.
Philip Cole was his last chance.

Andy Roswald put the kettle on and sat at the kitchen table to wait.

To wait for the kettle, to wait for Renee; it seemed that he was always waiting for something or other. The older he got the more waiting was going on and the less doing. It was frustrating.

Renee had passed him a message telepathically to say she was on her way home, so he had put the kettle on and prepared a sandwich for them both. They had fallen into this routine a few weeks ago; a night of healing followed by a light supper before bed. It had been soothing for a time after all the chaos of the months before but he was getting restless again. Especially now that she didn't need his help with the healing.

Renee would never fully recover from the trauma of her own murder and rebirth in faerie form, let alone from the loss of her baby. There were some things in life you couldn't just get over, no matter how much thoughtless-but-well-meaning friends and family might wish it.

The trick was to find meaning again; to find a purpose. And there was no better salve than helping others. Renee had been visiting the children's ward each day for the last couple of weeks, targeting one child, then another with her healing powers and slowly she was recognising the stages of healing, so she could perform the magic properly. When to pause; when to reduce pain; when to stop completely and let the child's own natural healing abilities take over. She had mastered the skill so well that Andy had not accompanied her for the last few trips. He had been able to leave her to it which meant that he was left twiddling his thumbs waiting for her to return. His best mate Bruce was away so he couldn't even wander down to the pub for a beer.

Training Renee in the faerie arts had been a salve to his own soul too. He had stopped moping about and started thinking about the future. For the first time in years, he had plans. He just needed to assess whether Renee was ready and willing to help him with them.

The pale green light flitting across the room roused him from his thoughts and he realised the kettle was already boiling and whistling. Renee appeared as he lifted it off the hob and turned off the gas.

'How did it go?' he asked, pouring the boiling water into the teapot.

'Good. Real good. She won't need me any more now. Everything is starting to heal of its own accord,' she said taking her seat at the table.

'Excellent.' He placed the mugs and the teapot on the table and handed her a sandwich.

For a few moments they enjoyed the hot tea and food, but he became conscious that Renee was looking at him curiously.

'What?' he asked.

'Penny for your thoughts,' she said.

'That obvious is it.'

'Umm, yes.'

'Well. I'm not sure where to start actually.'

'How about the beginning.'

He sat and looked at her, trying to gauge her strength. His plan was important, but he didn't want to put her in danger. If she wasn't ready, if it all went bad…

'Are you ready for another challenge? It could be really dangerous and it involves Queen Clio.'

'Absolutely. Besides, I owe you so much.'

'No. This is not about owing or debts — none of that is important. I need to know that you are ready. There are risks involved and I won't let you do this if I don't feel that you are ready.'

'You worry too much Andy. I am as OK as I ever will be. I'm ready. What do you need me to do?'

'Well, let me show you a story. Something that happened ten years ago.'

He had shown her his memories once before, so she knew exactly what she had to do. She brought her chair around the table and placed it next to him then she placed her hand on his forehead and closed her eyes.

The connection was instant. She could feel the power radiating from the filigree ring on his finger, drawing her into a part of his mind; reliving a memory in vibrant colour, smell and sound.

The first thing that hit her senses was the smell of rain. She was seeing through Andy's eyes and she could sense Nancy, Andy's wife, standing next to her holding his hand.

'What do you think she wants?' she heard Andy say to Nancy.

'God only knows,' said Nancy, her voice care-worn. 'It won't be anything we are prepared to give her.'

'No.'

'We have to stick to the plan. Lucy is the priority. We have to get her away. If one of us goes down, the other flees to fight another day. Agreed?'

'Agreed.'

They were in a deserted street, lined with old warehouses, a Sunday perhaps, the sun sinking low in the sky. The pavements were wet. The rain had stopped for now, but the air had the feel of an impending squall.

'What are we going to do if she breaks her word and brings the others?'

'The best we can. I can try a storm spell, but it will depend on where Lucy is. If she is in danger...'

They both knew that they had few options if Lucy was in danger.

There was a flit of red light; it circled above them and then landed on the other side of the road. The light shone brightly for a moment and the queen of the fairies, Queen Clio, appeared from its brilliance in a knee-length tunic of black silk, its hem and long sleeves adorned with red wasps. Over her torso she wore battle armour; a bustier made of a strange red metal.

Always the drama, Andy thought-spoke to Nancy.

Always, she replied, her thought-voice filled with scorn.

Clio walked towards them and stopped two metres in front of them. She looked directly at Nancy.

'You bring the human I see. Not wise.'

'I bring my husband. My equal. The father of our daughter. Where is she?'

'For the moment that is not your concern. You do not get to dictate the terms of this meeting.'

'I have nothing to say to you until I am sure that she is safe.'

Clio frowned. 'Be very, very careful. I can kill her in an instant if I don't like what I am hearing.'

Renee could feel Andy glowering at Clio.

'What do you want?' Andy asked her. He was trying to hold his temper, but the anger in his voice was unmistakable.

Staring directly at Andy, Clio said 'This is a conversation between faeries; between equals. If you speak again — I will kill you. Then I will kill your daughter.'

For a moment Renee thought that Andy was going to scream her down. She could sense every muscle in his body tensed to strike, but she could also feel a strength, a vast inner strength that she had never guessed at before, holding himself in check. She felt Nancy's hand tighten on his.

They waited.

Clio straightened her back and looked at Nancy again.

'You will come with me to my realm and you will live with your daughter. I have a use for your skills. Refuse and you die. Either way, Lucy stays with me. I have a use for her too.'

I'll bet you do, Andy thought to Nancy.

Hush! Nancy thought back.

Clio looked alarmed. She stared at Andy's fingers.

How can she know? Andy gasped.

'You have given him a filigree ring! A human!' she stared at Nancy, outraged. 'You betray our own kind?! For this creature! Do you know nothing of the history of the rings?'

'I know more of it than you could ever imagine,' Nancy said.

'And yet you still do this?'

Nancy had lost her patience, 'Where is my daughter? You want me to come, then show her to me. I will not come until I see she is safe.'

Renee could see that Clio was enraged and wondered why the ring had offended her so much. It obviously took a great deal of self-control for Clio to put the matter aside. A few moments later, Clio looked up to the roof of one of the warehouses and Renee felt a murmur.

'What was that?' Renee asked Andy in the real world.

'That's what it feels like when a faerie is thought-talking to someone nearby,' he replied, narrating over the top of the vision. 'We didn't know that before this moment; if we had, we would never have done it in front of Clio.'

A purple light drifted down from the roof and expanded to reveal a fairy with purple wings, her arm tied to that of a young girl.

'Mummm!' the girl screamed as soon as she laid eyes on Nancy. She strained against the rope. The purple fairy pushed a finger into the middle of the girl's forehead, subduing her with a spell.

Again, Renee felt the rage boil inside Andy.

'Here. She is safe, she is alive. Come with me now or die. Your choice.'

Renee felt Andy's hand slide into the pocket of his trousers and grab a something metal. Nancy squeezed his other hand twice.

The next few minutes were a scene of absolute chaos.

Andy pulled the metal ball from his pocket. It was woven from iron wire; its strands twisting in an intricate pattern to form a Celtic design. He hurled it at the purple-winged fairy and it expanded enormously, one side opening up as it grew until it surrounded the purple fairy in an iron cage, clamping shut and leaving Lucy outside but still tethered. Inside the cage, the purple fairy beat her hands on the metal, but where her skin touched the iron it sizzled. Her screams reverberated off the buildings. Nancy threw a storm spell at Clio creating a mini cyclone that knocked Clio backwards onto the ground.

Andy rushed to Lucy and cut the rope that was tethering her. They rushed back to Nancy's side ready to flee, but his legs went from underneath him. A rope was winding itself around his legs; a magical snake made of hemp. A yellow fairy had appeared from nowhere and was pulling the rope in, dragging Andy along the bitumen towards her. Andy grabbed the rope and, as his ring touched it, the rope jerked and pulled away. Fairies were arriving from everywhere. Andy got up but hesitated.

Nancy was trying to hold Clio down with the storm, but Clio was strong.

Go now. We agreed! Nancy thought to him. *Take Lucy and flee.*

Renee could feel the turmoil in him but sensed that Andy would keep his word.

'Where are your wings, Lucy?' Andy asked her.

'She has taken them from me!' the frightened girl replied.

'Can you shrink?'

'No daddy. She has taken all my powers!'

Nancy was knocked backwards and the swarm of fairies quickly surrounded the three of them.

Renee watched silently, knowing that all was lost.

Clio regained her feet and her composure, but her eyes were ferocious.

'Bring the rogue here.'

Nancy was pulled up by her arms and dragged in front of Clio.

A rumble of thunder filled the air and then it started to rain again. Clio looked up and smiled. She turned to Andy.

'You, human. Do you know what happens if a faerie dies in the rain?'

'No...'

'You are about to find out.' One of the fairies pushed Nancy to her to her knees in front of Clio.

Andy strained against the arms that were holding him down, thrashing madly.

The rain got heavier, soaking through his clothes. He was wet and slippery, but he could not break free.

Renee sat rigid in her chair in the real world. She didn't want to see any more.

She saw Clio pull the sword out of thin air, she saw the fairy that was restraining Nancy wrap her fingers in Nancy's hair and pull her head to one side, and she saw the sword come down on Nancy's exposed neck.

Nancy dissolved into a mass of golden sparks.

The sparks hovered in the air for a moment and then drifted upwards on the breeze, spreading out and disappearing into the night sky.

Renee gasped.

'Bring her,' Clio told the fairy holding Lucy.

Andy felt the arms release him and he looked up. Lucy was sobbing and screaming.

'Daddy! Daddy! Please, help me, daddy!'

Then two dozen lights of different colours disappeared into the darkness of the storm.

Andy sat on the wet road, rain running down his face.

It was then that Renee realised that the sobs she was hearing were not just in the memory.

She opened her eyes and took her hand from Andy's forehead.

'Oh…Andy…'

Words were useless. She wrapped him in her arms.

Ryan sat down in the white plastic chair and put his elbows on the table. It was a large room and there were several white tables placed around it, evenly spaced to give a modicum of privacy. It looked like a cut-price community hall. Only one of the other tables was occupied; the one furthest from him. The inmate, in bland prison greens, stood out starkly against the bright clothing of the visiting woman. Their conversation was in hushed tones; too low for him to catch the words.

He had signed in as Bill's work colleague, a fellow employee from the nursing home. It was not unreasonable for a workmate to visit a fallen co-worker, but he was worried it might raise suspicion. Johnny would probably curse him for taking the risk, but he had to see Bill. Things weren't the same without him and he had realised that the only reason he had gotten into this whole damn mess in the first place was to protect Bill. To protect Bill from himself, from Johnny, and from the whole mad fucking world.

It was another five minutes before Bill was brought into the room.

Once the guard had left him, Ryan sighed deeply and tried to smile.

'Still alive I see,' Ryan said.

'Yep.'

'Be careful, Bill. Johnny knows people in here, he might try to have you killed.'

'Yes, that's why I need to know what he is up to. I need you to keep me up to date.'

'I'll do what I can, mate, but Johnny doesn't let me know in advance who he is going to kill next.'

Bill nodded. 'Look after yourself too. You can't trust him. He has left me here to rot. I would never have thought he was capable of that…'

'No. Me neither.'

'Go to Blint, get yourself a new ID in case you have to jump ship; in case Johnny gets cagey. You can trust Blint — he's no friend of Johnny's and he will get you good papers. Does Johnny know you came here today?'

'No. I didn't tell him.'

'Then for Christ's sake tell him when you get back! Before his inside men do. Tell him I asked you to come and see me — to lend me some money and you told me to piss off, OK? You gotta show you are loyal to him. Ring him as soon as you are out of the building; act like you are giving him an update.'

'OK, OK!' Ryan said louder than he had intended. The couple at the next table glanced their way. One of the guards standing along the wall started watching them closely.

Ryan put his head in his hands. 'What are you going to do Bill?' he whispered. 'You have got to get out of here, man. I don't know what I will do if…'

'Don't worry about me. Just keep the information coming and I'll be fine.'

'I never thought for one moment that Johnny would turn on you like this. I mean…'

'I know, I know! I would never have picked it either. Just stay safe, man. And make up another ID for me too while you're at it. If things go pear-shaped in court, maybe I'll get a chance to make a break for it,' Bill said quietly.

'Johnny has shut down operations for a while. No babies, no tricks. I am just keeping the stock alive. Even the drug trade has been cut back to his most trusted sellers,' said Ryan.

'He's just being cautious. If the cops find the base, the whole operation is shot to shit. He's always made a big song and dance about establishing another base somewhere, but as far as I know, he never got off his arse and actually did it. If everything goes bad, head north. You know where. I will find a way to get the hell out of here and meet you there, OK?'

Ryan nodded.

'Blood brothers,' he said, looking Ryan straight in the eyes.

'Blood brothers,' Ryan repeated, meeting his gaze.

Tom sat at his desk looking at the photo on his computer screen. The administration area at the prison had been able to send it over within minutes of Gardiner's call. The phone records and visitor log were proving more difficult. Another area of the prison bureaucracy handled those; it was taking time.

The photo in front of him showed the pale underside of Bill's forearm. A large red welt standing out in sharp relief against the white skin. It was about as long and as wide as a woman's finger but, instead of being a single solid impression, it was a network of finer lines. A filigree pattern.

He had never seen anything like it.

The way the skin had healed, he guessed that it had been done a long time ago. Had he been branded by something? Was it the end product of a teenage initiation rite?

He leaned back in his chair and looked at the photo of Rebecca Cole sitting in a frame on his desk. It would remain there until her case had been solved. He owed her that much. There was another photo sitting next to it, a man and a woman smiling at the camera. He glanced at it for a moment and sighed. They had waited a long time, but they would have to wait a little longer.

He opened the computer file on Rebecca Cole and scrolled down to the folder containing the crime scene photos. Christmas beetles, blood and minuscule footprints. He looked at Rebecca's photo again. Last night he had sat at home and studied the video footage of the night that he had been shot. He had watched it over and over again to try and find a clue, something to tell him he wasn't losing his mind. No one in the police department had seen it; they all thought the footage had been destroyed along with his body camera in the gas explosion the day he had caught Bill.

He didn't believe in the paranormal or faeries, but now he had seen one with his own eyes. He had been healed by one and even though he knew it was real, and the faerie was definitely Rebecca Cole, he still kept looking for excuses not to believe it. The tiny footprints at the scene of her murder and the lack of a body made it that much harder.

So, assuming he wasn't crazy, how did an ordinary woman die and come back as a faerie? And who was Andy Roswald, really? How did he get involved with her?

What did she want? Was Bill's arrest enough? Or was it something more?

He was worried that this was becoming an obsession. He had to restrain himself from talking about it to other police officers; he knew they would have him certified if he did. There was no one he could confide in.

It was starting to wear him down. Sooner or later, he would have to seek Andy out and find some answers, or he was going to drive himself crazy.

It was late. He had to go home and get some sleep.

Tom drove out of the underground garage and headed towards the Sydney fish markets. Part way down the road he realised he was taking the long way home.

He couldn't help himself; he was a moth to a flame. He turned at the corner and travelled down the narrow road, slowing a little as he passed the run-down terrace house.

He had travelled this road numerous times since his return from the brink of death, and every time he cursed himself. He had never seen anything to make the trip worthwhile and each time he did it increased the chance that the old man would notice him driving by.

That would be a disaster. Andy Roswald was the only person who would be able to give him the answers he needed. Tom had to know why he had been saved from death by a faerie. He had to keep the old man on side, win his trust, and being caught spying would destroy that.

He cursed himself again and drove on hoping that, once again, his fleeting presence had not been noticed.

Sitting at the kitchen table the next morning, Andy and Renee were both feeling a little seedy. Last night they had cried and laughed and cried again and had downed copious quantities of wine in the process.

The kitchen was their sanctuary, their banquet hall, and their war cabinet. It was the room in which the past was assessed and the future planned.

Cups of tea in hand, they nutted out the way forward.

'Do you know if Lucy is still there, or still alive?'

'No. And that has to be the first step. There is no point walking into Clio's den if Lucy isn't there.'

Renee noticed that he didn't say *if she is dead.* Was it because he didn't want to acknowledge it as a possibility or was it because he could sense that Lucy was alive?

'There were hundreds of fairies living in the compound when Nancy and I went there,' he continued, 'and based on what I saw when Clio captured you and me, the numbers haven't changed much since then. I am hoping Gaia will agree to scout around and see if she can locate her.'

Gaia was a fairy with vivid pink wings. She lived in Queen Clio's realm and was one of Clio's most trusted guards. Many weeks ago, she had come to warn them that Queen Clio had ordered her to kill Andy. Together, they had created a ruse to fool Clio into believing that Gaia had carried out her orders. Gaia had agreed to keep them up to date on what Clio was up to in the hope of avoiding a fairy-human war.

'You don't think that Gaia will know Lucy?'

'It's possible, but I don't want to get my hopes up.'

'Okay, if Lucy is still there, what then?'

'Well, I suppose that depends on where she is being held and if she wants to leave.'

'You seriously think she would want to stay after all that?'

'I don't know. Clio filled her head with all sorts of lies before, she may have again.'

'How was she captured by Clio in the first place?'

'It's a long story. But the short version is, Lucy got careless and Clio sensed her. When Clio realised she was just a little girl, she befriended her. When she found out that she was our daughter...'

'You had already had dealings with Clio before this?'

'Oh, yes, many times,' he said pouring them more tea. 'The faerie war was over by this time, but Clio doesn't forgive and forget.'

'You were involved in the fairy war?'

'We didn't fight in the war but, whenever we came across refugees, we assisted them to escape. A lot of them had no idea how to live in the human world. We got them set up as far away from the battle zone as possible. Clio didn't like that. We were traitors as far as she was concerned.'

'But you never knew Gaia?'

'No. Clio didn't have a second in command back them. She didn't trust anyone.'

Renee sipped her tea and assessed the situation.

'So, it will be just you and me against the entire compound?'

'Almost. Bruce will help too — and Gaia hopefully.' Bruce was Andy's best mate. Renee had met him soon after becoming a fairy and had quickly realised that Andy and Bruce were inseparable and irrepressible; a grey haired dynamic duo.

'Have you spoken to Bruce about this?'

'Oh yes. He is actually away at the moment on a little scouting trip.'

'Scouting for what?'

'A faerie-free town. A refuge, in case we manage to get Lucy free. We won't be able to stay here anymore I'm afraid. Clio will not stop trying to find us if we manage to get Lucy. We will have to go into hiding.'

Renee hadn't thought about that. Of course they would have to leave. Clio found them before, she could find them again. Renee was still protected by the tree charm that Old Blue had put on her, but the concealment spell on Andy only worked against Clio, not against all her minions. Sooner or later Clio would realise that Andy was still alive and come after them. When that happened, Gaia would be in grave danger too, as she had lied to Clio, telling her that she had killed Andy.

Renee looked around the kitchen and felt a pang of sadness. This place had been her sanctuary for the last few months; leaving here would break her heart. But for Andy, this had been his home for years; the home he had shared with Nancy.

'How will you cope with leaving this place?' she asked him.

'Well, I won't say it will be easy, but I have to think of Lucy. And I have given Bruce strict instructions to find a house that is only a short stroll from a decent local pub!'

'What about Bruce?'

'He will be coming too. And you of course…You do want to come, don't you?'

'Well, of course.'

'Good. That part is settled at least,' he said taking a deep breath. She wondered if he had been bracing himself for her to say no.

'You said before that you helped to re-home refugee fairies. Would any of them be able to help us?'

'I don't know where any of them are any more. Some are dead; Clio managed to track them down and kill them after she won the war. Others were in touch with Nancy, but I have no way of communicating with them now.'

'Okay, what is our first step? Try and get in touch with Gaia?'

'No. Bruce will be back soon, I want to make sure our safe base is ready before we start talking to faeries again. If it all goes pear-shaped, we may need it. Our one advantage is that Clio didn't recognise me; she didn't realise that I am Lucy's dad. So, she won't be expecting you to launch a rescue mission after all this time.'

The guard walked Bill into the visiting area. It was his second personal visit in a week. That was unusual. There were no limitations on visits from lawyers or police, but personal visits were limited to one per week.

Philip Cole was already seated at the table waiting for Bill and he did not look impressed.

The guard pulled out the second chair.

'Sit,' the guard told Bill and then he leaned down to remove Bill's handcuffs. 'This visit has not happened. Understood?' the guard told him in a low voice.

Bill nodded, confused.

'I just got off the phone to Johnny. He is not happy that this meeting is occurring at all. If he had known earlier, he would have prevented it. But since Mr Cole is here and the visit has already been logged, it will be easier to delete it from the record after the fact than to raise suspicions by putting a stop to it now. You will advise your friend that he is not to come here again under any circumstances.'

Bill nodded again. So, Johnny did have a man inside.

The guard moved back to stand against the wall and Bill was acutely aware that he was still within hearing distance. Bill leaned back in his chair and composed himself.

'Who would have thought that a chance reunion would end up like this,' Bill said smugly.

'What do you want Bill?' Philip was in no mood for niceties.

'Just a chat. Reminisce…'

'Bull shit. What are you playing at? This is dangerous,' Philip hissed at him in an undertone.

'This is dangerous you think? I'll tell you about dangerous, you stuck-up son-of-a-bitch.' All the pretence was gone and his eyes were hard and angry even though he kept his voice low enough so he could not be heard by the guard. 'You don't know how lucky you are Sonny-Jim. Did you know that the boys at the garage had been done over?'

Philip started at this news.

'And they hadn't disposed of your little instruction sheet. Lucky for you, I like to keep things tidy.'

'I don't know what you are talking about.'

'No, of course, you don't,' said Bill sneering at him. 'But let's just say that I have a record of the business transaction you conducted with them, in your handwriting no less. There are a few people who would like to get their hands on that.' Bill let the implication of the statement hit fully home for a moment.

Philip went pale.

'What do you want Bill?' asked Philip, his voice a whisper.

'I need a lawyer. A damn fine lawyer, no less. I know how your little social circle works, Philip. You can get me one.'

'And who is going to pay them?'

'You are.'

'That would not look good. Not for you or for me,' he said coldly, before adding, 'Or Johnny.'

And there it was. The threat. What a god-damn fool he was.

'No. It wouldn't. But you remember Ryan?'

'Yes... Are you still in touch with him?' Philip asked, astounded.

Bill wanted to punch him then. Hard. So hard that Philip's chair would tip over and splatter his big ugly head on the cement floor. In school, this snobby bastard had thought Ryan was too good to hang out with the likes of Bill.

'Well as a matter of fact,' Bill said with a sarcastic smile, 'he and I are still close. Which is kind of lucky for you. You'll be able to associate with your elders and betters for a change. You are going to pay him and he will pay the lawyer.'

'And if I don't.'

'Do you really want to end up in here?' Bill asked smiling. 'With me?'

Tom pulled the canvas off the easel and set it against the wall. It wasn't finished, but he had other images in his mind at the moment.

An older painting lay propped next to it. He had never liked it. Tom picked it up and placed it on the easel. He obliterated the image under a coat of fresh white paint and then placed the roller in a bucket of water to soak.

He left the canvas to dry and wiped his hands on the old shirt that he used as a paint smock. There was a dark stain down one side of the shirt that no amount of washing would remove and a small round hole at chest height. It was the shirt he had worn when Bill shot him. He kept it as a reminder that life was short.

Tom's computer was already on in his study and he closed the document he had been working on earlier. He played the video recording of the day he was shot and watched it twice. The room had grown dark by the time he finished the second viewing and he got up and turned on the light.

He fast-forwarded the recording and paused it on the image of a glowing woman; he sent the image to his printer. The machine whirred to life. Tom paused the footage several more times; the printer spitting out image after image of the faerie woman. Finally, he got up and collected the images and returned to his studio. He pinned them to the cork board he used to display his reference material and began to paint.

Gaia's Mission

Gaia was dressed in jeans and a short-sleeved shirt. The starchy feel of the jeans on her legs was unfamiliar to her and irritating; she kept plucking at the material.

'You won't have to wear it for long, Gaia. We need to blend in,' Clio assured her.

They had just landed on the roof of an old building. It was three or four stories high and not far from the centre of the city. There was an outside patio with chairs and tables set up in groups. Gaia flew around the perimeter in miniature scouting for danger and when she gave the all clear, they assumed human size, hid their wings and adjusted their clothing.

A sign on the building declared that this was the Best Rest Backpacker Hostel. Whatever that was. Gaia wondered if backpackers were humans with a particular power or attribute that would aid Clio in her quest.

There were three of them on this expedition; herself, Queen Clio and a faerie called Elga with bright yellow wings. Gaia had wondered at the selection of Elga. She was not the sort of faerie that Gaia would have selected to infiltrate and spy on humans. Her intelligence was debatable and her subtlety non-existent. She also had no special magical talents to speak of.

Gaia had the distinct impression that Clio was keeping secrets from her. This was worrying. Did Clio suspect that her loyalty lay elsewhere? If so, her life and her role as a double-agent to the rebels was in great danger. Gaia had always played the loyal servant and she had taken pains to conceal her alliance with the rebels from everyone. But the fact remained; Clio was not confiding in her like she once did. She had given Gaia only the sketchiest details of today's mission.

Clio led the pair across the rooftop to a heavy door with an iron lock and handle. Clio stayed well back and gestured to Gaia to work her magic on it. Human locks, even iron ones, had never been a barrier to Gaia. They fell open when she prodded them with her mind. Using an oven glove as protection against the iron, she pushed the handle down and the door swung inward. Clio led them down a flight of cement stairs to a door on the third floor and gestured for Gaia to open it as well. They emerged into a dull hallway of soiled and chipped beige paint and brown patterned carpet. There were many doors, all closed, spaced along the hall.

'Wait here,' she said to Gaia, 'Guard our escape route.' Then Clio took Elga by the hand and guided her down the hall. It prickled Gaia's pride to have to wait in the hall while this imbecile was trusted with the secret of their mission.

Clio knocked on one of the doors and it was opened a moment later. Were they expected? Gaia heard a female voice greet them and invite them inside. Elga and Clio entered the room and the door was closed behind them. All was quiet once more.

It had been many weeks since Gaia had seen Renee and Andy, but she had been conversing with the rebels on a regular basis trying to keep them informed of Clio's actions. Something had changed in Clio's mind; something had spurred Clio to put her plans into action, and Gaia was completely in the dark as to the catalyst or the plans.

Clio thought that Andy was dead, that Gaia had executed him as Clio had ordered but, in reality, he was alive and well and, thanks to Gaia, he was permanently cloaked from Clio's perception. Clio had made it plain that she was expecting Renee to appear at the compound to avenge Andy. But that hadn't happened and, for a while, Clio had been in a state of anger and frustration, formulating and rejecting plan after plan to intimidate Renee into joining her in her fight against humanity. Then suddenly, the manic pacing and ranting had stopped.

'My queen?' Gaia had asked. 'You seem content today. Have you discovered a way to control the foreign faerie?'

'Gaia, thank you for your concern. I have made many discoveries and my path is clear. I no longer care if the rogue faerie joins me or not. She is irrelevant. At some point, she will join me or die, but I need her no more than I need a human. I have discovered things that would turn your hair grey, Gaia, powers that I have never dreamed of. And in good time, I will reveal them to the world and the world will never be the same again!'

She had been expecting Clio to order her to go and kill Renee. She was delighted that this was not the case, but she was alarmed at what this new development could mean. She had a hard time concealing her confusion and the dread had settled in her stomach like a stone.

Ever since this conversation, she had been trying to slip away to warn Renee and Andy that something big was coming, but she had been required to escort Clio on one mission after another. They had travelled all over the country and not once had Clio confided in her about the purpose of these trips.

She shook herself from her thoughts, realising that she had not been paying enough attention to her surroundings. They were in enemy territory, she could not afford to be lax.

Ten minutes later, still on high alert, Gaia was surprised by Clio's sudden appearance near her shoulder. She had not sensed her before her appearance.

'The job is complete, I left via the air vent. It is time to head back to the compound.'

They walked up the stairs to the roof again and Gaia could not contain her doubts.

'My queen, is it wise to trust Elga with such a mission? I fear she will not be an effective spy. Were there not more suitable candidates?'

'Ahh, Gaia! I would have a thousand of you if it were possible but, alas, that is not the case. Don't worry. Elga is amply qualified for the role she plays here; her lack of intellect will not be a concern. She has already served me well.'

Gaia did not pursue the conversation any further but wondered what possible benefit Elga could be to Clio's plans.

Tom had spent the day trawling through the police database looking at images of scars, brands and tattoos. He had seen hideous burns and scars from all sorts of injuries; both accidental and deliberately inflicted. He had seen brands used as punishment, scars resulting from bullet wounds and knife injuries and delicate tattoos that were artworks in miniature. The more he looked at the photo of the scar on Bill's inner forearm, the more convinced he was that there was some hidden meaning to it. It could be a link to the Stonefish or the other gang members.

He had been looking for any prisoners, past or present, with a similar scar, but his search had turned up nothing. It had been after nine before he had given up and gone home.

A quick dinner and then he had logged in at home to do another couple of searches. This time he targeted the missing persons' database.

It was after midnight before he gave up for the night. For a long time, he stood in the shower with the water running down his back, letting his mind go blank. It was his way of disengaging from his cases, to allow sleep to come naturally. It didn't always work but, sometimes, these failures were a blessing. Sometimes, just as he was drifting off to sleep his relaxed mind would throw an observation up from its mysterious depths; something that had been lingering in his subconscious waiting to be seen. These little insights often gave him a doorway to another line of investigation.

He stepped out of the shower and started to dry off. As he dragged the towel across his shoulders he caught his reflection in the mirror. On his left shoulder, there was a raised red welt the size of his hand. The skin was puckered and distorted.

He stood and stared at it. The dreams of the fire had been strong lately. The stories that he had been told, the few memories he had of it, the scar on his back — none of it matched what happened in his dreams. He had one small patch of scarred skin on his back yet, in his dream, he was entirely engulfed in flames. They had not licked him from the back; they had hit him full in the face.

He looked at his face. Not a scar; not a line. Nothing to give away the site of any ancient burns. His hair, his ears, his eyes, all would have been gone forever if the fire had embraced him as it did in his dream. He had seen plenty of corpses and crime scene photos of the damage that fire can do to a body. His memories made no sense at all.

He remembered being in the hospital, he remembered that as fact, and when he had been released it was into the care of his grandparents.

The photo on his desk leapt into his mind. The smiling couple.

If he did this, if he asked permission to review the police case files, he would never be able to picture them as they were in that photo again. He knew that. The crime scene photos would obliterate that; they would be forever embedded in his memory as blackened corpses.

But he owed them.

And he owed himself too.

There was another way. He could start with the record of the inquest. The photos would not be a part of the public record and he could request a copy of it without any special permission from his superiors. It may tell him what he wanted to know without the need to look at any autopsy photos.

He made a note in the journal he kept by the bed and turned off the light.

It was almost dinner time when there was a knock at the front door. Renee hid and Andy went to answer it. He re-entered the kitchen with Bruce in tow and Renee emerged from her hiding place.

'You've turned up just in time for dinner,' Andy said to him.

'Welcome back Bruce,' Renee said, 'make sure you take him out for a beer tomorrow — Andy has been going stir crazy for the last week,' Renee teased.

'Absolutely, those young-uns down at the pub have probably been up to all sorts of tricks without us around to keep them in line,' exclaimed Bruce. 'It's our public duty!'

'So how did it go?' Andy asked once Bruce was seated with a beer in front of him.

'Well. Very well. Are you sure you want to have this conversation right here, right now?'

'Oh yes. I've filled Renee in on the plan — such as it is so far — and she is coming with us.'

'Oh good. That's a relief,' said Bruce, turning to face Renee.

Renee smiled. It was nice to know that she really was a part of this strange little family.

'The town itself is not too small and not too big, easy enough to hide in plain sight — as long as we aren't followed getting there. There are no faeries about for miles.

'There are four or five reasonable houses up for sale; any of them would be fine for Lucy, not a lot of ironwork to worry about. The place has a nice pub and shops, and there is a fair-sized national park on the doorstep. Lots of lovely old-growth trees in there — in case Lucy feels the urge to get back to nature. You should feel right at home too,' he said nodding to Renee.

'How do you know there are no fairies about?' asked Renee.

'Well. My great, great grandmother was a faerie, would you believe? And although I have absolutely no faerie abilities, I do have one little trick up my sleeve that has come in handy from time to time.'

'What?'

'I can smell you.'

'What?' Renee asked, surprised.

'I can smell when faeries are about. And I don't just mean when a faerie is standing right in front of me. It's more like a dog; I can smell where faeries have been.'

Renee was a little shocked by this.

'I took a wander up and down every street in that town,' continued Bruce, 'and there was not even the faintest trace of faerie pong.'

'Pong? Do we smell bad?'

'As ripe as a rotten prawn.'

'Oh…' Renee looked downcast and wondered if there was a way to disguise the odour.

Andy laughed at her reaction.

'Don't worry Renee; he's having a lend of you,' Andy said. 'Any more of that nonsense and you won't be getting any dinner you daft old bugger,' he said with pretend brusqueness to Bruce.

Bruce laughed heartily. 'Sorry, Renee. It was just a joke; you don't stink. Faeries actually smell a bit like rose petals and old paper. Quite pleasant, now I think about it.'

Renee looked at him with an exasperated smile. 'I don't know why I fall for it — I should know by now that you are eighty percent bull shit.'

'Ninety-nine percent would be closer,' added Andy.

Bruce raised his glass in a mock salute.

After dinner, Renee sat in her room and contemplated what she would take and what she would leave behind when they made their way to their new home. She didn't have much. She hadn't even had clothes on her back when Andy had found her. That made her laugh a little and then blush. She had never thought about that — she had been as naked as a newborn babe when Andy had found her — she had been so shocked and distressed at her predicament that her nakedness hadn't even entered her head.

Some time ago, she returned to her apartment to retrieve her most valued possessions; shrinking each in turn and placing it in a backpack, but she had been interrupted by the arrival of the policeman, Tom. One thing and another had happened in quick succession and her belongings had gone completely out of her mind. The bag still sat in the wardrobe where she had left it, untouched.

She retrieved it now and pulled out the antique grandfather clock and the two jewellery boxes; all she had managed to grab before Tom's arrival. She left the clock as it was, it would be easier to transport in miniature, but she increased the size of the two jewellery boxes. She remembered that she had been looking for the necklace her parents had given to her when she was just a baby. She opened the first box and remembered that the necklace had not been in it. She turned to the second; she had not had time to open it at the time she grabbed it. She did now and, to her dismay, found that the necklace was not there either.

It must be still back at the flat somewhere. This was probably her last chance; if they left town she might never get the chance to get it back.

She flew out the window and through the darkness to her old apartment. For the next two hours, she turned the place upside down.

It wasn't there. She swore.

The necklace was her good luck charm, her last link to her parents and her most treasured possession. Before she was murdered, it was part of her morning ritual to put it on before she went to work. What if she had been wearing it on the day that she was killed…

Johnny Black

Gardiner, Peale and Tom sat around the table in Tom's office. Piles of printouts and notes were stacked on every surface.

'So that's it then?' asked Gardiner, looking at Peale.

'Yep. The last file has been read and there is nothing to add.'

'Shit,' said Gardiner.

'Well, Mr Layton has provided us with some very useful information, we shouldn't be surprised that he wasn't quite stupid enough to record the details of the Stonefish and the den. It's quite possible he didn't know that much anyway,' said Tom.

'So, what do we do now?' asked Peale.

'Peale, I would like you to find out who this shady character is,' Tom said, passing him a photo of a man sitting on park bench.

'Where did this come from?' Peale asked.

'Some time ago, a little birdy — who shall remain nameless for the time being — gave me this picture and told me that this man is an associate of our dear old friend Bill. I want to know who he is, where he lives and then, I think we will start some surveillance. I believe he is a safe-cracker or a thief of some kind so, I would check the database first and see what you come up with. If we can't get the information we need from Bill, we might be able to get it from this guy.'

Peale took the photo and went back to his desk.

'Gardiner, I still think that Bill's scar has some kind of significance,' Tom said, stretching his arms and then lacing his fingers behind his head as a pillow. 'If it is a gang mark, there may be a few unidentified bodies floating about with the same type of scar. I want you to do a search of the John Doe database and see if any of the unidentified corpses recorded in it have any brands or scars that are similar to Bill's. I've already checked missing persons – but no luck there. You'd better have your lunch first; you aren't going to want it after you've waded through that lot.'

Gardiner laughed and left the room.

While they were busy combing those particular databases, he decided to would log into the New South Wales Coroner's Court database and do some searches on the inquest records. If it *was* a gang mark, there may be some mention of a scar in the inquest of a gang member. It was a long shot, but sometimes long shots paid off.

He logged in and narrowed his search criteria to the last thirty years. Since Gardiner was looking at unidentified bodies, he decided to concentrate on the named ones, then he narrowed the search further to only return inquests that had returned a finding of murder or probable murder.

He scanned the list, recognising some of the cases and dismissing them instantly, others he made a note of for further research. He was about half-way down the first page when a name hit him hard in the stomach. Gregory Thomas Hayes, died 12th October 1988.

He clicked on the link to see where the record was held. The file had not been digitised yet. It was still stored as a paper copy in the court archive.

He leaned back in his chair. Bill's scar faded into insignificance for the moment. He forced himself to look at the photo of the smiling couple on his desk. For some reason, he had expected them to be looking at him in disapproval. They weren't of course; their smiles were the same as always. He wasn't sure if that was a comfort or not.

He didn't believe in fate but, sometimes, it was very hard not to. Before he could procrastinate, he sent an email to the records office to request a copy of the file. He had just hit "send" when his phone rang.

'Tom Hayes,' he said as he picked it up.

He listened to the voice on the other end for a few minutes and then sighed.

'OK, I'll head over there now.'

He put down the phone and grabbed his coat.

'Peale! Gardiner! Drop everything and meet me at the car in five.'

They nodded in response and he made his way down to the underground car park.

The nursing home was a posh one with plenty of visitor parking. It was boom-gated to keep out the unwashed public with their never-ending thirst for free parking. Johnny Black owned this particular establishment, but he took little interest in its day to day operations.

Johnny stepped out of the Ferrari and reached for the bouquet of tulips lying on the front passenger seat. They were red. Blood red. He locked the car and wandered up the path to the main reception building.

Neat flower gardens bordered each side of the paved path. The bricks were of varying colours and arranged in art deco patterns. One part of the building was old; older than the oldest resident. It had been a convent at one point in its history; a fact that never failed to amuse him. It was certainly de-consecrated now.

The lawns and rose gardens reminded him of a memorial garden. He knew for a fact that there were a few former residents scattered amongst the rose bushes. They weren't the only ones either. The ashes from the main furnace were scattered in the gardens too, so there were at least ten women and five men secretly recycling their organic matter. He smiled.

As he entered the main administration area, the bored receptionist brightened.

'Oh Sir, she is going to love those! It's not her birthday is it?'

'No, no,' he said smiling, 'I just thought she would like them.'

The woman was good looking (and had fantastic legs). He would have liked to treat himself — introduce her to his own special brand of amusement — but a disappearance this close to home would be unwise.

'Did you want to take them to her now or would you like me to put them in a vase?'

'A vase would be excellent, thank you. I have an appointment with Mr Evans.'

'Yes, go straight up, he is expecting you.'

Johnny walked towards the lifts. As he passed a door, he heard a familiar voice and backtracked. The doctor was providing instructions to a nurse on the care of an elderly resident. When the doctor saw Johnny in the doorway, he finished up and went to greet him.

'Nice to see you, Mr Black. Have you dropped in to see your mother yet today?'

'No Dr Porter, I have an appointment with the administrator now, but I will be dropping in to see her after that. Once my meeting is over would you mind giving me an update on her condition?'

'Of course.'

'Wonderful. The meeting should be no more than fifteen minutes.'

'I will see you then, Mr Black.'

Johnny Black nodded and continued to the lifts.

Doctor Ryan Porter seemed to be holding up well. This was good. He had been afraid that Bill's internment would rattle him; make him lose his cool. So far, so good.

The nursing home had been an expensive investment. But what it had cost in renovation and restoration had been more than covered by the outrageous fees charged to the clientele. He had not believed it possible; he had been more than happy to make a loss on the venture, it was, after all, just an elaborate but respectable front for his main business.

He was the respectable businessman renovating and setting up a quality nursing home so that he could house his own mother in comfort in her old age. It gave him a saintly reputation within the walls of the establishment. Well, his next move might tarnish that a little, but he was prepared to wear it to keep his business safe.

He knocked once on Mr Evan's door and entered.

Mr Evans was a stiff and imposing gentleman. More old school headmaster than a nursing home administrator, but he got the job done. Placements were steady, costs down and profit up.

'Mr Black, wonderful to see you.'

'Thank you so much for finding the time to see me, I know you are a busy man.'

'Any time, Mr Black, any time. Please, take a seat. What can I do for you?'

'Well, no doubt you have heard the disgraceful news about my cousin, Mr Bill Doyle?'

'Yes. I am afraid I have.'

'Well, from all accounts, he is absolutely guilty. I don't know what to say I am afraid. You warned me of his tardiness just months ago and now, he has been arrested for abduction and murder.'

'Murder? Good gracious, I wasn't aware of that.'

'He hasn't been charged yet, but it appears that he has killed an old homeless woman.'

'Oh. That is bad but not the worst crime on the scale I suppose.'

'Yes, quite but, nevertheless, not something we want to have associated with this establishment.'

'Oh, I quite agree. What do you recommend?'

'As far as I am concerned, I have repaid my debt to him and he has no further claim to my good graces. Do you have enough on file to sack him for insubordination?'

'I'm sure I can manage that. If it isn't fully documented, it will be soon.'

'Excellent. No doubt the police will come sniffing around here at some point and although I want you to cooperate with them as much as possible, I think for the sake of our reputation, it would be better if they were not aware that he is the cousin of the owner. It may come out at some point, of course, but if you could ensure that there is nothing in the paperwork about my recommending his employment or any indication that we are related, I think that would be a good thing.'

'Absolutely sir, much better if our hiring processes appear transparent and unbiased.'

'Excellent. We understand each other. One rotten apple can be binned without a fuss.'

'Ah, now that does raise the question of Doctor Ryan Porter, however.'

'Yes, I can understand your concern, they have been friends for some time, and I did request Ryan's appointment. However, I can assure you that Doctor Porter was not involved in any of Bill's tawdry affairs and while I have been blind in regard to my own cousin, which is hardly surprising really, I can say with absolute certainty that Doctor Porter is a man of complete integrity.'

'That *is* a relief. He is quite popular with our patients and your mother in particular. It would have been a terrible shame to lose him.'

'Well, I think we are in agreement, so I will leave you to it.'

'It's been a pleasure sir, anytime I can be of assistance, don't hesitate to call.'

He left the office and walked down the stairs to his mother's room. When he reached room 116, he knocked lightly and entered. The old woman was sitting propped up in bed, hands neatly folded in her lap, staring out the window at the garden.

'Hi Mum,' he said as he bent and kissed her forehead. She turned and looked at him without recognition. The vase of red tulips had been placed on the bedside table for her.

'Hope you like the flowers I brought you.'

Her eyes moved over to the vase and, as if seeing them for the first time, her eyes lit up.

'Can't stay — but I thought you'd like these — still your favourites obviously.'

She turned and smiled at him and then her gaze returned to the brilliant red flowers in the vase. He patted her hand in a distracted way and turned as Ryan entered the room.

He couldn't remember which gutter they had pulled the old lady out of, but she was getting three meals a day and a warm bed, medication and regular flowers, so the demented old bag had nothing to complain about. She was a convenient alibi for his visits; her room was on the same hall as the concealed entrance to the basement. It was an easy way for him to meet with Ryan without raising suspicion.

'How are things going downstairs?'

'They are all fed and secured. We don't have any babies on the way, so I don't need to go down too often, but we are going to be months behind on our orders.'

'Yes, but until things blow over, I am not risking the whole operation for a couple of baby sales.'

'One of our regular customers has been getting upset. He has become quite attached to one of the boys and he is not taking the break in services very well.'

'We can't take the chance at the moment. He will have to wait. Let him know we will be back up and running next month and he can have four visits on the house.'

'Okay. I take it that we are not doing any transplants for the time being either?'

'No way. Just keep the stock alive. I'll look after everything else. The drug money will keep us going for the time being.'

'Ryan dear, could you get me a glass of water please?'

Johnny started at the sound of the old woman's voice.

'Sure, Mrs Black,' Ryan said to the old woman and she smiled at him. 'I'll be back in a minute, I'd better get her tablets sorted too,' he said and left the room.

It was the first time that Johnny had heard the old lady speak; she had always been too drugged or vacant when he was there. It sent a chill up his spine.

She was looking at him now. But this time she was completely lucid. Her eyes were bright and clear; they were focused completely on him.

'Where is Bill?' she asked him. 'He always reads to me in the afternoon.'

'I'm afraid he doesn't work here anymore, mum.' He was strangely worried that she might call him out on the 'mum'. That could be awkward. The lie was necessary, but he found playing the part of the dutiful son grating at times.

She looked at him sternly.

'John Denny, you aren't getting Ryan into trouble, are you? He has grown into such a lovely young man, and he takes such good care of me.'

'No...'

'And have you been looking after William?'

'William...?'

'Yes, John — William! Goodness! Who else would I mean? Are you looking after your baby brother?'

He nodded, stunned. He scanned her face, searching for something familiar — anything.

'Good,' she said, but her look was one of doubt. 'Your father isn't causing you trouble again, is he?'

Johnny was silent.

'I went home, looking for you, but you weren't there. I have been looking for you for so long and here you are safe and sound,' the old woman said smiling. 'It's so nice that you and Bill and Ryan are all together. I was so worried about all of you, but here you all are, so it all turned out alright in the end, didn't it! You are such good boys looking after me like this.'

She looked back at the flowers.

He stood motionless, hands clenched into tight fists.

When she turned back to face him again, the fog of dementia had claimed her once more.

There had been another murder and Tom and his team had been assigned to the case. The room and the adjoining hallway had already been taped off when Tom and the two constables arrived at the backpackers' hostel. The forensic team were still going over the scene, so they waited in the hall.

Five minutes later a troupe of white-clad forensic offices emerged and ducked under the tape. George removed his face mask and walked over to Tom.

'If you throw on these,' he said handing Tom a coverall, gloves and shoe covers, 'I can show you the highlights now.'

'Okay, you two wait here,' he said to Gardiner and Peale.

He wriggled into the gear and followed George into the room. The room contained a bunk bed and an old wardrobe; it was one of many in the cheap backpackers' hotel near the city centre.

The main feature of the very bare, drab room was the woman draped across the bed, her head and her long dark hair dangling off one edge. The blood had already pooled in her head turning her face a mottled purple and it was starting to seep from her open eyes. It made him think of an old B grade vampire movie. Funny how your mind tried to distract you from the horrors, even after so many years of dealing with this shit.

'Any idea how long she's been here?'

'Not long. Day at most would be my guess without doing all the tests.'

'Any obvious cause of death?'

'No. No obvious markings; we might find something when we do the autopsy.'

'Is it just me or is she glowing?'

George looked at Tom curiously and then bent over and examined the woman's skin.

'Hang on a minute.' George walked over to the window and pulled the curtains shut. He flicked off the light and observed the woman again in the dim light filtering into the room.

The yellow glow was much clearer now. The whole body was surrounded by a brilliant yellow halo.

'Nope. I think you have been hitting the coffee too hard, Tom.' George said and turned the light back on.

Tom was stunned. How could George not see that?

It was the same sort of glow that had emanated from the Fae woman. Bill's gunshot would have killed him if not for her. Surely there had to be a Fae connection in all this. Was this dead woman actually a faerie? But why could he see the glow and George not?

George opened the curtains again.

'Who rang it in?' Tom asked him, resorting to procedure to try and hide his confusion.

'Her roommate. She was out all night partying and couldn't get in this morning when she came home. The door was locked and jammed shut from the inside. The uniforms had to break the door off its hinges.'

Tom looked at the shattered door leaning back against the wall. He hadn't noticed it when he had entered, the woman on the bed had held his attention. There were two wooden wedges sitting on the floor next to it.

Tom walked over to the window and looked out. Two story drop straight down; no balcony. It had a sliding window fitted with a fly screen, which was still intact. It also had a metal clamp fitted to the lower frame to stop the window being opened more than a few centimetres. He had seen them before; it was a cheap way to make windows a little more child safe or, in this case, drunken-youth-proof. The gap was too small for someone to climb out and do themselves an injury but large enough to let some air circulate.

He checked under the bed and in the wardrobe. There wasn't much to see. Certainly not anything that would provide any kind of explanation.

'No drugs?'

'Nothing on any of the preliminary swabs taken from the body. There are low levels all over the room, but that is hardly surprising. She may have died from a medical condition, but she is pretty young and appears to be pretty fit, so I would say the chance of that is on the low side.'

'So, a locked room with a dead body,' Tom said to George.

'Yep. A classic whodunnit case for you to pull your hair out over.'

'Any thoughts?'

'Better you than me.'

'Gee, thanks.'

'Any time. I'll let you know when we get the lab results back.'

'Is the roommate still around?'

'Yeah. One of the boys in blue is talking to her in the next room.'

'You finished in here?'

'Yeah, we are just waiting for the morgue van to arrive and then we will be packing everything up.'

Tom took one final look around the room and realising there was nothing left to see, he walked out of the room and ducked under the police tape. He was glad to strip off the coverall; he always felt a little contaminated after visiting a crime scene.

He gestured to Peale; Gardner was nowhere in sight.

'Where's Gardiner?'

'In with the roommate,' Peale said, gesturing to the next room. 'Constable Lee was having trouble getting any sense out of her, she's in quite a state. Gardiner is talking to her woman-to-woman.'

'Goodo. The room itself is pretty clean. I don't think we'll be getting any clues from there. We are going to have to wait for the autopsy results for this one.'

Gardiner emerged from the next room and came over to them.

'A counsellor is going to be here soon and Constable Lee has arranged for one of Nicole's friends to come and pick her up. The hostel offered her another room, but she doesn't want to stay here anymore. Can't blame her.'

'Did you get anything of interest?'

'No, it was all pretty routine. The deceased is Amanda Redding from London, UK. The roommate is Nicole Jenner, also from London. The two of them had been travelling around Australia for the last two months doing bar work and fruit picking. Nothing unusual has happened during their trip so far. No threats, drugs, run-ins or stalkers. Nothing medical that she knew of. Nicole is really shocked by Amanda's death.'

'Did you get both of their next of kin details?'

'Yeah. Both girls have parents in London; I've got contact details for them.'

'Alright. Well at this stage it is an unexplained death and until we get some results back from George, there is nothing more for us to do here. Let's head back to base and get the unpleasant formalities out of the way.'

Renee's Secret

Tom called the police in England and was put through to the station in the town where Amanda's parents lived. The local bobbies went over in person to break the news to them. Two hours later Tom spoke to the grieving mother and father by phone, knowing that there would be questions they would want answered. It was the part he hated above all else, but he also wanted it done right. He had seen the body and so was able to answer all their initial questions honestly and sympathetically. There was so little that he could tell them, but he understood their shock, anger, frustration and sorrow because he had seen it before in all kinds of combinations. Everyone reacted in their own personal way when their world fell to pieces.

Until they knew the cause of death, the case was in limbo. If it turned out to be natural causes, Amanda's body would be shipped home to her parents. If it was murder, well, murder changes everything.

He had wanted to talk to the fae woman ever since she had healed him. Now he had two reasons to do so. Firstly, there was Bill's den. They had combed through every piece of evidence that Jeff Layton had left behind and they were still no closer to finding it or the identity of the Stonefish. He had thought about enlisting the help of Andy Roswald and his faerie friend for some time but had not wanted to approach them until all their 'normal' options had been exhausted.

Weeks ago, Andy Roswald had lured Tom to a pub with a bright green light — the light that Tom had encountered at the scene of Rebecca Cole's murder and at the garage where the mechanics had been turned to ash. Andy had been waiting for him and suggested that the light was a supernatural being; his other-worldly helper, if you like. At the pub that night Andy had presented him information about Bill's criminal activities and the photo of the thief — an associate of Bill's. So far, Tom and his team had found nothing on him; this guy was very much under the radar. The faerie had helped Andy to find the thief once; perhaps she could find him again?

The other reason he wanted to approach Andy was the new case. Perhaps the faerie knew the dead woman or could tell him more about the strange glow. Something wasn't right and he had no way of defining those feelings in a way that anyone else on the force would take seriously. He had a bad feeling about this one. Really bad.

He would be placing his trust in an old man and a fae creature that he knew nothing about. Assuming of course that he wasn't going mad. He kept asking himself that, over and over again. His torn, bloody shirt and the video footage of the fae woman bending over him were physical evidence that he really had been brought back from the edge of death by a faerie, but a part of him still believed that he was being deceived or deluded, or he was suffering from a mental illness.

Well, mentally ill or not, he needed answers and they seemed to be the only people that had them.

He walked down the stairs to his car.

He felt like he was on autopilot. How many times had he driven this exact route over the last few months? This time though, he didn't care if they saw him. This time, he was going to stop and knock at the door.

He parked out the front and locked the car. The house was old and in need of a few repairs but, given its age, that was hardly surprising. He guessed it would have been built around 1930. It was a terrace house with wooden fretwork decorating the edge of the verandah roof. The path was made of worn and cracked patterned tiles faded by many summers. The front fence and gate were made of widely spaced wooden palings with the tops cut into a decorative curve.

As he approached the front door, he noticed that the door handle was made of polished timber. The door knocker and the latch were brass. He wondered if there was any iron in the house at all and if the old tales of faeries not liking iron had some truth in them.

He took a deep breath and tapped the knocker three times.

Within a minute he heard footsteps coming down the hall. There was no point in trying to pretend that he was comfortable with the situation.

He suspected that the old man would see right through any kind of pretence.

The door opened and Andy Roswald stood looking at him over his reading glasses.

'Wondered when you would turn up,' the old man said. 'You'd better come in,' he said holding the door open and allowing Tom to pass. 'Kitchen is straight ahead.'

The old man followed him into the kitchen and motioned Tom to a chair.

'Tea?'

'Thanks.'

Tom sat down and looked around him. The kitchen was old but clean. A sturdy kitchen table and four chairs sat at one end of the kitchen and a bench and cupboards ran along the opposite wall. Andy placed the kettle on the gas stove to boil and retrieved a couple of mugs and a biscuit tin from the cupboard.

'What brings you here now that Bill Doyle is safely in gaol?'

'We haven't been able to find his den, but we've found enough information to know that it actually exists.'

'Damn,' said Andy. He made the tea and came and sat down opposite Tom.

'We are trying to find out who the thief is, the man you photographed meeting Bill. Whoever he is, he doesn't seem to have a criminal record in Australia and we can't find him on any watch list either.'

'A low-flier.'

'Yep.'

'Do you think he might know where the den is?' Andy asked.

'That's what I'm hoping. Now that Bill is locked up, I might be able to pressure the thief into helping us.'

Andy nodded.

'He broke into the safe at the garage. It was papers mostly, by the sound of it,' said Andy.

'Papers? Do you know where they ended up?'

'Yeah. The thief delivered them to Bill. Met with him at the Rose and Crown.'

'I don't suppose the faerie would be able to get them back or get me a copy of them. Is she here?' Tom asked looking around the room.

Andy leaned back in his chair and folded his arms across his chest. He stared at Tom.

'I don't recall mentioning anything about a faerie,' he said quietly.

'She didn't tell you...?' Tom wasn't expecting this.

'Didn't tell me what?'

'Look, I know about the faerie, okay. Bill shot me. I was as good as dead. She pulled out the bullet and patched me up. She was pretty drained by the end of it.'

Andy looked surprised and worried.

'Is she okay?' Tom continued. 'Have you seen her since then?'

'She's not here at the moment but, don't worry, Renee is fine.'

'Don't you mean Rebecca?'

'No, Renee; she is Renee now. Did she tell you who she was?'

'No. But I put two and two together. She didn't actually speak to me at all. I was chasing Bill, and he pulled a gun out of nowhere. Didn't even stop to aim, just turned and fired; got me right in the chest. He was about to finish me off with a bullet to the head when there was a massive explosion. I think she blew up the gas barbecues. I was dying. There was no way an ambulance was going to get to me in time,' he paused for a moment to gather himself.

'Renee brought me back from the edge of death. I didn't get to thank her. Please, when you see her, thank her for me. If she hadn't…'

Andy nodded, looking at him closely. He appeared to be thinking things over.

'You haven't told anyone about any of this?' asked Andy.

'No of course not. I'd be certified insane if I did.'

Andy nodded and sighed.

'I was hoping to keep you out of all this faerie stuff, but Renee has had other ideas, obviously. Look, we will help you as much as we can, but you can't put all your chips on us. We might not find anything,' Andy said.

'I appreciate that, but any little detail might provide a missing link. Anything you can tell me might help the investigation.'

'Alright, but, like I said in the pub, I will not get on any witness stand.'

'Understood.'

Andy sipped his tea.

'We don't know where the den is, we were hoping you'd be able to get that out of Bill,' Andy said. 'We can have a look around and see what we can find, but that's about as good as it gets.'

'What about the thief? Have you seen him around since he handed the papers over?'

'No, but we haven't been looking either. The Rose and Crown, the garage and the park were where he used to meet Bill — those are the only places we have seen him. With Bill in gaol, the pub is probably the only one of those he might return to. But you can probably stake it out better than we can.'

'True. I will get someone onto that. I don't suppose Renee knows what was in the papers?'

'No. She didn't get a close look.'

'Well, whatever it was, they wanted it locked up tight.'

'There was some jewellery as well; the thief took that.'

'Probably going to pawn it. I will keep an eye on the local pawn shops. You never heard a name?'

'No. It was Renee doing all the snooping. I wasn't with her, but she has a good ear for details. She would have told me if she had discovered his name.'

'How did this happen? Renee, I mean. Was she always a faerie?'

'No… It's a mystery to all of us. Last year she was a normal woman minding her own business and now, here she is — a super faerie.'

'A super faerie? As opposed to an ordinary faerie?' Tom said with a wry smile.

'Well, that's a bit of an exaggeration, but she can do things that other faeries can't.'

'Like turning men to ashes?'

'I never said she did that!'

'You didn't have to.'

'Well. That wasn't what I was referring to, but her abilities are none of your business and if you are going to make trouble…'

'I am not trying to cause trouble for her,' Tom said, holding up his hands, 'I owe her my life! I'm just curious.'

'Well you know what they say about cats and curiosity,' Andy grumbled.

'I'm sorry. I won't ask any more about that. But can I ask how you got involved in all this?'

'Long story. I've known about the little folk since I was a lad. Tuned into them you might say.'

'Umm. Well, there might be something else you can help me with. I think it might be faerie-related. Have you ever heard of a dead body glowing like a faerie?'

'Glowing? Like Renee does?'

'Yes. But yellow instead of green.'

'No. I haven't.'

'The forensic guys couldn't see it. I don't understand why I could. Is it possible that the dead girl is a faerie?'

'Unlikely. Faeries have protections to hide them if they die in public places. They certainly don't light up like candles. I'm not sure why you would be able to see it and not the others though,' he said looking at Tom curiously.

'No. I thought I was going mad when the forensic guy told me he couldn't see it. I was wondering if Renee passed on some kind of faerie sight to me when she healed me?'

'Possibly. Some people can sense when a person has been touched by a faerie; perhaps some of the magic goes the other way too?'

'This is a big ask, but I was wondering if you and Renee could come to the morgue and view the body. We don't know much yet. If she was murdered, there are no signs of foul play, but something just isn't right. I could set up a visit tomorrow night when there aren't many people about.'

'Doesn't matter what time, I can smuggle her in without anyone seeing her if I need to. I will talk to Renee and I'll give you a call. I want to see this. I don't like the sound of it and I dare say Renee will agree with me.'

Two hours after Tom left, there was another knock on Andy's door.

'Bloody hell,' he muttered, 'It's like Central Station here today.'

He opened the door to find Bruce.

'Ahh, you must have read my mind. I was going to wander down and pay you a visit later, come in, I'll get the kettle on again. You're my second unexpected visitor today.'

'Oh. And who was your first?'

'The tall detective.'

'So, he knows where you live?'

'I would've thought much less of him if he hadn't been able to figure that one out.'

'Very true. I have news too but I'm not sure you're going to like it.'

Over tea, Andy filled him in on the incident between Renee and Tom.

'So,' Bruce said, 'she saved his life.'

'I don't know whether to yell at her or applaud her. That was a terrible risk she took,' he said shaking his head. 'He is in her debt now. That might be a good thing but he is also mighty curious about her and that is never good in my experience.'

'Rubbish! Andy, you are forgetting your own history! You were the curious one, always sniffing around in faerie affairs, just like me. Do you really think either one of us has been a thorn to the fae?'

'To Clio maybe, but, no, not to the fae in general,' he conceded.

'And speaking of Clio — that was why I came here in the first place. I have been in touch with some of my faerie kin and they are getting very nervous about Clio.'

'Why's that?'

'She's been travelling, exploring, all over the country.'

'What? Clio? That's not like her. She usually stays pretty close to her swarm.'

'Yes. And that's not all. The places she goes; there has been magic used. My cousin took me to one of the sites. I don't know what kind of magic it is, but it smells bad.'

'Have there been any deaths?'

Bruce looked surprised.

'I don't think so. Not that I have heard about.'

'Well, there might have been one here, in Sydney. The young copper, he told me about a woman that he has in the morgue — she is glowing, Bruce.'

'Oh my god. I really need to see her, Andy.'

'Yes. As soon as Renee gets back I am going to call the copper and he is going to take us to see the body. I think you'd better come along.'

'Do you think she is setting up for another war?'

'I don't know what she is up to, but the sooner we find Lucy and get her the hell out of there the better.'

'Are you sure Lucy is still alive?' Bruce asked quietly.

'Yes. I can feel it in my bones.'

Bruce nodded.

Bones were bones; there was no arguing with bones.

Renee was in Northern New South Wales; there had been a mine collapse and several men were still trapped. The top levels of the mine and all the administration buildings had been evacuated and a rescue team had taken over the lunch room. Men in fluorescent yellow emergency clothes were waiting to be briefed on the situation; rows of air tanks were stacked along the wall. She hid on top of a light fitting to watch.

'The engineer is looking at the damage from this side now. All communication to the western end of the mine has been lost,' he said, pointing to a diagram of the mine pinned to the wall.

'The lift goes down 100 metres and then opens on to the main tunnel. The tunnel continues west for two kilometres,' he said tracing the route on the map with his finger. 'The collapse occurred here, just outside G heading,' he said pointing to a large bay cut into the coal, 'and has blocked access to all the headings to the north-west of it. We have nine men missing.'

She didn't wait to hear more. She flew to the building that housed the lift that would take her down to the lower levels. It was a metal cage with a solid floor, but there was plenty of room to slip down the side of it and into the lift well. She flew down the empty shaft until she reached the tunnel leading to the trapped men. It was dark and the swirling coal dust made her cough. She should have thought of that. She couldn't see anyone nearby so she increased her glow to give her some light. To one side of the tunnel was a large green sign with a white cross on it; a first aid room. Perhaps there would be a face mask in there.

There was more than that. There were all kinds of safety equipment and a full medical examination room to one side. There were also air tanks and breathing apparatus. She increased her size long enough to kit herself out with oxygen and a face mask and then flew in miniature towards the rock fall to see if there was anything she could do.

The dust had started to settle when she reached the site of the collapse and in the reflected light from her fairy glow, she could see a mass of rock and coal tumbled together into a gigantic slope stretching up to the roof of the cavern. There was no way in for a human, but a creature as small as she was could find a passage through the tiniest of cracks. She was able to crawl, slip and squeeze through one gap after another until she was on the other side of the rubble.

The first man she encountered was half buried under the fall of rocks. He was dead. There was nothing she could do for him except to gently close his eyes. She could not linger, there were others who may need her help.

Further along the mass of rocks, she found a second man; unconscious and half buried. She dimmed her glow and returned to human size. Once she had cleared the rubble off him, she could see that he had a broken leg and several cuts. His breathing was slow but steady and he should be okay once the rescue team got him out. She gently dragged him away from the rubble so that he would not be endangered if it collapsed during the rescue operation.

She shrank herself again and moved further down the passage. Three men sat in a huddle near an enormous mining truck. One sat quietly with his head leaning on one hand, another was leaning back against the wall with his eyes shut. The last man was sitting with his arms wrapped around his legs, rocking back and forward, moaning.

'Calm down Benny,' the one with the closed eyes said. 'You're alive. They'll get us out.'

The moaning stopped, but the rocking did not.

None of them seemed badly injured so she left them and moved further on. There were still four men unaccounted for.

There had been a second collapse further along the tunnel. A huge piece of the ceiling had come down and there was a mass of smaller rock tumbled around it. There was a tiny opening along one edge of the monolith and she flitted inside. There were two men lying beneath it. She checked for vital signs but found none. She brushed the tears from her eyes and sat for a moment to calm herself.

The opening she was in stretched to the other edge of the monolith. She mentally pulled herself back together and flew along the gap. She was in luck; it continued all the way through the rubble to the chamber on the other side.

Here she found two men, one sitting with is back against a wall of rock, the other lying on his side with his head resting on the first man's lap. The side of the prone man's head was caved in. There was a battery-operated lamp on the ground next to them providing some light.

'You'll be okay mate,' the first said.

'Bull shit,' said the second; his voice weak.

This was going to be a challenge. If only she could knock them both out for a while without causing any further harm.

Well… Why not? She could see into bodies, maybe she could see into brains too.

She flew behind the sitting man and rested a tiny hand onto the back of his head. The jumble of electrical impulses was awe inspiring. This is how a brain works, she thought. She would have to shut down the senses without shutting down the vital functions. She found the parts that controlled sight, hearing, touch and movement but could not work out which part was the conscious mind. It would be frightening for them for a while, but it would have to do. The injured man needed her help now.

She blocked the man's brain waves from reaching his senses then checked his heart and breathing. He was okay at the moment. There was no panic.

She flew straight to the second man and repeated the brain manipulation, then she returned to full size and got to work on the side of his head. The injured man was in a bad way. She placed her hands on each side of the man's head and using her mind, she pulled the splinters of bone out of the head wound; they hovered over the injury like tiny satellites. She stopped the bleeding and the swelling in his brain and then, like a jigsaw puzzle she slotted the slivers of bone back into place, reforming his skull. She did not heal the wound entirely but left a minor fracture and laceration that would heal themselves in time but also explain the blood all over his clothes. The head complete, she moved to his heart. It was stressed. The blood flow was back to normal and she suspected that his sensory deprivation might be the problem. She looked at the brain again and saw a flare of activity. She shrank herself and placed her hands on his head again. She returned his hearing first and then slowly returned his movement, feeling and sight. The activity in his brain slowed and his heart began to regain its proper rhythm. His companion was probably in a similar state.

She flew behind the sitting man and looked inside his brain. It was strangely quiet. For a terrible moment she thought he was dead, but then she sensed his heart, slow and steady, as was his breathing. He was asleep. She returned his senses to normal and the sudden light on his eyelids made him stir.

'You still with me?' The man on the floor asked in a panicked voice.

'Hmm, Yeah, sorry. I dozed off for a minute there.'

'Nearly gave me a heart attack you bloody numpty.'

'Well, I can see you're feeling better. You can get your fat head off me now. My bloody legs have gone to sleep.'

She left them arguing and rearranging themselves and flew back the way she had come. She left the breathing apparatus on the floor in the first aid room and flew back to the lift well.

The lift was on its way down and she waited until all the rescuers had disembarked before catching a lift with it back to the surface. Another group of rescuers was waiting for its return and she flitted over their heads unseen and began the long journey home.

She was exhausted.

It was late in the afternoon when she returned home and Andy was sitting at the kitchen table waiting for her when she entered the kitchen. She could tell by the look on his face that he was not happy.

'What's happened?' she asked.

'If you were my daughter, I would be seriously tempted to ground you for life, young madam!'

'I beg your pardon?' Renee exclaimed.

'I had a visit today from none other than Detective Inspector Tom Hayes; the man with the baby blue eyes,' he growled at her. 'Are you insane?'

Renee grimaced.

'What did he say?' she asked, already expecting the worst.

'That you showed yourself to him, in faerie form no less, and healed him. Brought him back from the point of death! He sends his thanks by the way.'

She sat down heavily.

'I had meant to tell you about that.'

'Oh really, and when were you planning to tell me? When hell froze over?'

'Oh, come on,' she said, 'what was I supposed to do? Let him die? He was about to capture Bill and the bastard shot him. He was doing this for me and my baby!'

'You can't go around saving everyone and showing yourself to the world. This isn't just about you — it's about the safety of every faerie on the planet! Do you understand that?'

'Of course, I understand that! But I wasn't showing myself to the world, I was showing myself to one man, one good man — a man that I can trust!'

'How do you *know* that you can trust him?'

'I don't know! I just know that I know. The same way that I knew that I could trust you,' she said heatedly. 'You aren't my father, Andy, and I am not a child. I have to make my own calls on who I can trust and who I can't. I let one man push me around for years and I am not going to allow anyone to manipulate me like that again! He destroyed my self-confidence, made me doubt my own instincts — made me doubt my own reality!'

'I am not trying to make you doubt yourself and I am not trying to dictate to you. I am just trying to make sure you have thought this through. Tom was doing his job, it's a tough job and he knows it. The risk of being shot is a part of that job. What if he reveals you?'

'Tom helped me. I couldn't let him die. If he says anything, people will say he is crazy. I know this is dangerous, but I am prepared to take a risk here. And if worst comes to worst I can disappear. Besides he has the same feeling that you and Bruce have — it's like an aura of familiarity.'

'A sense of knowing him?'

'No. I hardly know anything about him — it's more like a sense of family, of unity, of belonging.'

'And Bruce and I feel the same way?' asked Andy, his curiosity overwhelming his anger.

'Yes.'

'I wish Nancy was here,' he said quietly. 'She would tell me straight away what this is. I just don't know. Look, I'm afraid for you, okay? It is really hard to pack up and start over and it's not always possible,' he sighed.

'I'm sorry I didn't tell you straight away. That was wrong of me. I just wasn't sure how to tell you.'

Andy nodded. 'No more secrets, okay?' he said.

'No more secrets,' she agreed. 'So... is Tom okay? He recovered properly?'

'Yes, yes, he's fine.' He looked at her slyly. 'You aren't getting sucked in by his big blue eyes, are you?'

'NO!'

'Alright, alright, no need to get titchy.'

A Conflict of Interest

Renee had been buzzing from one place to another in fairy form for weeks and she never thought she would say it but she was sick of it. She was ready to look like and act like a human again.

She stood in front of the full-length mirror in her room and willed her wings to shrink. Once they had become tiny dots on her back, she changed them to look like small brown freckles. Next, her hair was shortened to a crop cut and its colour changed from auburn to light brown. Then, she changed her eyes from their bright green opal colour to a muted brown. Months ago, she had decided on this as her default "look", one that she could use in public. A small tweak to the shape of her nose and eyes and she had become Renee Roswald, daughter of Andy Roswald. No one could recognise her in this disguise, which was a good thing because the missing person posters for Rebecca Cole were still scattered all over Sydney.

As she entered the kitchen, she heard Andy on the phone.

'Yep. We'll be there, tomorrow at 5 pm. Okay, bye.'

'Who was that?'

'Detective Inspector Tom Hayes,' he said. 'We are going to meet him at the morgue tomorrow afternoon. Not a great first date but you can't have everything.'

'Oh really. Aren't you afraid I might drown in his big blue eyes?'

'Yes, alright, very funny. This is serious though. Bruce thinks so too; he's coming as well. When Hayes came over this morning, you weren't the only thing he wanted to talk about.'

Renee rolled her eyes.

'I told Bruce to meet us at the pub for dinner. There are things I forgot to tell him this morning; it's been a busy day. I'll fill you both in at the same time.'

The Contented Soul was a short stroll down the road. The night was pleasantly warm, and in this part of the city, where the buildings were shorter and the street lights fewer, the stars could be seen shining brightly in a clear black sky.

Bruce had already claimed their favourite table and their usual tipples were waiting for them when they arrived.

'Excellent,' said Andy downing half his Guinness in one go, 'it's been a thirsty day.'

'Have you spoken to the copper?'

'Aye. We're going to visit him at the morgue at 5 pm tomorrow. You okay with that?'

'Absolutely.'

'What is going on at the morgue?' asked Renee.

'Hayes said there was a backpacker that died a couple of days ago. He says she is glowing.'

'Glowing?'

'Yep. But the forensic guys couldn't see it. Just him. He's worried that you have infected him with something,' Andy laughed at her and winked.

'Oh, pleaaaasse,' said Renee.

'But that's not all. Bruce told me this morning that Clio has been travelling far and wide, performing bad magic. We think she is up to something and this poor dead girl might have got caught up in it.'

'So, the three of us are going to go and have a look at the body and see what we can see,' added Bruce.

'Probably better if you come in your human form for this visit,' said Andy. 'He has arranged for us to visit when one of his mates is on duty; avoid too many awkward questions.

'There is something else he told me too — I forgot to mention it to you, Bruce,' Andy continued. 'Bill's den is real.'

'Oh shit,' said Bruce. 'I was hoping that it was just an urban legend.'

'Yeah. But the coppers don't know where it is. Bill isn't talking and Hayes hasn't been able to identify the thief. I gave him a few leads, but we all need to keep our eyes out for him. Hayes needs a name — and an address if we can get it. He thinks he might be able to pressure the thief into telling him where the den is now that Bill is in gaol.'

'I haven't seen him since he dropped the papers to Bill,' said Renee.

'Have you got a photo of him?' asked Bruce.

Andy flicked through the photos on his mobile phone and handed it to Bruce.

'Ahh. I've seen this toss-pot around. I don't know his name but, yeah, I'm sure I can find something out.' Bruce forwarded the photo to his own phone. 'I'll look into it tomorrow morning. There are a couple of people I know who might be able to shed some light.'

'Good. Because the other thing is about the Stonefish. It ain't Bill.'

'Boy, you are a bearer of good news tonight, aren't you?' Bruce sighed and polished off his beer.

Renee looked at them both silently. She had been an idiot to think that Bill's capture meant this was over.

'Do they know who the Stonefish is?' she asked, subdued.

'No,' said Andy quietly, sensing the change in her mood. 'They have found plenty of references to a bigger boss, sometimes they even call him the Stonefish but never a real name. They were probably too scared to put his name in writing.'

'Andy! The people... The victims... With Bill in gaol...?'

'Yeah, I know, I know. I hope Bill wasn't the only gaoler,' said Andy.

'Oh, Christ! I never thought of that,' said Bruce, suddenly solemn.

'We have to help Tom find them.' said Renee.

'We have to help Hayes find the thief, then it is up to him to do his detecting-thing. We are talking needle in a haystack here. If we hear something, we pass it on, but there is not much else we can do. We have to focus our attention on Clio. If she is gearing up for a war, we have to help put a stop to it. We are the only ones that even know she exists. Humans will be slaughtered en masse if she has her way,' argued Andy.

'That may be true, Andy, but the inmates in the den are suffering now. We don't even know what Clio is up to yet. Are you letting your own interests cloud your judgement here, Andy?' Bruce asked pointedly.

'Of course, I am! What fool wouldn't put the safety of his own family above that of complete strangers? I am not saying we abandon them, Bruce. But I am saying we have other priorities — for now. If Clio is planning a war against humanity — which was what she said when Renee and I were taken prisoner — then I have to get Lucy the hell out of there. We have to stick with the plan. If those poor bastards in the den were left to rot — then they are already dead, Bruce. It has been weeks since Bill was arrested.'

'I can't agree with you there, Andy. Some of the kids that disappeared off the streets — I knew them. Maybe Bill grabbed them and maybe they moved on. I don't know. But this is still a priority for me. I am not going to sit here and do nothing. I am going to help you get Lucy back any way I can, but I am not giving up on them.'

'I am not saying we give up on them,' said Andy. 'They still could be alive; the Stonefish could well have provided them with another gaoler. But they are not MY priority.'

'Then we are agreed. You can concentrate on Lucy and I'll concentrate on the den. What about you, Renee?' asked Bruce.

'I'm sorry, Andy,' Renee said looking at Andy, 'but it has to be both. These monsters killed my baby and god knows how many others. This is personal. But Andy, you've kept me safe and taught me everything I know about being a fairy so I can't walk away from you and Lucy either. All I can promise is to do the best I can on both fronts.'

Andy shrugged and smiled.

'I can't ask more than that.'

Andy had not slept well. He wandered out to the kitchen in his dressing gown and slippers.

He was torn. He could empathise with Renee and Bruce wanting to find the den, but he could not resist his desire to rescue Lucy first. He had mulled over how to rescue her for the past ten years, ever since she had been abducted, but he had never had the means to piece together a reasonable plan. Now with Bruce and Renee, and possibly even Gaia, there was a real chance of succeeding.

The dead backpacker made him nervous. Clio was up to something.

The knock at the door startled him out of his reverie.

Who the hell would be knocking at his door at this time of the morning? Renee wasn't even up yet.

He shuffled to the door, uncaring that his hair stood up in unruly clumps. If someone was going to knock this early they deserved an eyeful of him in all his morning glory.

It was Bruce.

'Ahh, good. The day is too fine for sleeping,' Bruce said and walked past him to the kitchen.

'What the hell are you doing up this early, ya daft old bugger?'

'I haven't been to bed yet, actually.'

'What?'

'I called in to see an old friend of mine on the way home from the pub last night and well, we got to talkin' and one thing led to another...'

'So, an old girlfriend was it?' Andy asked, exasperated.

'Hehehe,' giggled Bruce. 'I've still got it you know!'

'Well don't give it to me.'

Bruce flopped into a chair; he was grinning like an imp.

'So, you decided to come over here and wake me up so you could brag about it?'

'Well, that was part of the plan, but since you were already up, you kinda ruined that bit,' he said.

Andy rolled his eyes and went to put the kettle on.

'That's not all I have to brag about though,' said Bruce.

'Oh, here we go!' said Andy, expecting a tall tale.

'I have the name of the thief.'

'What?! How?'

'My lady friend isn't just a pretty face. She knows people,' he said and passed Andy a note.

Andy held the note out at arm's length, squinting to focus without his reading glasses. 'Tim Crace; otherwise known as "Cracker". Seriously? Cracker?'

'Advertising perhaps?' suggested Bruce.

'That he is good in bed, or that he cracks safes?'

'Bit of both maybe,' said Bruce winking.

'You sure this is legit?'

'Absolutely. I've got his address too. I was staking his place out last night. He came home about 3 am. It's him alright.'

'Perfect. We can hand this over to Hayes tonight at the morgue.'

'My thinking exactly. And if he can get this guy to talk, we'll be free to get on with rescuing Lucy,' Bruce said.

Andy beamed. Perhaps today wasn't going to be so bad after all.

The Morgue

At 4:50 PM Tom was waiting outside the entrance to the morgue. George had already arrived and gone in to prepare for the viewing.

At 5 pm an old Morris Minor trundled slowly into the car park and pulled up. An old man climbed out of the driver's side and was followed by Andy and a woman that Tom had never seen before. She was wearing blue jeans and a white halter neck top.

As they approached, Tom recognised the driver as one of the men that he had spoken to at the scene of Rebecca Cole's murder.

'Hope you don't mind me bringing Bruce along,' Andy said nodding towards him, 'he has a few tricks up his sleeve that might come in handy.'

'Under the circumstances, I won't say no.' Tom shook his hand in greeting and then turned towards the woman. He looked at her curiously.

For a moment her face seemed to flicker and he saw the features of Rebecca Cole before him and then the green flash of the fae woman's eyes. Those eyes. God, he had dreamed about those eyes. Conscious of the fact that he was staring at her, he forced himself back into the present.

'That must come in handy,' he said as her face returned to its previous state.

'Incredibly,' she responded.

He noticed that she seemed as nervous as he was. There was so much he wanted to ask her, but now was not the time or the place. He settled on, 'Thank you.'

'Don't mention it,' she said with a Mona Lisa smile.

'Right!' said Andy, breaking the mood, 'Where is the glowing lady?'

'I'll take you in to meet George and see the body now, but please don't mention any glowing in front of George or the morgue staff.'

'No; probably wise,' agreed Andy.

The room smelled strongly of disinfectant and formaldehyde and it was extremely cold. George nodded in greeting and ushered them over to a steel gurney; the body lay covered with a sheet.

'Normal practice is to sign in all visitors in the book before a viewing, but since you are escorting them, Tom, I assume you will be happy to sign in on their behalf?' George said.

George could be very perceptive at times. It was unusual to have non-family members view a body, but Tom knew that George trusted his judgement.

'Yes, that would be a good idea,' said Tom.

George handed him a clipboard and once the paperwork was complete, he moved over to the deceased and gently folded the sheet down to reveal the dead woman's face.

She was young.

She was still glowing.

'Have you completed the autopsy?' Tom asked.

'Yes, just waiting on toxicology to come back; that will take a few weeks.'

Bruce was staring at her, so was Renee. Andy just looked sad.

'Any findings so far?' asked Tom.

George raised his eyebrows and looked towards the three standing beside the gurney.

'It's okay — they are cleared for this. They are helping me with the investigation. I'd rather you didn't mention that to anybody else, though.'

'No problem. You know your business better than I do,' said George.

'I think this one is going to end up in your unexplained basket — along with the three dead mechanics,' he said flipping over a page on the clipboard he held. 'I am one hundred percent sure of the cause of death — catastrophic heart failure.'

Bruce walked over to her and bent down to examine her face and hair.

'What caused it in a woman this young? No idea yet,' George continued. 'Her entire heart exploded inside her chest.'

'Exploded?' Bruce jolted upright again.

'Yep. Never seen anything like it. Pieces of it acted like shrapnel and tore her other organs to pieces in the process.'

'How is that even possible?' asked Tom amazed.

Andy and Renee were staring at George with looks of disbelief.

'Well, I have one theory — but this is pure speculation, mind you. I think her heart was frozen solid first and then it exploded, so the frozen pieces acted like knives.'

Renee had gone white and Tom wondered for a moment if she was going to faint. Andy seemed to be thinking the same thing as he moved a little closer to her.

'Are there any signs that the rest of her was frozen?' asked Tom.

'Nope. I can't even be sure that the heart was frozen — it is so badly damaged. But to find a piece of heart buried like a bullet deep inside a lung? With a matching entry wound? I have no idea how that could happen unless the heart was frozen at the time. But then, that doesn't add up either, because the blast was contained inside her — her whole torso should have exploded if that was the case,' said George. 'And how you could make a heart explode at all — well that's beyond me.'

'Does she have any tattoos or strange markings?' Tom asked.

'A small rose tattoo on her arm, pretty standard fare these days. Nothing else remarkable. There are no other injuries, no bruising, and no signs of sexual assault. Nothing, except of course that her heart became a shrapnel bomb.'

Tom looked at the dead woman's face again. It never got any easier to see young people dead. You learnt how to hide the outward expression of your feelings, but they were still there, lying in wait, ready to wake you up in the middle of the night. He turned to the three observers.

'Is there anything else you want to see before we go?' he asked them.

'Nope, I've seen enough,' said Andy in a voice that sounded like he was coming up for air.

Bruce and Renee shook their heads, they both looked shocked.

'Thanks George,' Tom said. He guided the three of them back to the car park.

'Back to Andy's now,' said Bruce. 'Not a word until we get there. You're coming too,' he said looking at Tom.

There was no arguing with a face like that.

'Tea?' asked Andy as they entered the old kitchen.

'I need something stronger, Andy,' said Bruce.

'Me too,' said Renee.

'That makes three,' said Tom.

Andy played host and got them all settled with scotch whiskey.

'What did you see?' Tom asked Bruce.

'What you did. Yellow glow fit to light up a town,' said Bruce.

'What?' said Andy. 'You saw it too?'

'Yes. I take it you didn't?' said Bruce.

'No.'

'What about you Renee?' Bruce asked.

'Yes. A very yellow glow,' said Renee.

'And you could still see it, Tom?' Bruce asked.

'Yes. Same as before.'

'Now that is strange,' said Andy. 'If it was Renee's healing that made you able to see it, then I should have been able to see it too.'

'So being healed by a faerie isn't enough,' said Bruce, 'Something else is happening here.'

'What did it look like?' Andy asked Bruce.

'Like a faerie with their glow on full blast. A yellow faerie. But she wasn't a faerie, Andy. She didn't smell like one, but I could smell faerie in her hair. She has been near one recently.'

Tom didn't even bother to ask how Bruce could smell faerie; it seemed like every day there was a new revelation.

'Do you think a faerie killed her?' Tom asked.

'Certain of it. And I would be so bold as to guess which one too.'

'Clio,' said Andy.

'Would bet my life on it,' said Bruce.

'Who is Clio?'

'The queen of the Australian faerie colony,' said Andy. 'If it was her, you have no hope of making an arrest or stopping her for that matter. You are going to have to leave this one to us.'

Tom leaned back in his chair and looked them over. Only a fool would judge them by their outward appearance. Two old men, pushing eighty would be Tom's guess, but as switched on and sprightly as men of fifty (the effect of being touched by faeries no doubt) and a nondescript woman who was actually a fae creature who could change her appearance at will and bring people back from the edge of death.

They were right, of course, this copper was no match for them when it came to a battle with the fae.

'I suspect you're right.'

Andy looked surprised. Perhaps he was expecting an arm-wrestling match, thought Tom.

'I will pass on anything I can that might help, but faerie murderers are outside my experience, knowledge and jurisdiction. I have to concentrate on cases that I have a snowflake's chance in hell of solving. Like finding Bill's den. I don't suppose you have any word on the identity of the thief?'

'As a matter of fact, we do,' said Bruce, handing him the note he had shown Andy earlier. 'A friend of a friend gave me a tip and I saw him turn up at this apartment at about 3 AM with my own eyes.'

'Awesome!' said Tom, reading the note.

'What will happen to the girl's body?' Renee asked. She had been subdued since they returned from the morgue.

'Once the autopsy report is finalised, the coroner will decide whether or not her body can be released to her parents before the inquest. I am guessing the inquest, when it finally happens, will return an open finding. I think Rebecca Cole's inquest will end up the same way.'

Renee looked at him and nodded in agreement.

'Would you two mind if I had a word with Renee, alone?' asked Tom.

Andy's face instantly changed to a protective parent expression and he turned to face Renee.

'It's okay Andy, there are a few questions I would like to ask Tom, too.' She looked at Tom quickly and then away again. Nervous? he thought.

'You're sure?' asked Andy.

'Yes, I'm sure. Why don't you two go down to the pub and I'll meet you there in a while?'

'Come on Andy,' said Bruce, nudging Andy's arm, 'I owe you a beer.'

Andy didn't appear very happy, but he got up and followed Bruce.

'You know what to do if you need me?' he asked as he reached the kitchen door.

'Yes, Andy, but I'll be fine.'

He harrumphed one last time and left the room. A moment later they heard the front door close.

'You really are Rebecca Cole, aren't you?' asked Tom.

'I was, yes,' she said. She allowed her body to assume its natural fairy shape. 'I am Renee now.'

Apart from her wings and her eyes, she was the image of Rebecca Cole. She was tall and slender with long auburn hair. She was very beautiful. Her eyes were hypnotic and he was worried that he was staring. He decided it was safer to look at her wings.

'But you weren't always a faerie, were you?'

'No. I don't know how that happened. No one else seems to know either. As far as I can tell this has never happened before.'

'You don't think Clio was involved somehow, do you?'

'I don't think so. She thinks that I came across from the old country. She doesn't know that I only became a fairy recently.'

'You have met her?'

'Yes, and once was definitely enough. She wants to start a war on humanity. She tried to recruit me.'

'You aren't looking for a war then?'

'When has war ever solved anything?'

'Never... Glad to hear you feel the same way,' he paused for a moment and rested his chin in his hand. He let his eyes meet hers and as gently as he could, he said: 'I need to know how you died, Rebecca. It might prevent it from happening again.'

'Yes... I understand,' she said. She took a deep breath and looked down at the floor.

'I didn't remember at first. I woke up as a fairy in a pool of blood. I didn't know who I was, or where I was; I just was. Weeks later, it all came back to me in a rush.'

He nodded, encouraging her to go on.

'The day I died, I had been waiting for my husband, Philip, at a cafe. We were meeting to try and finalise our separation. He was late. Then I started to feel really sick and I wondered if everything was okay with the baby.' She glanced up to meet his eyes. 'A man, a stranger, offered to help me. I had a bad feeling about him and I tried to say no, but I couldn't speak, I felt like I was going to pass out.'

He listened quietly, not wanting to interrupt her.

She looked away again.

'I couldn't stop him, he got an arm around me and pulled me out of my chair. I could hardly walk, he sort of half walked and half dragged me down the street. I couldn't do anything.

'Then I remember being in a car and my foot was twisted and wedged; it was hurting. And then I woke up again and the floor was really cold underneath me and then...'

She gasped, her eyes enlarging; she was distressed. Now was the time to interrupt.

'Did you know the man?' he said quietly.

She turned to look at him, her eyes scanning his face. Her breathing slowed.

'No. There were three of them and I didn't know any of them. I had never seen them before.

'Why?' she said. 'Why would anyone do this to someone? How could anyone do this — just for money? What sort of monster kills a woman for her baby?'

'They didn't mean to kill you,' Tom said gently.

'What...'

'They messed up. The doctor who was going to sew you up afterwards got cold feet and didn't show. They were going to take you as well.'

'Oh my god...' he heard her sharp intake of breath as her hand moved to cover her mouth.

'Some of the papers we found...' he said.

Renee put her face in her hands.

'...they were planning to take you to the den once they had the baby.'

She looked up at him again. There were tears streaming silently down her face.

'We have to find it; we have to free the others,' she said.

'Yes,' he said.

'Do you think the thief will lead you there?'

'I hope so, but if he doesn't I may need to ask for your help again.'

She nodded.

'The men from the garage...' he said.

She chewed her lip.

'...was it you?' he asked.

'I didn't mean to. I didn't know I was capable of that! I was so angry and it just came out of me; a huge blast of flame! When I saw what I had done...'

'Can all faeries do that?'

'No, thank god! And I won't be doing it ever again either — I can control it now. Andy showed me how.'

'How does Andy know...?'

'You would have to ask Andy that.' It was said politely but firmly.

He nodded, he couldn't blame her for being loyal to Andy.

'How did you end up here?' Tom asked glancing at the old kitchen.

'Andy found me hiding in a shed. I was a bit of a mess. He brought me here and calmed me down. He has been good to me. More than I deserve.'

'You didn't deserve any of this Renee.'

She nodded, calm again, but she didn't look convinced.

'How is Philip?' she asked

That question took him by surprise. And was that a tinge of jealousy?

'He's been better, I suppose you would say. He's coping a bit better now than he was.'

She nodded.

'Why do you do this?' she asked. 'Why do you spend your life cleaning up after the scum of the earth?'

'Someone has to do it. Imagine if all that scum was left to fester.'

'But you put your life on the line, every day, to try and save people you don't even know.'

'Well, why did you do it?'

'When I saved you? … I suppose it was my way of getting revenge on Bill for my son. I wanted him to be caught and I didn't want him to hurt anyone else. Especially not you,' he thought she might have blushed then, but it was hard to tell in the dim light of the kitchen.

'I suppose I'm the same,' he said. When I was ten, both my parents died in a house fire. I didn't find out until years later that the fire was deliberately lit.'

'They were murdered?' Renee asked, horrified.

'Yes.'

'Did you find out who did it?'

'Not yet. My grandmother wanted me to drop it. I think she was afraid that I might find something that I wouldn't like. Out of respect for her, I didn't pursue it. I didn't want to upset her. But she died last year, so nothing I find is going to hurt her any more. I suppose I always knew that I was going to chase it up when she was gone and that's why I joined the force, not just to help others but to find out as much as I can about my own family too.'

'But surely they won't let you investigate it yourself?'

'Officially, no. But they might let me look over the case files and if I find something to help kick-start the case, they might agree to let the cold case team take it on. I have already requested the inquest papers from the court archive, I don't need special permission to view those.'

'Are you sure you want to know?'

'Yes. Absolutely no doubt about it.'

The stars were twinkling brightly in the clear night sky by the time she walked Tom out to the front verandah.

'I said thank you before, but it doesn't really cut it. I wouldn't be here if you hadn't turned up. If you need help, if there is anything I can do, at any time…'

'No. You aren't in my debt. I did it because I wanted to; because it was the right thing to do. Pass it forward. Try to find those poor people trapped in Bill's den.'

'I will.'

His eyes really were magnetic. She had to keep reminding herself to look away. What would he think of her? God! She was acting like a smitten schoolgirl.

He made his way down the path to his car and she waved as he pulled away from the curve.

She watched him drive away and then she pulled the front door closed behind her and made her way down the front path. The night was cool but not cold. The fresh air and the walk would do her good.

Technically she was still a married woman. Although, technically, she was also dead. She wasn't sure which was trumps.

Tom was attractive, there was no doubt about that, but she hardly knew him, and she had no idea what he thought of her. She had jumped into a relationship with Philip before she got to know him properly and it had ended in disaster. She was not going to do that again. Besides, she would be moving away from Sydney soon — it just wouldn't work.

When she pulled herself out of her musings she realised she had just walked past the front door of the pub and she had to backtrack a bit. She hoped that Andy and Bruce hadn't seen her. She felt like a bit of a dill.

They were at their usual table and had a glass of wine waiting for her. Unfortunately, they had both seen her gaffe and took delight in ribbing her about overshooting the entrance, suggesting that perhaps she shouldn't have a drink tonight after all.

It was well after ten by the time Renee and Andy started the walk back to their humble terrace house. Bruce had already called it a night as he had things he wanted to do in the morning.

They were not even halfway home when the call reached them. A low rumbling, murmuring through their consciousness.

'It's Old Pepper,' said Andy, stopping suddenly.

'Do you think Gaia is back?'

'That would be my guess. Let's go see.'

Renee sent a small tremor through the earth, back towards the old peppercorn tree — *On our way* — in tree-speak.

The street was dark and there was no one about. Renee held a hand out to Andy and as soon as he took hold, she shrank him to the size of a beetle and placed him in the small satchel she carried over her shoulder. It was clipped to her belt to hold it steady when she flew. She had designed and made the bag herself. On one side there was a small plastic panel and behind it, inside the bag, was a pocket made of stiff fabric. This little room held a fabric sling just the right size for a miniature Andy to sit in, with a tiny safety harness that was stitched to the lining. Now he could fly with her in safety and comfort. She shrank to travel size and flew towards the call.

They passed the overgrown park and gave the dark Moreton Bay Fig tree a wide berth. Neither of them were inclined to go close to Old Kraken. Nancy had been afraid of him too and had warned Andy to stay well away from him. While most of the fairy trees were old and friendly, Kraken was a monster. Before she became a fairy, when she was still a young child, she had made the mistake of climbing into his branches to escape her sister. Her hands had stuck to him and she had heard his evil laugh. If she hadn't fallen to the ground, she was sure that Kraken would have absorbed her — drawn her into himself. She shuddered at the thought.

Old Pepper was another sort of tree entirely. She was a knobbly old peppercorn tree who liked to speak her mind and had a wicked sense of humour. Inside her grizzled exterior, she held a fairy doorway that led to Old Blue, a magnificently tall Blue Gum who lived deep in the forests of the Blue Mountains to the north west of Sydney. Old Blue was an old friend of Andy's and since he was only a couple of kilometres from Clio's compound he was an excellent staging point for their secret dealings with Gaia.

It took less than ten minutes to fly to Old Pepper; much faster than walking.

The old tree stood silently in the grounds of the Sydney botanical gardens. There were flying foxes and possums scrabbling about in the trees nearby, but they gave Old Pepper a wide berth. She had told Renee once that she had frightened them off because she did not like the feel of their claws on her bark (or their excrement for that matter).

Renee landed on a thick branch.

'There you are,' the old tree said. 'I've been calling you for ages.' The voice travelled through the wood at Renee's feet and straight into her mind.

'Sorry Old Pepper, we couldn't hear you until we got out in the open, we were chatting to Bruce at the pub. There are strange things going on,' she replied, sending the words back through the wood without opening her lips.

'Yes, very strange, and Gaia is here to tell you more. Come in! Come in!'

Renee walked along the branch to a knothole in the trunk of the old tree. Inside was a warm, dimly lit chamber and Renee dropped down to the floor. Gaia was already seated on a wooden ledge.

Renee took Andy out of her bag and increased his size to match theirs.

'Good to see you again,' Renee said as she walked over to Gaia and sat down next to her.

'I wish it was in better circumstances,' Gaia replied.

'What's wrong?' Andy asked, 'Is Clio causing trouble?'

'Not yet, but I think she will soon. She is up to something, but I don't know what. She is not confiding in me at the moment and that worries me.'

'Do you think she suspects you?'

'I'm not sure. She is acting very strangely. In the last few months, she has been travelling all over the country, even as far as Perth. She makes me escort her and always takes a single faerie with us, then she leaves that faerie behind when we leave. A couple of times I have had the opportunity to ask them what Clio wants them to do, but the answer is always the same — they don't know, Clio will tell them when the time is right. I think she must be installing faerie spies all over the country but, if she is, she is not choosing her spies very well.'

'What do you mean?' asked Andy.

'Well, to put it bluntly, she seems to be choosing the faeries with the weakest minds. I would think they would all be destined to fail and, potentially, even expose faeries to the human world. These faeries should not be out in the wider world at all, let alone out by themselves.'

'Do you think it is because they will obey her blindly?' asked Renee.

'Possibly. But even blind allegiance isn't going to save them. I just don't see what benefit they could be. She is planning a trip to Darwin soon. I have tried to ask her about her plans, but she always tells me the same thing — all in good time.'

'Well, she might not be telling you much, but the fact that she takes you with her when she is obviously up to something, makes me think she still trusts you. Up to a point anyway,' said Renee.

'Yes, I suppose you are right. Unless, of course, it is a trap.'

'Who knows why she does anything. That faerie is crazy,' said Andy in disgust.

'If she finds out that Andy is still alive, that you didn't kill him, you will have to run. Where will you go?' asked Renee.

'To the rebels. They will keep me safe. I have been feeding them information to help them plot her overthrow. And Clio still hasn't given up on you yet, Renee. She is still expecting you to return to the compound.'

'Seriously! She thinks that killing Andy would make me want to join her?'

'I told you she was crazy,' said Andy.

'She is half expecting you to turn up and try to kill her, I think. She wants action and if you did attack her she would have a story to twist to her advantage. I am sure she would paint you as a friend of humans and try to get everyone to follow her on a crusade against humanity.'

Renee tried to imagine what a fairy war would look like but, never having been involved in a war of any kind before, she struggled. Andy and Gaia had no such problems.

'When did you say she was going to Darwin?' asked Andy.

'In a couple of weeks. She is busy deciding which faerie she will take with us.'

'That could be the perfect time for us to act, Renee. To get Lucy,' Andy said.

Renee pondered this.

'Lucy? Who is Lucy?' asked Gaia.

'My daughter. Clio took her from me a long time ago.'

'Lucy of the kitchen? The cornucopia faerie?'

'You do know her! Thank god! Is she alright?' Andy asked.

'If it is her, she is alive and healthy, but she is not treated very well. She is a kitchen slave.'

'And a cornucopia fairy does what exactly…?' Renee asked.

'Food. Created from whatever comes to hand. Old leaves, sticks, bones, anything that was once living matter. She can re-order its structure so it becomes ambrosia, fruit or bread. It is a rare talent and one that makes it much easier to survive in a hostile land,' said Gaia.

'How many cornucopia fairies does Clio have?'

'One… Lucy.'

'Oh.'

'The compound has become dependent on Lucy. Clio refuses to allow raiding parties or trading anymore. All the food we have comes from our garden or from the leaves that the others gather for Lucy to convert to palatable food. Clio won't give her up without a fight.'

'How many people is Lucy feeding? She must be draining her powers dry every day!' said Andy.

'Clio only allows her chosen ones to dine in the great hall. But even that gives Lucy very little time or energy for anything else.'

'Are you one of the few?' Renee asked, worried.

'Yes. But I will not stop you from saving Lucy. I can get my own food, my own way. But it might turn a lot of the faeries against you if you take Lucy. Food will be scarce.'

'Do you think that it might inspire a rebellion against Clio?'

'Perhaps... I will have to think about it. If you are going to rescue Lucy, you will need to plan carefully, she is well guarded. Give me some time to scout out the kitchens and study her routines and we might be able to work something out.'

'There is something else we need to ask you about, too. A woman was killed in Sydney a few days ago, in a backpacker hostel. When I looked at her body, it was glowing like a fairy — but she was not a fairy and Andy couldn't see the glow.'

'A backpacker hostel? Where was this place?' Gaia said surprised.

'It was called the Best Rest Backpacker Hostel, right near the centre of the city.'

Gaia looked stunned.

'What did the woman look like?'

'She was young, maybe twenty, with long black hair.'

Gaia relaxed a little.

'And she definitely wasn't a faerie?'

'No.'

'Clio took me to this place a few days ago. She took a faerie named Elga as well and left her there. For a moment I thought the dead woman might have been her. Perhaps Elga killed her? But why, I couldn't guess. If Elga was supposed to be a spy, it looks like she has messed things up already.'

'Do you have any idea why the dead woman might be glowing?'

'No. None. I have never heard of a human glowing before and a dead faerie loses her glow.'

'Yes, that's true — I hadn't thought of that,' said Andy.

'Do you think Clio would have wanted Elga to kill the woman?' asked Renee.

'I don't think so. It would draw attention. Whatever it is that Clio is doing, it isn't finished yet.'

'So, what on earth is Clio up to?' pondered Andy.

An Autopsy and an Inquest

Tom pulled over and left the car on the main street outside a takeaway shop. It was dark and the glaring red and blue neon lights on the "open" sign were reflecting off his white, unmarked police car.

Inside the takeaway, a TV murmured, its sound muffled by the closed door and the grimy glass. Behind the counter, the proprietor flashed back and forth from deep fryer to grill, turning meat patties and deep-frying potato chips. A single customer sat on one of the metal chairs, a newspaper spread before him as he waited for his order; the pre-season AFL match on the TV was ignored by both.

The street was quiet. Tom walked past the takeaway and continued past a row of small businesses closed up for the night. Dew was beginning to form on the cars parked in the street and the air had an autumn chill.

Tom walked slowly and quietly down the street, not wanting to draw attention to himself. He turned a corner and continued towards a block of flats further down the road. He walked past the flats never changing his stride, his eyes scanning left and right.

A little further on, there was a single-story house with a for sale sign in the front yard; its windows were dark and quiet. He turned and walked up the driveway into the empty carport. A low brick wall on one side of the carport provided a place to sit and wait.

From his vantage point, he could see the entire front of the block of flats. It was a concrete structure with large glass windows running down the centre. The harsh fluorescent lights revealed a central staircase servicing three floors. Each floor had two apartments; one on either side of the stairs. There were lights on in the windows of two of the apartments; the rest were in darkness. From where Tom sat, he could see the carport at the front of the building. There were six car spaces, but only two of them contained cars. Each space had a brass numeral attached to the roof above it. Number 6 was one of the empty ones. Tim Crace was not at home.

It was half-past eleven. Based on what Bruce had told him, he decided to wait until half past three to see if the thief would come home tonight. He didn't doubt Bruce's intent, but if Bruce had made a mistake, if this Tim Crace wasn't the man they were looking for, it would be better to work it out now before they started trawling through the man's records.

He sat and waited; his mind revisiting the last few days. The backpacker was going to be another unsolved case, he knew that already. It grated, but there was nothing he could do about it. At least not now.

Bill and his cronies were another matter. The more of them he could lock away the better. Especially if it meant finding the den and releasing the captives. It could be that the business had been shut down already, that the prisoners were already dead or had been moved on to another pimp. They would not have been released alive.

Was he spending his time searching for a mass grave? If he was, then that was terrible but necessary. He still hoped to find them alive of course and based on the information in Layton's papers, it had been a fair-sized operation. It was unlikely that the Stonefish and Bill were the only ones running the den.

There would have been at least one medical person involved for the births and transplants and probably a full-time gaoler — which couldn't have been Bill — he already had a full-time job and a drug run to look after. Tom guessed there were at least four in the racket, the thief might be one of them, or he might be sub-contracted as needed.

They hadn't had any luck chasing down any of the baby buyers; Layton hadn't been involved in that side of things. At least he wasn't until they decided to attack Rebecca Cole. That in itself was a bit of a mystery. Up until they attacked her, they had only been involved in drugs and snatching runaways; not selling babies. They were complete amateurs with no medical experience (Layton had admitted as much in his notes). Layton had noted how Rebecca died, that the deal had gone sour and that the baby was just a stinking nuisance to them. Their payday had not arrived as expected and they were all pissed off about it. Tom was oddly relieved that the cold callousness of these notes had sickened him; his police work had not turned him into an unfeeling machine yet.

Tom felt like his head was going to explode. Trying to deal with faeries, dead backpackers and baby dealers, returning from the brink of death and investigating the murder of his parents, he knew he was in danger of burning out. But he couldn't stop. It was like a drug.

Tom sat and breathed in the cool night air to clear his head. He knew that he was placing a lot of hope on this man, Tim Crace, to give him some answers. He would need to do some research and find a pressure point if he was going to get anything out of the thief anytime soon.

It was almost midnight when he heard a motorbike approach. It drove into carport number 6 and the rider parked and kicked the stand down. Tom left his perch and headed over to the building entrance, walking straight past the carports and glancing at the rider in passing. He was amused to see the man wrapping a chain through the wheel of his bike and fitting an anti-theft device to the handlebars.

Tom slowed down his pace a little to make sure he wouldn't outstrip the rider too much. When he reached the front door, he heard footsteps behind him; by the time he was through the door and up the first flight of stairs, he heard the outer door open again. When he reached the landing of the third floor Tom pulled an old envelope out of his pocket and knocked on the door of number 5. The sound reverberated in the stairwell. He already knew that no one was home.

Tom turned to watch the rider climb the last few stairs. He had taken his helmet off and in the bright lights of the stairwell, Tom could see him clearly. The rider looked at Tom with wary eyes.

'You don't know where he is, do you?' Tom said nodding toward number 5. 'I have a message for him.' Tom fiddled with the envelope in his hands.

'Nah. I can give it to him if you like,' he said. The man looked tense; ready for a confrontation.

'No thanks, I owe him money. I'll come back later.'

'Suit yourself,' the rider said and shrugged, but Tom noticed that the man kept his back to the door. As Tom descended the stairs he caught the man's reflection in the stairwell windows; he was still standing outside his apartment watching Tom descend. It was only after Tom had left the top flight of stairs and started down the next that he heard the door to the apartment close above him.

Bingo.

Constables Peale and Gardiner were already at their desks when Tom arrived the next morning. It had been after 1 AM by the time he got home from casing Tim Crace's flat and he hadn't slept well.

'You look like shit,' Peale said.

'I may look like shit but I smell like a rose. I have the home address of our mystery thief and hopefully a legitimate name to go with it.'

He handed the details to Peale.

'Cracker? Seriously?'

'Oh yes, and a very dodgy nickname. I want you to do a full search on the address, find out the registered phone number for it and get an approval to obtain a copy of his phone records. Then see what you can find against his name and the nickname.'

'On it.'

'Gardiner, we still haven't received anything from the gaol about Bill, have we?'

'No Sir,' she said, following him into his office.

'Right, I want you to get on to that, I want a list of all his phone calls in and out and all of his visitors. If the guy on the desk is being obstructive, go higher. If you don't get anywhere, I will have a chat with the Chief Inspector and get him to kick some arse over there,' he collapsed into his chair. 'Once Peale has the phone records for Crace, do a compare with Bill's home phone, mobile and the gaol. If we have proof that they have been in contact, we might be able to get approval for a phone tap on Mr Crace.'

'No problem,' she said and went off to get started.

The three of them made a good team, he thought to himself as she left the room. Hopefully, the powers that be would let him keep the two constables under his wing after this case was closed. It was good experience for them and they both seemed to be mentally suited to the work and the odd hours. It would be a shame for them to end up back on the beat.

He needed coffee, but it would have to wait. He scanned his emails and then opened the file on the backpacker death. Administratively, there was nothing he could do about it until all the medical findings were returned. Over the last couple of days, the team, with help from some beat cops had interviewed every witness, friend and acquaintance of the dead girl that they could find. They had turned up nothing. At the moment, the medical findings were pointing to some kind of bizarre health condition, not murder. Once all the forensic tests came back the coroner would review the case and try to determine the cause of death. If there was a murder case to answer, his team would be tasked with the investigation. He both hoped and suspected that the findings would be inconclusive. If they were, the case would be put on the back burner until some new evidence came to light. Which would probably never happen. How can you pin down a murderous faerie when the world doesn't believe they exist?

It was times like this that he doubted his own sanity. He had seen her, he had spoken to her, but tonight, in spite of that, he knew that he would go home and watch the faerie footage again and try to find holes in it. Then he would give up and admit that, yes, he did believe in faeries and if that meant that he was insane, then so be it.

The knock at the door startled him out of his thoughts.

'Delivery,' Peale said passing him a buff coloured envelope.

'Ta.' Tom turned it over to check the sender's address.

N.S.W. court archive.

Peale was already out the door.

Now that he held the package in his hands, he wasn't sure that this was what he wanted. He had felt so sure yesterday when he had spoken to Renee about his parents, but now, holding a physical weight in his hands, everything seemed different.

He put the package to one side and tried to get on with the day's work.

For the rest of the day, the package sat in the corner of his eye like an annoying dust mote.

By five o'clock Tom was exhausted. The late night, poor sleep and the nagging worry of that package on his desk had drained him. He said goodnight to his team went home.

Dinner was cooked, served and eaten, accompanied by a glass of wine. The dishes were washed, dried and put away. He was avoiding the issue, he knew that. He had looked through hundreds of autopsy reports and coroner's reports; he knew the sort of information he would find inside.

Finally, he refilled his glass and sat down on the couch.

Get it over with.

He ripped open the parcel and tipped the contents out. A wad of papers fastened by a bull-dog clip slipped out of the envelope, landing on the table with a dull thunk. There were several photocopied documents clipped together and he unfastened them and sorted through them. The first was the coroner's report. A second was the sworn statements of the police. A third held the transcribed testimony of the witnesses. A fourth was the summary of the autopsy of Gregory Thomas Hayes.

That was it. He flicked quickly through each document to make sure that another set of papers had not been caught inside them. Nothing.

There was no autopsy report for his mother.

First, he read the witness statements.

'I was asleep in my bed when I heard this god-almighty scream. Threw me awake so fast my head was dizzy. The fire was lighting up my bedroom. I was out in a shot and got my hose going. Mrs Jones from across the street was already there with their hose and her hubby was trying to break down the front door. He couldn't get in, but that was probably a good thing; the fire was too intense. Not too much later the firemen came and got the fire under control, although at one point I thought my house was going to go up too because they aimed their hoses at one side of the fire and a huge tower of golden sparks flew straight up into the air. Thankfully, they didn't come down again, they just drifted off into the night. It would have been beautiful if it wasn't so awful.'
Peter Craig, aged 63

'I was just coming home from the night shift when I saw these strange little lights drift out of the neighbour's house. They were pink and red. I think now that they must have been embers, but at the time I didn't know what they were. I stopped and stood in the driveway and watched them drift away, and then I heard the flames. I ran inside as fast as I could and called triple zero and woke the missus. She got the hose going and I went over and tried to get inside the house. All I could think of was their little boy, Tom. Then we heard the scream, and I just flipped out and started trying to shoulder charge the door but it was no use; I ended up dislocating my shoulder...' Les Jones, aged 45

'... Les woke me up and I don't know what came over me, it was like I was on auto-pilot. I didn't even care that I was still in my nightie, I grabbed the hose and tried to get to little Tommy's window, but the whole house was going up. I will never forget when the fireman brought the poor little boy out, I thought to myself — he is a goner. Better that he dies now than suffers for months in the hospital; there is no way he is going to survive this — his whole face was just melted!' Mary Jones, aged 42

The police statements covered much the same territory with the addition of information about the family. The fire had started in the middle of the night on a quiet suburban street. It was only by chance that Mr Jones had been on his way home from his night shift and had seen the strange red and pink lights. The injured boy and the body of his father had been recovered from the blaze, but there had been no other remains found. The mother was missing.

She had been seen at the house earlier in the day and none of her neighbours were aware of any travel plans. She had no known friends or family outside her immediate family and her neighbours. No trace of her had been found since. The police had not been able to establish her full name or her background. The pair were not married and no one seemed to know the woman's full name. The boy's paternal grandparents had only met her once and it had not gone well. All anyone knew was that she was known as Willow and for some strange reason, her son was known as Tom Willow. The locals believed her to be a hippy and thought her strange but likable. The boy was well known and liked in the small community, as was his father, Gregory Hayes, a local teacher.

The coroner had summed up various local theories and discredited them one by one as implausible or unsubstantiated. There was speculation that the young boy had been playing with fireworks in his room but the physical evidence for that was lacking. The fire had been started in the ceiling and the crawl space at the same time, indicating not only that it was deliberate but that more than one person had been involved. The one thing that the coroner kept coming back to was the missing mother. It was unclear if she had been abducted and her family attacked or if she had played a role in the burning of the house. The coroner noted for the record that the woman known as Willow may know more about the case if she was still alive and marked her down as a person of interest. The finding was left open.

Now he knew why his grandmother had not wanted him to look into the death of his parents. She had thought that his mother, Willow, was responsible.

Thinking back, she had always tried to discourage him from talking about his mother and father when he was a boy, especially in front of his grandfather. His grandfather had no time for weeping, the mere mention of Tom's parents was enough to send his grandfather into a roiling rage.

And that was why they had changed his name to Tom Hayes.

He wished he had known all this sooner.

He had hardly known his grandparents when he had gone to live with them. His father had only taken him to visit them a couple of times. Tom did not realise, until he was much older, that his grandparents had never liked his mother. She didn't fit their mould.

The one thing he could remember, above all else, from the time before the fire, was how happy he had been with his mother and father and how he had never doubted their love for one another or for himself. Whatever it was that had happened, he knew in his heart that his mother, Willow, had not been responsible.

But was she still alive?

A Spoon and a Fork

Johnny sat next to the old woman's bed and studied her face. It was deeply lined; ravaged by years of hard living on the streets. Ryan had once told him that she had been close to liver failure when he had pulled her out of the gutter. She had been sedated for weeks while they weaned her off the booze and got her back to reasonable health.

She had been a random drunk, living rough on the streets. A means to an end.

Now he wasn't so sure.

He pulled a vial from his jacket and moved closer to the bed. The old woman was snoring loudly, her mouth slack. He watched in revulsion as a single strand of drool slid from her gaping mouth and dropped onto the bedsheets. Her breath was like a sewer.

He removed the long-handled swab from the vial and slid it into her open mouth, scrapping it against the inside of her cheek. She did not stir. He slipped the sample back into the vial and closed it securely. He was seated again with the vial safely back in his pocket when Ryan appeared.

He nodded a greeting and Ryan dropped into the seat next to him. Johnny glanced over at the door; it was all quiet.

'Where exactly did you find Mrs Black again?' he asked.

'She was sleeping under a bridge near Babayaga's lot. Out like a light; chronic alcoholic. She didn't come without a fight, we had to keep her sedated until she was weaned off the booze.'

'Is she still sedated now?'

'No. We don't need to anymore, she's settled down. She's taken a fancy to me, and Bill. She seems happy to stay put now. She has severe dementia, so no worries about her saying anything, everyone knows she spouts absolute rubbish.'

Johnny nodded; gazing at her lost in thought.

'I have rounds to do, so I will catch you later,' said Ryan.

'Yep,' Johnny said, his eyes never leaving the old woman's face.

Ten minutes later he shook himself back to the present.

He pulled his mobile phone out of his pocket and speed-dialed a number.

'I need you to come and meet me. Usual place.'

He ended the call and left the building.

Johnny parked his car in the supermarket carpark and waited. He watched the mothers struggling with their prams and trolleys and screaming children.

Who the fuck would want that? he thought to himself.

The front passenger door opened and a dark-haired man slouched into the passenger seat.

Johnny took two vials from the glove box and handed them over to him.

'I need you to get a DNA analysis done on these. I want to know if there is any relationship between them.'

'Give me two weeks.'

'You've got one.'

The man tucked the vials into his coat pocket and climbed out of the car.

Tom closed the door behind him and exhaled. He felt like he had been holding his breath for an eternity, but he had been in the Chief Inspector's office for ten minutes at most. Once he was sure that he wasn't shaking, he walked down the hallway to the elevator. In his hand, he held a signed "Permission to enquire" form.

Two days ago, Tom had surprised the Chief Inspector by requesting access to the police files on the deaths of his parents. The Chief Inspector had not been aware of the case and since he was no fool, he had been unwilling to give his permission straight away without knowing all the details. He didn't want any scandals on his watch.

Today, he had called Tom into his office to inform him that he could see no reason why Tom shouldn't see the files; Tom was, after all, a child at the time and it was pretty clear that he could not have been directly involved in what happened.

Tom had been given clear warnings and boundaries. He had permission to speak to any of the investigating officers who had worked on the case but was not to interview anyone outside the police force. If he found anything of interest, he was to present his finding to the cold case team. Under no circumstances was he to progress the case on his own; the risk of contaminating evidence or prejudicing a court case was too great. His would be a research and quality assurance role only.

Well, that suited him fine. He knew the rules and he would play by them. For now.

He made his way down to the cold case team to inform them of his interest and request copies of the original files. There was no turning back now.

Wattle Ridge, population ten thousand, was a slightly scruffy country town on the edge of a large national park and a forestry plantation. Timber, dairy and sheep farming were the main sources of income for the mid-sized town. The people and the buildings had a relaxed, settled feel to them as if they had been draped onto the land like a cosy blanket.

Renee liked the place at once, and even Andy, who had been a Sydneysider for decades, said that he thought he could get used to it.

Bruce took them on a guided tour of the town and the houses that were up for sale. The real estate agent was kind enough to show them through three places even though they did not have an appointment. By lunchtime, they were seated in the pub having a counter lunch deciding on which house they would choose. Somehow all three had agreed without any words exchanged, that this town would be their new home. Now they just needed to sort out the details.

The house closest to the pub won out in the end, Andy not willing to forgo his evening saunter for a beverage, even though the house would need a little work. Andy and Bruce were both keen to tackle the renovations as both were experienced home handymen.

By the late afternoon, a deposit had been paid and the purchase was underway. Being a small town and quite a distance from any of the major cities, the price of the house was much lower than similar properties in Sydney. The sale of Andy's place and the money taken from various drug dealers over the years would more than cover the purchase and the renovations. There was nothing to prevent them moving in once the sale was finalised.

Now they just had to get Lucy back.

Tom sat on the couch in his lounge room.

Another glass of wine, another packet of papers he didn't want to open. For the second time in a week, he sat staring at a buff coloured envelope. It was thick and it was heavy.

He drained his glass and tore the envelope open.

There were two files inside; the top-most file had a note clipped to it:

Tom,

you will notice that I have not made copies of the photos in packet C45. It contained the autopsy photos of your dad. There is nothing in the photos that is not already detailed in the autopsy report. If you must see them, call me.

Janice.

He could have kissed her.

It took him two hours to read through the first file. It was a slightly more detailed version of the information that had been presented to the coroner. There wasn't anything in it of any importance that he didn't already know.

He took a break and stretched his legs. He retrieved the bottle of wine from the kitchen bench and refilled his glass.

The second file was smaller. He flicked to the oldest papers and began to read.

After the inquest had returned its findings, further attempts had been made by the police to track down Willow. She had been listed as a missing person and a reward offered for information about her whereabouts. One enterprising police officer had gone on a trek to all the known hippie communes in the area asked for help. He received a mixed response but no information of any value.

There were a couple of calls from the public, but the information turned out to be bogus; nutters and reward seekers. There was absolutely nothing to go on. She had vanished without a trace.

The last two pages were a report about the death of an old homeless man in a park. It had occurred two years after the fire. At first, he thought Janice had accidentally mixed these papers in from another file that she was copying; then he saw the photographs on the second page. Several were of the old man's body and two were of the spoon found in his pocket.

Sleep was impossible. Tom tossed and turned. By 5 AM he had given up and was sitting in his home office at his computer.

The file he had read the previous night had been nagging him.

The report on the death of the old man had been placed in the file about his father's death because of the spoon. Engraved on the back of the spoon were an address, a date and a time. It was his parents' address — the house that had been destroyed by the fire — and it was the date and the time that it had burnt down; killing his father and scarring him.

Why would an old homeless man have a spoon commemorating the death of Tom's father? He could not begin to understand it.

It was an antique spoon, possibly ancient, definitely European. Its handle was made in an intricate filigree pattern. The photos of the old man's body showed that at some point, long before his death, the old man had been branded with it. The scar, pink and puckered, was on the inside of his left forearm in the same position as the scar on Bill's arm. Was Bill branded at the same time as the old man? He compared the photos of the scars and the spoon. He was sure it was the implement that had been used to brand both of them.

Somewhere there was a link between Bill, the death of his parents and the death of this old man. What were the chances of such a link, let alone him (of all people) stumbling upon it? It must be millions or billions to one. Fate? Impossible. But then he had thought that about faeries too at one point...

He scoured the police database for any information on the death of the old man. There wasn't much to see. The body had never been identified. He had been buried in a pauper's grave almost twenty years ago.

Were Bill and the old man both part of the same gang? Was he related to Bill? A DNA test might be in order (if there was anything left to test). DNA testing was in its infancy in Australia at the time the old man died. It was unlikely that any biological material would have been kept. Still, it was worth a look.

There were witnesses to the old man's death who said that the old man had been harassed by a gang of youths before he had his heart attack. The coroner had returned a verdict of misadventure. The single paragraph written by the police and the single sentence recorded by the coroner, reflected the lack of care or concern so often displayed about the death of homeless people.

He wondered which policeman had made the connection between the engraving on the spoon and the death of his father. There was no note to show who had placed the report into the file and nothing to say if they had done any further research.

Tom had been investigating Bill Doyle for months, but he had found very little information about him. There was a registered birth certificate for Bill and then nothing for eighteen years until he obtained a driver's licence. In the years after that bank accounts were obtained and tax returns were filed. He was born in a time of paper records, most of which had never been digitised or added to the police or government computer databases.

Bill had no living relatives. There was no one he could interview to find out about his youth. He would have been a teenager when the old homeless man died in the park. Did they know each other? Was Bill a member of the gang that attacked the old man? If Bill had ever been in a gang, there was no record. He had never been prosecuted for anything; his criminal record had been squeaky clean until now.

But there was something else that was nagging at him.

He had seen this spoon before, or something very similar, quite recently. It was something he had barely noticed as it had not been important at the time. Now, he was picking his brains desperately trying to remember where he had seen it.

He went and put the kettle on and climbed into the shower.

As the warm water ran over him he went through the cases he had been working on recently in his head. Rebecca Cole, Jeff Layton and the other dead mechanics, Babayaga, the backpacker (Amanda Redding). He worked his mind through Rebecca's apartment, then Philip's house trying to recall the contents of their kitchens and display cabinets. No and No. Jeff Layton hadn't been into antiques and the other mechanics had been complete bogans so they were unlikely candidates. Babayaga didn't own anything, so it couldn't have been her and Amanda's room at the backpacker hostel had been devoid of cutlery and antique finery.

He stepped out of the shower and wrapped a towel around his waist. He dripped his way into the kitchen and poured himself a coffee.

Photos. He would go through all the evidence photos for all these cases. He took his coffee back to his computer and opened up the photos for the Rebecca Cole case. Nothing.

A sudden thought occurred to him. Bill had murdered Babayaga, the homeless woman who had helped Tom with information many times in the past. That was a fact. And now Bill was linked to another homeless person by his scar. Did Babayaga have a scar too? He had not looked at the autopsy photos closely. It was hard to see those kinds of photos when it was someone you cared about.

He pulled up her file and read through the description of the injuries and markings found on Babayaga's body. Apart from the wounds that had killed her, there was nothing. Not... a... thing. She was the most unblemished person he had ever seen, especially given her age and lifestyle. He flicked through the remaining evidence photos but stopped when he saw a photo of her nest. Sitting among the blankets, partly hidden, was an enamel mug and bowl. And a fork. A fork with a filigree handle. He flicked through the other documents looking for a description and analysis of the fork. Nothing. Had it been kept as evidence? God, he hoped so.

He dressed quickly and drove to the office.

Tom looked at his watch; it was seven thirty in the morning. He entered the building but didn't bother going to his desk; he went straight down to forensics in the basement.

'Oh, hello. Suffering from insomnia, are we?' George said looking up from the plaster cast he was working on.

'Do you still have all the evidence from Babayaga's murder here?'

'Yep. Haven't finished cataloguing it yet. Unfortunately, as far as the current bureaucracy is concerned, our dear dead homeless are way below second priority,' he said with a scowl, 'even someone like Babayaga.'

Yes. That made Tom angry too.

'Anything, in particular, you're after? Not that she had much.'

'A fork.'

'Righty-o.' George said, unfazed and he disappeared into a storage room off to one side of the workshop. Through the open door, Tom could see row upon row of shelves stacked with brown evidence boxes. There was a large cool room at the back for heat sensitive items. There were no bodies stored here, they were all kept at the morgue. Tom was glad of that, even though he had been a police officer for over ten years, he still was a little bit uncomfortable being around cadavers.

George returned with a large cardboard box and pulled on a pair of gloves, Tom followed suit. George proceeded to remove items sealed in labelled paper evidence bags. An enamel bowl, a baked bean tin, a comb, a swiss army knife, and then the fork.

'Has it been processed yet?' Tom asked, excited.

'Let me check.' George pulled up a file on his computer and scanned through the work record for Babayaga's belongings.

'Print analysis has been done. Some smeared fingerprints and one good print that matched Babayaga. No chemical analysis done yet, it looks pretty clean, so we might not get anything off it. Each of the items has been photographed, but the pictures haven't been uploaded to the computer file yet, so I'll get Samantha to do that this morning.'

'Has there been any analysis on the forks age and origin?'

'No. Unless it was a crucial piece of evidence, we wouldn't go to the expense of having it assayed.' George placed both his hands against his temples and closed his eyes, 'I'm getting a premonition here — I'm predicting that you are about to tell me that this is important.'

'You are a genuine clairvoyant,' Tom said, grinning at him.

'I need a reason,' George said, opening his eyes and looking at Tom seriously. 'Gotta justify the expense. And before you ask — a hunch won't cut it.'

'Bill Doyle has a brand on his arm that was made by this fork or one just like it.'

'Okay, we're getting warmer.'

'And there is a dead homeless person, a John Doe, who had the same brand on their wrist. They also had a spoon in their pocket with the same filigree handle as this fork. The analysis of the spoon said it was of European origin and that it was extremely old.'

'So, you want to see if there is a connection between the two.'

'Yep.'

'My memory is pretty good, but I don't remember this other case. Was it local?'

'Yes, but it happened twenty years ago. When Bill was a teenager.'

'And it was murder?'

'Witnesses said the old man had been assaulted by a group of teenagers, but the inquest took less than ten minutes to return a finding of death by misadventure.'

'Why does that not surprise me? Have you obtained the spoon from that case?'

'Not yet. I am going to go and have a look in the evidence archives and see if I can get access to it and any DNA evidence.'

'Alright. Let me know if you have any luck. If you find the spoon, I'll order the assessment of the fork. If not, it's probably not worth the time and money,' George placed the fork back in the evidence box.

Tom went straight over to archive. There was always someone in early over there. He knew that he was stretching the boundaries a little with this one, after all, there was the possibility that the old homeless man was involved in the deaths of his parents. However, for the time being, the link to the case against Bill gave him ample reason to access the old homeless man's records.

The truth was, he wanted to find out as much as he could before he passed his parents' case on to the cold case team. He wanted to make sure that there was enough evidence for them to take the case seriously. If a link was found between Bill and the death of his father Tom would have to be removed from the case against Bill. That would be annoying, but he would rather Bill was put away for good than have the case fall over because of a conflict of interest.

'Hi, Janice.'

'Back already! What can I do for you?'

'I am working on the murder of Babayaga and I have discovered a possible link to a much older case. I need to find out what evidence we have in storage for this case number,' he said passing over a sticky note with the file reference scribbled on it.

'Okay. Let me have a look.' She fired up her computer and quickly found the record.

'Well, no one is assigned to this case at the moment and there is a box reference listed here, but none of the details have been entered in the database. It looks like it was pre-database days so only the bare minimum of information has been entered. Come and we'll check out the paper index cards, they might tell us a bit more.' She led him over to a set of wooden drawers marked with a series of numbers. He was not familiar with their filing system and wondered how anyone could find anything in this lot.

She opened a drawer and rifled through the index cards, finding what she was after within seconds.

'Here we go. The box is in the archive room and it contains one set of very dirty clothes — hat, jacket, shoes etc — one pocket knife, a spoon and a hair sample.'

'A hair sample, seriously? That's awesome.'

'It became policy in the late 80's to collect hair samples from John Does. Proper DNA testing wasn't available to us then, but the science was going gangbusters and some forward-thinking fellow in the forensics team decided to plan for the future. But don't get too excited yet. Just because the cards say it exists, doesn't mean we will be able to find it. There have been a few moves over the years and things get mixed up sometimes.'

The evidence archive was a dusty room filled with boxes upon boxes in all shapes and sizes. Each row of shelves was labelled with more of the code numbers. The box they wanted was right at the top; a shower of dust came down with it as Janice eased it off the shelf and climbed down the ladder. She placed it on the floor and opened the lid.

'Well, since you are interested in this one, it's time it got entered into the evidence database. You can have a quick look now, but you won't be able to take anything away until I have documented it.'

He carried the box out to a large workbench. Janice pulled on a set of gloves and passed a pair to him. She began to lay the items out one by one on the bench. Tom couldn't help but smile when she pulled the spoon out. The plastic bag containing it was beginning to crack with age. She handed it to him and he took it gently in his gloved hands. He turned it over and read the inscription. It was still in good condition, the writing clear, the intricate handle undamaged. He had the photos for now, but he would ask George to have this spoon and Babayaga's fork assessed side by side. He passed it back to her and she placed it into a new paper evidence bag.

'Some of this other stuff will need to be properly repackaged before anyone handles it. We don't use plastic bags for long-term storage anymore, it can cause mould problems. There are tests that George might want to carry out that weren't available the last time this stuff saw the light of day.'

Next Janice pulled out a vial containing several strands of hair.

'Can I have a couple of those for George to analyse now?' Tom asked.

'Is it just the spoon and the hair that you are interested in?'

'For the moment, yes.'

'I'll document them now and send them up to George before I start repacking all the other bits and pieces. He should have them around lunchtime if nothing urgent comes up.'

Gardiner was at work and already on the phone when Tom walked past her desk to his office, she nodded a hello in his direction and he waved in acknowledgement.

He went into his office and sat down at his computer. There was an email from George to let him know the photos of Babayaga's belongings had been added to her computer file, so he opened it up and looked at the fork again.

He wondered what Bill's reaction would be if he showed it to him.

His phone beeped, the signal for an internal call.

'Tom Hayes,' he said.

'Guv, I've got the police liaison officer from Long Bay Gaol on the line. It's about the phone records for Bill Doyle,' it was Gardiner.

'Oh yes. This should be good. Put him through.'

'Connecting you now, Sir,' she said and he heard the line click and reconnect.

'Hello, this is Detective Inspector Tom Hayes.'

'Hello D.I. Hayes, this is Charles Gordon from Police relations at Long Bay Gaol. I understand you have been having some difficulty obtaining the call records for Bill Doyle?'

'That would be a bit of an understatement. He's been in there for almost two months now and we have not received a single notification of any of his calls or visits. I am assuming he hasn't been kept in isolation this entire time?'

'No. No, I am afraid there has been a rather large lapse in protocol in Mr Doyle's case and the security team are trying to get to the bottom of it as we speak. I have been able to recover the recordings of all his phone calls — they were about to be deleted I'm afraid, so that was a close thing — and we are piecing together the visitor log now. Again, the records are in rather shabby condition, I'm afraid. We are investigating whether it is negligence or deliberate obstruction.'

'You think he has a man on the staff?' asked Tom.

'Our screening processes usually preclude that kind of thing, but Bill Doyle appears to be a bit of an unusual criminal, so I'm afraid it is a possibility.

'I have made a copy of the phone recordings. Would you like me to send it over?'

'Actually, I need to have a word with Mr Doyle so I will come over and pick it up in person.'

'Not a problem. I can leave it at the guard desk for you.'

'I'd rather pick it up from you; it might get conveniently lost if it goes to the guard desk.'

'Well, I don't think things are quite that bad, but I see your point.'

Queen Clio took the last slice of nectarine from her plate savouring its juicy sweetness. She rose from her seat and Gaia moved to follow her.

'Not tonight Gaia. I am tired. The rest of our preparations can wait until tomorrow. You can have the rest of the night off.'

Gaia bowed and left the room. A little too eager to go, thought Clio. Perhaps it was wise not to trust Gaia with this secret; she seemed preoccupied of late.

Once Gaia closed the door Clio moved over to the fireplace and stroked the ring on her finger. It flared into brilliant light. She sent a thought-message out into the darkness and then paced the floor impatiently.

A few minutes later a faerie, not much more than a child, appeared at her side and bowed. A pretty thing thought Clio. The woman-child had glittering dark blue wings and eyes. She gazed at Clio in reverential awe.

'Tonight, you shall play your part in the freedom of your people. The task you perform tonight will go down in history and you will be remembered and honoured for all time.'

'Yes, my queen,' the faerie said, an anxious frown appearing on her face. 'I came straight away, as you said, and told no one. My mother will worry if I am gone too long…'

'Never fear, it will be done quickly and she will be none the wiser.'

The girl took comfort at this.

Such a simple girl, thought Clio.

She took the girls hand and together they flew off into the night.

They flew out through the gate-tree and into the forest, undetected by the guards on duty; her concealment spells shielding them both. Secrecy was essential.

Not far from her realm, a river ran through a green valley and they landed in the soft grass at its edge. There were fewer trees here and the stars shone brightly above.

The girl turned suddenly when she heard a strange moaning sound in the long grass to one side of them.

'It's alright, you can go and look if you like,' said Clio, gesturing to the place where the noise had come from.

The girl walked over and looked down into the grass. She froze.

'What…?' she asked.

'A spell as powerful as the one I am about to perform requires energy. He will provide that.'

'He works in the town, at the bakery,' the girl said.

'Not anymore.'

'He is only young; like me…'

'He is a human.'

The girl looked confused.

'Here,' said Clio passing the girl a beautiful porcelain doll. 'As I promised.'

The girl took the doll, but her eyes did not leave those of the boy hidden in the grass.

Clio started chanting strange high-pitched words and the girl turned towards her. At that moment the eyes of the doll glowed a deep, dark blue, the colour of the secret places of the ocean. The girl looked into the eyes of the doll and found that she could not look away, not even when she heard the boy scream behind her.

Sometime later, Clio picked up the doll from the grass. The doll's hair had been reduced to a burnt, straggly mange and the porcelain made strange pinging noises as it cooled. The once clear face was sooty and cracked. The doll glowed.

Clio ordered the earth to part in front of her and she placed the doll into the fissure. She clapped her hands together and the earth reformed as if it had never been disturbed. With a thought she moved a large rock over the burial and dragged her finger across its surface, effortlessly carving an intricate curling symbol.

Clio flew back to her castle alone.

Philip

Gaia had been looking for an excuse to slip away from Clio for over a week, so her early dismissal had come as a welcome surprise. She needed to talk to Andy and Renee; Clio's plans for her trip to Darwin were well underway; it was only a matter of days until they left.

As soon as she closed the door to the grand hall she left the compound and flew straight to Old Blue. When she landed on one of his branches she could sense that he was sleeping so she slipped quietly into the knothole entrance and down onto the floor of the chamber inside. There was a warm glow coming from the doorway through to Old Pepper and she hoped that she would not wake him by passing through its glistening wobbly surface.

She passed through the water-like barrier and emerged into a similar chamber within Old Pepper.

'Oh hello, Missy. Back again already?'

Gaia had noticed that Old Pepper was awake more often these days. All the faerie activity had stimulated her growth and her mind.

'Hi, Old Pepper. Your girth has expanded a little since I last saw you!'

'You cheeky beggar, I bet you say that to all the trees.'

Gaia laughed.

'You need Andy and Renee, I suppose?' Old Pepper asked.

'Yes please.'

Gaia laid her hands on the woody walls of the interior chamber and released a stream of faerie energy into the old tree.

'Ahh… That does wonders for my aching branches,' Old Pepper sighed.

Gaia heard the low thrum begin to pulse out into the ground. Andy and Renee should be here soon. She settled herself onto her favourite ledge to wait.

Twenty minutes later she was awoken from a light doze by the sound of faerie feet on the branch outside. Renee dropped down from the entrance and helped Andy from her bag.

'We head to Darwin the day after tomorrow,' Gaia told them.

'So soon! We haven't got everything ready yet!' Renee exclaimed.

'Don't worry Renee, we'll manage,' said Andy. 'The safe house isn't ready yet, but I'm sure we'll be able to conceal Lucy at the house for a while. The main thing is that we get her out of there,' said Andy.

'Are you still willing to help us?' Renee asked Gaia.

'Yes. We will manage without Lucy. Some of Clio's inner circle might be more willing to turn against her when they have to eat the same food day-in-day-out as the rest of the faeries do.'

'Okay, so how are we going to get her?' Renee asked.

'I have watched her on and off over the last few days,' said Gaia. 'Lucy cannot fly. She has no wings. They keep her within the castle grounds mostly, but she is allowed to venture into the faerie village when the cook allows it.'

'The last time I saw Lucy, Clio had taken her wings away,' said Andy. 'She has probably wound that spell into a ring to keep her flightless. If you remove the ring her wings will come back but, if Lucy hasn't used her wings for years, she won't be strong enough to fly. You will have to shrink her and carry her,' he said to Renee.

'I can take my travel bag. She'll be safe in there,' said Renee

'She sleeps in the servants' quarters,' Gaia continued, 'you won't be able to take her from there — it is too heavily guarded. But each day she is sent to feed the prisoners in the dungeon. The only guard is at the entrance to the cell block; Clio stupidly thinks that the cells are secure enough. That will be the place to approach her. If she agrees to go, she can walk out of the cells and back toward the kitchen as usual. Then you can shrink her and fly out with her.'

'What do I do if she doesn't agree to go?'

'Tell her we will come one more time, when she has had some time to think. If she refuses again, well, that's it I suppose,' said Andy.

'She may not believe that you have sent me. Do you have something that I can take as proof?' asked Renee.

'There's her old teddy bear. I still have it. She will recognise that,' said Andy.

'What time does Lucy feed the prisoners?' Renee asked.

'Once a day. Around midday. Clio and I will be leaving at dawn.'

'Alright. I think we can do this,' said Andy. 'Are you up for another trip into the lion's den?'

'If the lion isn't home, absolutely,' said Renee.

D.I. Tom Hayes and Constable Leia Gardiner met Mr Gordon in his office at Concord Gaol later that morning.

He was neatly dressed in an unremarkable suit and tie; the prison pass clipped to the pocket of his coat was the only thing that distinguished him from any other white-collar worker.

He ushered them in and passed Tom a computer disc in a clear plastic case.

'These are the phone recordings; it looks like we got them all before they were deleted. I also have a list of the numbers that he called,' he said, passing Tom a sheet of paper. 'Some of these aren't on his approved caller list, so we don't have the names to go with them — I am not sure how that happened.'

Tom looked at the bureaucrat with contempt.

'Anything else you haven't told us?'

'Well, I did mention that the visitor records were patchy and I am afraid it is pretty clear now that they have been deliberately tampered with. We have managed to recover the dates and times of visits but not the names of the visitors. I do, however, have the footage from the visiting area for those times and I have added it to the disc. Perhaps you will be able to identify them from that?' he said hopefully.

Great, thought Tom, more hide and seek. Tom had glacial patience in most circumstances; he was known for his ability to slowly wear things down, especially dodgy witnesses, but today his patience had gone to the Bahamas for the winter.

'Well, it's better than nothing I suppose but not much. I am assuming that your processes have been tightened up now and that we will be receiving regular reports on Mr Doyle's contact with the outside world from now on?'

'Oh yes. I am overseeing it myself. There will not be any further breaches I can assure you,' Mr Gordon said, his face red.

'Glad to hear it,' Tom said with a brittle smile that didn't reach his eyes. He stalked out of the office. Gardiner walked beside him and he could see that she was silently fuming. Once they were well away from Mr Gordon's office, she vented.

'Does he have any fucking idea what kind of monster Bill Doyle is? Seriously? He is treating this like a mix-up with a pizza delivery or something!'

'Yes. My faith in Mr Gordon and the rest of the staff at this prison is pretty low at the moment,' Tom said quietly, 'I want you to do daily check-ins with Mr Gordon — keep the pressure on. I am going to be prodding Bill again today and I want to know if he runs screaming to anyone in the next few days. Get it?'

'Got it.'

'Good.'

They entered the interview room and Gardiner set up the recorder.

Tom pulled a manila file from his satchel and placed in on the table.

A few minutes later Bill was escorted in and his cuffs removed. Tom noticed that Bill was quick to adjust his sleeves once the cuffs were taken off; he was not giving Tom the opportunity to see his scar again.

Gardiner did the introductions for the tape and Tom leaned back in his chair and looked Bill over.

He was looking thin in the face. Strained. Either the prison food wasn't agreeing with him or he was starting to stew.

'Nice to see you again Bill. You've been in here a while now, settling in okay?'

'Fuck off.'

'My gran used to wash my mouth out with soap if I said that, Bill. Politeness doesn't cost anything you know,' Tom said with a smirk.

Bill turned away with a sour look on his face.

'You still haven't told me much, Bill, and there are so many things I want to know. I notice you still don't have a lawyer.'

'Don't you worry about that. That will be sorted soon enough and then you will have to watch yourself you fucking pig.'

'Tut, tut, Bill. Well never mind. I suspect that your new lawyer will tell you to cooperate more, Bill, if you ever want to see the light of day again. But in the meantime, I have something to show you,' Tom reached into the file in front of him and pulled out a large photograph. He slid it in front of Bill, watching Bill's face for a reaction.

Tom almost laughed. Bill went from cocky-aggressive to wet-yourself-white in seconds.

'So, you recognise it, I see.' The photo of Babayaga's filigree fork had been enlarged to show the detail on the handle.

Bill sat back in his chair and folded his arms.

'Did it hurt when you were branded by it?' Tom continued, 'I bet it did. Did you scream like a baby, Bill?'

Bill's mouth moved, Tom figured he was trying to frame a vulgar retort, but Bill's vocal chords did not seem to be cooperating.

Bill recovered himself a little and sat back in sullen silence and stared at the wall.

'How about these?' asked Tom.

Tom slid the photos of the front and the back of the old man's filigree spoon across the table.

Bill picked them both up and looked at them closely; he looked both curious and confused at the same time.

'Where is this from?' he asked.

'You've never seen it before?'

'No.'

'Well, it certainly seems to be the partner of the fork, don't you think?'

Bill put the two side by side and regarded the handles.

'Dunno. S'pose it looks the same. But I've never seen this one before,' he said looking at the spoon.'

'But you have seen the fork before, haven't you?'

Bill's face reddened and he looked like he wanted to strangle Tom.

'And while we are having such a lovely time, how about this one Bill.'

Tom slid a photo of the dead homeless man across the table.

Bill looked and looked. He didn't stop looking. The thing that surprised Tom, however, was that he was not looking at the scar on the old man's arm, he was looking at the man's face, with a look that Tom could only describe as dread.

'Do you know this man, Bill?'

'No.'

'But you've seen him before, haven't you? A long time ago.'

Bill looked completely rattled.

It could be a time to push ahead and try to get something out of him, or it could be a time to sit back and let him stew some more; let Bill's mind leap to its own conclusions, let the pressure build in his head all by itself. Everyone was different and judging the cracking point was never easy.

Bill sat up straight in his chair.

'Not saying anything until I get my new lawyer.'

'Atta boy Bill. You keep on swimming. The further out you swim, the deeper you will go down. And boy, are you going down.'

Tom, Gardiner and Peale sat in Tom's office watching the video projected onto his wall from his computer.

They had not gone through the phone records yet, Tom wanted to see the video first. Bill and his cronies had taken the greatest pains to delete the history of his prison visits, so that was where they would look first.

The footage had been filmed from a camera mounted high on the wall of the visiting area. White plastic chairs surrounded sturdy tables that were bolted to the floor. Mr Gordon had not been particularly good at editing the film and had left a lot of unrelated footage at the beginning of each snippet.

They fast forwarded the clip, the figures racing madly about in front of them, moving to and from the tables in a macabre dance.

'Stop there,' Peale said suddenly.

They saw Bill enter the room with a prison guard and move toward a table at the far end of the room where a man was already seated.

'Who is that?' asked Gardiner.

'Back it up a bit, to where the seated guy comes in,' Tom said.

Gardiner complied and they watched the scene play out in high-speed reverse and then play again in real time. A man in a suit entered the room and glanced warily at the camera before moving to the table on the other side of the room.

'I know him. We interviewed him. He's from the nursing home.' Peale said.

'Doctor Ryan Porter,' said Gardiner.

'One of Bill's workmates?'

'Yeah. Though they look as thick as thieves here,' said Peale as they watched the pair whispering at the table.

'What did he say at the interview?' asked Tom. He had not been present for that one.

'Not much. He said he'd worked with Bill for a few years, they got along okay, had a beer after work every now and then, but he had no idea he was into anything dodgy. He seemed pretty legit to me,' said Peale.

'Yeah, it didn't ring any alarm bells with me either,' agreed Gardiner, 'but this certainly doesn't look kosher.'

'No. It doesn't. Make a note and let's see if he turns up again — then we'll check his phone records.'

The recording continued and all three of them exclaimed in surprise.

'Oh my god. Philip Cole,' exclaimed Gardiner.

'Yes. I think I will go and have a chat with Mr Cole,' said Tom. 'Visiting the man who is accused of murdering your wife. That is more than a little suspect, especially considering the details of the visit were deleted. I think it is time to have another look at Philip's phone records too.'

Johnny sat in a lounge chair in the hidden basement of the nursing home. He was flicking through the report he held in his hands, reading and re-reading each section over and over again to make sure.

Yes. He was sure. There was absolutely no doubt.

He went over to the fridge and got himself a beer.

A few moments later he heard footsteps coming down the stairs and there were a series of distant shouts, muffled by heavy doors.

'Shut the fuck up,' he heard Ryan yell from the hallway and abruptly the noise ceased.

Ryan entered looking a little haggard.

'You look like shit,' said Johnny.

'Yeah, well I feel like it too. I was up half the night stitching up one of the breeders. She managed to rip a hole in her arm with her teeth. I have her in a mouth brace now. We need another gaoler Johnny. I can't cope with this and the day job.'

'I'm working on it. It won't be too much longer. But that's not what I came for. I need you to do something upstairs for me.'

'What?'

'It's time for mother to pass away.'

'What?! She's just getting manageable. Why?'

'She knows too much. The other day, she was completely lucid and she repeated some of the things we had been talking about. I know that everyone thinks she's demented, but this is getting too risky.'

'Shit. You don't want me to just sedate her again?'

'No. She has to go. She knows too much. Especially now, with Bill in gaol, if the police come sniffing around again interviewing staff, we just can't risk it.'

'No. I suppose not. It's a shame, though. She's one of my favourite patients.'

'Do it tonight. Make it look natural and then sign the body over to our special undertakers okay?'

'Okay. Are you going to pay for a funeral and everything?'

'No. It's going to be a private family affair.'

'You want me to keep the furnace going?'

'No. I don't want our furnace used for any disposals at the moment, it might draw unwanted attention.'

Ryan watched Johnny leave the room and sat in sullen silence for a while. He really did like the old woman. She reminded him of Johnny's mother. His own mother hadn't been particularly loving to him as a child, but Johnny's mother had always had a smile and a kind word for him. Until she left. Everything went bad after that.

Why was he even doing this shit? Bill was in Gaol, he was working fifteen-hour shifts and for what? All the proceeds had dried up now that they were in shut down mode. How did he ever get dragged into this bloody mess?

He sighed and got up to make preparations.

Tom left work and drove over to Philip Cole's house. It was after six. He was pretty sure Philip would be home by now. Nothing like an unannounced visit from the police to put the wind up you.

As he pulled over and parked outside the house, he noticed that there was a car parked in Philip's driveway, a car that he didn't recognise.

He pulled out his mobile phone and called Peale; he hoped he was still on duty.

Peale answered straight away.

'Peale, Tom here. Can you run a plate through the database for me please?'

'Sure, fire away.'

Tom read out the digits and heard Peale tapping away in the background.

'Vivienne Scott — lives in Redfern. I know that name from somewhere.'

'Yes. She's Philip's secretary. This could be interesting. I'll fill you in tomorrow.'

He ended the call and climbed out of the car. Of course, it could be completely innocent...

He knocked on the door. There was silence.

He knocked again, three times, hard. It was the knock of someone who was not messing about.

This time he heard the sound of feet hurrying to the door.

Tom heard the latch being turned and Philip appeared in a dressing gown, his hair dishevelled.

Oh dear. What have we been up to? Tom thought to himself.

'Mr Cole.'

'D.I. Hayes, I wasn't expecting you.'

'No. Obviously. May I come in?'

'It's not really a good time.'

'I'm afraid this is important.'

He could almost see the wheels turning in Philip's head.

Finally, Philip moved aside, holding the door open to allow him to enter.

'Um, please, go through to the lounge room,' Philip said, pointing to the left.

It was a lot cleaner than the last time he had visited and there was a subtle hint of perfume in the air. Tom took a seat on the couch and Philip took a seat opposite him.

'Do you have visitors, Mr Cole? I noticed your secretary's car outside.'

Philip's mouth hung open for just a second before his brain engaged.

'Yes... I'm borrowing it from her at the moment. My car is out of action.'

'How nice to have such accommodating employees.'

'Well, she doesn't need it at the moment so it was no trouble.'

'Does she have a second car?'

'Oh, no, she's away...travelling. I drove her to the airport.'

'Oh, on holidays, I see. Going somewhere nice?'

'I don't know to be honest. Other people's holidays don't really interest me.'

'It must be difficult without her.'

'Pardon?'

'In the office.'

'Oh, yes. But she won't be gone for long so we can cope for a while.'

'She's due back soon?'

'Yes, day after tomorrow.'

He made a mental note to check on her comings and goings. Hopefully, there was a CCTV camera somewhere near the office.

'Well, the reason I came tonight was to ask you about Bill Doyle. The man we have arrested in connection with your wife's murder.'

'Do you have enough on him to charge him with that yet?' Philip asked.

'No. Not yet, but we have charged him with several other offences, so he won't be going anywhere any time soon.'

Philip nodded, he had regained his calm very quickly. Too quickly perhaps thought Tom, especially since Tom was sure that Philip's secretary was hiding in the bedroom, probably in a similar state of undress. Mr Cole was quite an actor. How long had the affair been going on, Tom wondered.

'I was a little surprised to discover that Bill had called you from prison,' Tom said.

Philip blanched.

'And that you paid him a visit,' Tom continued.

'I know this seems bad, but I can assure you, it isn't what it seems...' said Philip.

'Oh really? So why did you go to see Bill Doyle, Mr Cole?'

'He called me. He said he needed my help. I know him from school. At the time I didn't even realise that he was the man you had arrested for Rebecca's murder,' said Philip.

'So, it was all just a coincidence was it?'

'Well, no. I think Bill knew exactly what he was doing. He wanted to make it look like I was involved in the whole thing so he could blackmail me for legal help.'

'Mr Doyle has been blackmailing you and you didn't think to tell us?'

'Well, no. I mean yes... Look, it's not quite like that. He threatened to bring up the fact that we used to go to school together and make it look like we were bosom buddies unless I organised one of my lawyer friends to represent him. I told him to piss off and I haven't heard from him since, so I figured no harm done.'

Tom leaned back in the couch.

'You do realise that by not telling us this, you have made yourself look very bad indeed?'

'I guess I wasn't thinking. I just wanted it all to go away.'

'Mr Doyle went to school with you.'

'Yes.'

'Which school was that and when were you there?'

'Camperdown High School during the late 80's. I went on to University after that and I haven't seen him since.'

'And is there anything else you should be telling me about Mr Doyle?'

'No. That's everything, I swear.'

Tom leaned back and looked at Philip, his face unreadable.

'Should you think of anything else, anything at all, I would advise you to call me straight away — day or night. I will be looking into your association with Bill Doyle very closely, so don't think for a minute that I won't find anything you are trying to hide.'

Philip nodded again but said nothing.

'Goodbye, for now, Mr Cole.'

Tom walked up the hall to the front door and avoided the temptation to steal a look in the master bedroom. He closed the front door behind him and crossed the road to his car, climbing in and then looking into his rear-view mirror. Philip was watching him from the front door.

Tom drove around the corner and turned onto the connecting road. Philip lived on a crescent, both ends of the road connecting to the road Tom was driving down now. He drove until he reached the other connection and then headed back towards Philip's house from the opposite direction. He parked behind another car, far enough down the road that he could not be seen from Philip's doorstep. He turned on his dash cam and directed it at Vivienne's car.

Sure enough, twenty minutes later Vivienne emerged from the house and climbed into her car. Philip was at least smart enough not to go out and kiss her goodbye.

He debated whether he should follow her and pull her up for a routine traffic inspection but decided he didn't want Philip that edgy just yet. A phone tap and some surveillance might prove useful.

Magick Most Evil

Bill woke suddenly. A guard was shaking him; one burly hand on his shoulder the other over his mouth. When the guard saw that Bill was awake he removed his hand from Bill's shoulder and put a finger to his lips. He looked over at Bill's sleeping roommate.

The guard was big. Bill was scanning for a weak spot when the man whispered in his ear, 'Johnny's here to see you.'

Relief washed over Bill, the thought that Johnny was prepared to risk one of his insiders to bust him out made his heart glow for a moment.

The guard led him silently through the corridors and the small device attached to the guard's shirt collar emitted a low hum. Bill had used one before and knew that each camera they approached was going offline before they were identifiable, then flicking back into life as they passed out of range. A small blip in the transmission. Unless someone was examining that particular recording at normal speed, it would not be noticed.

The guard led Bill into an interview room and gestured for him to take a seat. It wasn't one of the normal visiting rooms and he wondered what the next step of the plan would be. There was no surveillance camera.

Johnny entered.

'Bill, this is my man, Trevor.'

Bill turned to him and nodded. Trevor did not move. He stood with his arms crossed behind Bill's chair.

'This little meeting did not happen. I was never here. Understood.'

Bill nodded, suddenly wary. That didn't sound like he was getting out of gaol anytime soon. What was this?

'Thanks to your fuck-ups, I've had to close down the business for a while. I may have to set up a new lair, thanks to you. Ryan is keeping the breeders fed and quiet, but all other activities have ceased. Do you realise how much money you have cost me?'

'Don't bitch to me, man! I'm the one taking all the risks and you're the one taking all the cream. I thought this was a bust out not a take-down. Are you leaving me here to rot?'

'Yep. 'Bout time you copped your fair share of the crap. I've been risking my neck since you were in nappies and not once have I been caught. Why is that do you think? Do you have any idea how much I hated wiping your snotty nose and keeping you fed? Do you have any idea what I gave up to keep you alive? You ungrateful little shit.'

Bill was flabbergasted. He had never heard his big brother speak like this before.

'Always the big man weren't you, out rolling drunks,' Johnny continued, 'but too weak to come to my aid when our old man was laying into me.'

'What the hell are you talking about? Who was it that finished the old bastard off once and for all?'

'Yep, you even took away my revenge you little prick. I had it all planned. Then you came in swinging and screwed everything up.'

'Plan, what plan? You never told me about any plan.'

'Of course not. You would have fucked it up if I told you.'

Johnny stared at his brother in grim silence for a while.

'You always believed she was going to come back, didn't you?' said Johnny. 'But why would she? She had escaped him and was finally free of you. And so, I copped the crap from him instead. Well, she didn't escape me in the end.'

'What?'

'Dear old mum was right under our noses the whole time. The old drunk woman that Ryan picked up as my cover story at the nursing home; your favourite patient. The old crone that reminded Ryan of our dear old mother. Turns out she really *was* our dear old mother. Ryan killed her last night — but I haven't told him who she was yet.'

'You…'

'Yep.'

Bill was white. His face crumpled. He was shaking his head in disbelief.

'And you know what I've decided to do? Since she managed to escape our dear old father in life and left us to rot, she is going to rot right next to dear old dad. I'm going to bury her with him. She won't be able to escape him in death!' Johnny began to laugh, loud and fierce.

'No. Johnny! You can't…Johnny, no!' Bill stood up suddenly, but Trevor pushed him firmly back into his seat. Johnny leaned down into his face and Bill's expression changed to fear.

'You still don't get it, do you? If she had stayed, none of this would have happened,' snarled Johnny.

'How could she stay?' asked Bill.

'How could she leave and not take us with her! Tell me that!' Johnny yelled at him.

'She couldn't…'

'Bull shit. And now I am free of my entire loser family. Don't expect another visit bro. You're on your own.'

As Johnny left the room he nodded to the guard. Trevor nodded once in return, lifted his shirt and removed a length of electrical cord that had been wrapped around his waist.

The sky was already beginning to lighten in the east as Renee and Andy reached Old Pepper. Renee walked along the branch toward the knot-hole entrance and heard Old Pepper give a long loud tree-yawn. Renee dropped into the hollow inside and lifted Andy out of her bag.

Once she had increased him to full size she asked him again:

'You are absolutely sure about this Andy? If something happens to me, you will be stuck in here forever.'

'Rubbish. Gaia knows I'm here. Something would have to happen to both of you. Stop worrying. I'll be fine.'

'Okay. I'll stay here as long as I can.'

'Stick to the plan. Go now. That way Gaia has a chance to warn you if something is amiss,' Andy said.

'Alright, alright. You're right of course,' Renee replied, 'Look after him, Old Pepper. I'll be back as soon as I can.'

'Don't worry Renee, Andy and I will have a lovely chat, won't we,' said Old Pepper.

'Course we will,' said Andy rolling his eyes. Old Pepper was a consummate flirt. Renee couldn't imagine being stuck inside a tree for the rest of your life, especially not with Old Pepper, but she held her tongue.

She took a deep breath and pushed through the magical doorway into Old Blue.

Just before midday, Renee said goodbye to Old Blue and disguised herself as a Christmas beetle. She flew through the trees, over the ridge and towards Clio's realm.

As she approached the gate tree that was the entrance to the compound she scanned the ground, looking for a sign. There! Just outside the entrance was a large granite boulder. Carved into its surface was an ornate Celtic pattern and lying at its base was a small black stone; Gaia's sign. It meant that Gaia and Clio had started their journey to Darwin.

She felt enormous relief. She had been dreading the idea that she would have to enter the fairy realm with Clio still inside. She sent a quick thought message to Andy to let him know that the rescue was on, then flew through the entrance, undetected by the guard; she still wore Old Blue's enchantment.

She flew along the paved path through the centre of the village and up to the foot of the imposing steps that lead into the castle. Behind the castle was a walled enclosure containing the servants' quarters and kitchen and she flew over the wall and into the grounds. She was hoping to find Lucy in the kitchens and follow her down to the cells but when she reached the kitchen it was empty. There were signs that a meal had just been prepared so she continued into the castle and down to the dungeons, remembering the way from her last visit with Andy. Just inside the doorway to the cells, the guard was dozing at his post, an empty plate on the floor beside his chair. She slipped past him and down the long flight of stairs to the basement below.

There was a narrow hallway with three doors coming off it. The first two were closed and she could see that each of the doors had a viewing hatch at head height; both doors were closed. The third door stood open and there was light spilling into the passage.

She moved over to it and inside she could see a female figure moving cautiously towards a set of chains bolted to the wall. The other end of these chains was levitating a foot from the floor as if chained to an invisible animal. In one hand the woman held a bowl of food, in the other, a long staff. The woman stopped a few feet from the chains and put the bowl of food on the floor, then she used the staff to push the bowl closer to the floating chains.

Renee watched as the chains clanked and the bowl rose into the air. Its contents were poured out and almost instantly disappeared as if being poured into a space-time wormhole. The woman watched as the bowl was placed gently back on the ground. She used the stick to reach out and pull it back toward herself.

She picked the bowl up and backed away slowly. When she was well out of the creature's reach, she turned and started with surprise when she saw Renee standing behind her.

'What are you doing here? No one is allowed down here! If Clio finds out you will be severely punished!'

Lucy was just as Gaia had described her, pale skin, blonde hair and very thin. She had no wings. Lucy was probably only a few years younger than Renee, but she was so thin, it made her appear younger. She was obviously not getting enough to eat.

'My name is Renee. I have come to get you. Your father, Andy, wants you to come home.'

'My father is dead. Clio killed him.'

'No, he isn't.'

The chains behind them began to crash about as if a desperate ghost was trying to break free. Lucy looked terrified; Renee was only curious. Something was very wrong here.

'Stop! You have to go. The creature is upset, you will get us both killed.'

The crashing stopped suddenly and Lucy looked towards it, wary.

'What is the creature?' Renee asked.

'I don't know. It is my punishment to feed it every day. Clio hopes that one day it will eat me. She says it is what I deserve.'

'Why would you deserve that?'

'Because I am a child of the enemy. She says it is only because she is merciful that she has allowed me to live in slavery rather than kill me,' the woman said, her eyes moistening.

'Your father *is* alive and he wants to take you home. Do you remember your home?'

'Yes, I hold it in my heart.'

'The little house with a front verandah and the green door. The wooden handle and the brass knocker?'

'Yes!' Lucy exclaimed, her face lighting up. 'I remember those. But how? Where did you come from? Clio told me she killed my father. How do you know my father?'

'I am an enemy of Clio and a friend of your father. Here, he gave me this to bring to you.' Renee removed a small brown bear from her satchel.

Lucy was no child, she was at least twenty, but her hands shook as she reached out and tenderly took the little bear.

The chains clanked twice and then stopped.

Renee's attention strayed to the chained animal. She walked towards it.

'What are you doing! Stay back or it will kill you!' Lucy exclaimed, grabbing her arm.

'Has it ever tried to harm you?'

'It grabbed me once, but I screamed and fought and I got away.'

'Maybe it was just trying to communicate?'

'I don't think so,' Lucy said, her eyes fearful.

Renee turned her attention back to Lucy.

'Will you come with me? Will you return to your father's house?'

'Away from this? Yes! God yes.'

The chains rattled again.

Renee turned to look at them again.

'If you can understand me, rattle your chains three times,' said Renee.

One, two, three.

Lucy's eyes were wide.

'Rattle once for yes and two for no. Do you understand me?'

One shake.

'Did Clio make you invisible.'

Shake.

'Are you human.'

Shake, shake.

'Are you a fairy?'

Shake.

'Can anyone other than Clio see you.'

Shake, shake.

'How long has the fairy been here?' Renee asked, turning to Lucy.

'I don't know. Clio has made me feed it for the last ten years.'

'Oh my god. Over ten years,' Renee said, turning back toward the prisoner. 'Those chains are iron, aren't they?'

Shake.

'Are you in pain?'

Shake.

'I am going to try and break the spell so I can see you, then I'll try and get you out of there, but we are going to have to work quickly before Lucy is missed from the kitchen.

'Promise me you will not try to hurt me, Lucy or anyone else and I will try to get you out of here and to a safe place. Do you promise?'

Shake.

She did not doubt it for an instant. The chained fairy had the same scent of familiarity emanating from it that she had sensed with Andy, Bruce and Tom. The sense that they were somehow bonded.

'OK. I need to touch you. Can you hold out your hand?'

Renee moved forward and stretched her hand toward the chains that were hovering above the ground. She made contact and felt fingers entwine her own. She held the hand gently in both of hers.

Lucy was standing near the door, still too terrified of the fairy to come any closer. Renee bent forward and whispered to the prisoner, 'Squeeze my hand once for yes and twice for no. You reacted when I told Lucy that Andy was alive.'

Squeeze.

'Do you know Andy?'

Squeeze.

'Right, we'd better get a move on.' She closed her eyes and concentrated on the feel of the hand in hers. It was small, but the skin felt dry and cracked. She pushed her fairy healing into the hand and it coursed out like a golden glow in her mind, and for a moment she saw the outline of a female fairy kneeling before her. She sent her mind swirling into the fairy's body trying to sense where the invisibility spell was anchored, but she could not find the source.

'I think this will take longer than we have,' she told the fairy. 'I am going to break your chains and then we will work on breaking the spell once we are safe. Once you are free you must stay close to me or I will lose you.'

'I don't know if that's a good idea,' said Lucy.

'She is in pain and she is Clio's prisoner. We have to help her. The three of us will be out of Clio's reach in a few minutes.'

Lucy looked worried but nodded her agreement.

Renee slid the filigree fire ring from her finger, the ring that kept her power of fire under control. She imagined a thin, powerful line of fire emerging from her finger and a split second later the fire obeyed. Frightened that she would hurt the fairy, she traced this fire quickly across the clasp of the cuffs, trying to avoid contact with the invisible fairy. She breathed a grateful sigh when the chains fell away and she sensed with her healing powers that she had not done her any further damage.

'Hold my arm,' Renee said to the fairy and she felt a gentle grip on her forearm.

'Okay, are you strong enough to shrink?'

One squeeze.

'If I hold my hand out, can you shrink and fly onto it?'

Another squeeze. A moment later Renee felt a tiny pressure on her palm. With her other hand, she opened her bag.

'See that little compartment. I want you to fly in there and strap yourself in, it could get a little rough.'

She felt the pressure leave her hand.

'I'm going to put my hand in the bag, tap it three times if you are ready to go.' Renee lowered her hand into the little compartment.

One, two, three taps on her finger.

'Okay Lucy, we have to go now,' she said and guided her out the door.

'We have to get past the guard. I am going to shrink and fly into your hair. I want you to walk up the stairs and past the guard like it is a normal day.'

'I would normally go to the kitchen after this.'

'Alright, that's what we'll do then. Be as normal as you can, don't let the guard suspect anything is wrong.'

'I need the bowl,' she said and ducked back into the cell to retrieve it.

When she returned, Renee shrank and flew up into her hair, hiding just behind her left ear.

'Let's go,' she whispered to Lucy once she was in position.

Lucy walked up the stairs and stooped to retrieve the guard's plate as she passed him. He was still sleeping. No one approached her as she walked towards the kitchen.

The kitchen was empty.

'The cook isn't here. Probably slacking off, since Clio is away. Normally I would go and collect vegetables from the garden for lunch.'

'Good. Stick to the routine for now.'

They went out the back door of the kitchen and into the sunshine. Lucy walked down a gravel path to a series of raised garden beds behind the castle. A low wall surrounded the kitchen garden in a half circle and joined onto the taller outside walls of the castle. There was a gate in one side of the wall leading to the heart of the village. A guard stood on duty next to it.

'Are you free to go into the village when you want to?'

'I can when the cook sends me to get supplies.'

'Right, let's go then.'

Lucy was not challenged as she walked out the gate and down toward the village.

'How about leaving the compound and going into the forest?'

'No. I am not allowed out without a chaperone.'

'I want you to get as close to the gateway as possible without raising suspicion. Then, I am going to try to shrink you.'

'The guard will sense me, even if I am tiny.'

'If we wait until someone else is coming in, he might not notice us. Head behind the last house — the one with the black door.'

The last house in the village was twenty feet from the entrance. A large stone wall enclosed the entire compound and a single arch provided access to the gate tree and the forest outside. There was a guard on either side of the opening.

Lucy continued on towards the archway and then turned down the laneway between the last two houses. Renee felt a sudden jolt through her body as if she had walked through a powerful electrical field.

'Did you feel that? What was it?'

'I don't know!' Lucy said in alarm.

Lucy peered back between the buildings towards the gate. The guards were at attention. Something was wrong.

'Oh my god! Look!' said Lucy.

Renee looked back towards the castle, a stream of guards was pouring out and running towards the gate.

'We have to go now! Something has alerted them.'

Renee returned to full size and before Lucy could argue she shrank Lucy to beetle size and enclosed her in her hands.

'My concealment charm should hide you while you are in my hands she whispered through her fingers.'

Renee shrank to the size of a beetle, but kept her fairy form, holding Lucy safe within her hands.

The soldiers stood in rows in front of the gate.

Renee flew up to avoid the running fairies and flew as fast as she could towards the entrance. Below her, a fairy with purple wings was also running toward the gates. The purple fairy has her hands raised and Renee could see that the entrance was shrinking. The arch was getting smaller and smaller, the view of the trees outside becoming less and less.

Renee darted past the ear of one of the guards, ducking and weaving through the raised spears of the guards behind him, the hole was closing fast, she accelerated and made herself smaller again, flashing through the opening just before it crashed closed behind her.

She looked back, and all she could see was a large gum tree with a hole right through the middle of it. The village inside was no longer visible, all that could be seen through the hole was the forest on the other side. The door to Clio's realm had been closed.

They didn't have much time; Clio's guards would realise their mistake and open the portal again soon. She had to get to Old Blue before the swarm of guards came after them.

She flew down the side of a hill and into a green valley; there was a small river trickling through the centre of it. They just had to get over the next ridge and they would be safe.

A strange dark blue light appeared on their right. There was a fairy stone there and the Celtic pattern engraved into its surface was glowing a dark midnight blue. Suddenly Clio and Gaia stood before it and the glow receded.

'Oh my god!' Renee exclaimed and darted to the left.

'After them!' Clio roared, 'Don't let them escape!'

Gaia pursued them and Clio set off at a tangent; Renee suspected she was trying to cut them off. Somehow, even though she was tiny and still wearing the concealment charm, Clio and Gaia could sense exactly where she was.

The ring! Lucy was still wearing the ring!

She could not go to Old Blue; that was too dangerous. Clio would have the old tree destroyed if she found out it was a fairy tree. She had to shake them off.

Up ahead she saw an old farm shed surrounded by an acre of old rusting ploughs and farm machinery. Renee had an idea. She hoped she would not hurt her two companions in the process, but it was the best she could come up with at short notice.

She flew around the old machines, hoping the iron would interfere with the senses of her two pursuers and then she plunged directly into the hopper of an old threshing machine. She hid deep inside and found a bolt hole to peer out of.

She saw the red and pink lights approach and then veer away suddenly. They circled, staying a good ten feet from the iron machinery at all times. They were searching for her but not finding. The iron was shielding her.

Lucy moaned in her hands.

'What's wrong?' Renee asked through her fingers.

'Iron! I can feel iron. My head hurts.'

'We won't be here long. I just need to wait until Clio and Gaia move away a bit.'

She wasn't sure if they would sense her if she moved outside the protection of the hopper.

'Do all fairies hurt the same way from iron?'

'Yes. Everyone.'

'So how close to iron do you need to be for it to disrupt your senses?'

'"Two cubits will bring on fits". You never learnt that? A cubit is two feet.'

'So, four feet will mess things up? Well, they aren't even coming within ten feet so, I think we can do this.'

The pink and red glows had moved to the other side of the farm, circling the discarded farm machinery at a distance. Renee slipped out of the hopper and flew close to a plough, a tractor, a harvester and then slipped the last three feet across open ground into the enormous machinery shed. Its walls and roof were made of corrugated iron sheeting.

In the very centre of the shed she landed and grew to human size. The roof was more than ten feet above her and the walls at least six feet away in all directions.

'How's the head now?'

'Better.'

She placed Lucy on the ground and increased her size to match her own.

'We have to get that ring off you. My concealment charm should work if you aren't wearing it.'

'But I will lose all my powers forever if I remove it!'

'No. You won't. That is just another of Clio's lies to keep people under control. She tried it on me. I lost my powers for about twelve hours, then I was back to normal again. You will be fine. And you will be free of her.'

Lucy looked doubtful but pulled her ring off. It unravelled and turned into a long black hair. She dropped it in disgust.

'Feel any different?' asked Renee.

'No. But then, Clio had already taken all my powers away anyway — except for cornucopia of course.'

'All right, we should be able to fly out of here without them noticing.'

'Hang on. What about the creature? She might have a ring.'

'Crap. You're right.'

Renee opened the bag and lowered one of her fingers into the compartment.

'Are you still in there?'

She felt a tap on her finger.

'Thank goodness. One tap for yes, two for no — are you wearing one of Clio's rings?'

Tap, tap.

'Good. Anything else that might give us away?'

Tap, tap.

'Are you ready to try and get out of here.'

Tap.

'Okay. How about you Lucy? Ready?'

'As I'll ever be.'

Renee closed the bag and passed it to Lucy.

'You carry it and I will shrink you both,' Renee said.

She shrank Lucy to beetle size and put her hand down to allow Lucy to climb onto it. Once Lucy was caged inside her cupped hands Renee shrank herself and flew to the doorway. She flew until she was over one of the metal wrecks and heard Lucy groan from her hands. She was going to be careful this time. She flew fifteen feet straight up into the air. If they sensed her, she could dive straight back down again and lose them in the scrap heap again. She turned slowly on the spot, searching for them.

There. Two flashes of light bobbing at the edge of the machinery. Then she saw more, six, seven, dozens! All different colours, all swirling at the edge of the heap of iron. She focused on the ones closest to her. There was no sudden movement; they continued to fly on their chosen paths. Renee flew to the edge of the heap and turned to look again. Nothing.

Finally, she flew to the nearest tree and stopped to watch.

She saw a red and pink light come together for a moment and then a squadron of coloured lights formed behind the pink. Then the pink light and her followers flew away from the farm and onward in the direction of the original chase.

Finally, Clio, accompanied by a purple and a yellow light, flew back in the direction of the compound.

Now that the way was clear, Renee took the opportunity and flew straight to Old Blue.

Gaia led her troops further south, scouting around the valleys and ridges for the next hour. She was sure that Renee and Lucy had slipped away but had no idea how or where they had gone. She assumed that they would head to Old Blue at some point, so she made sure to avoid that area entirely.

She had only half her mind on the chase, the rest was trying to process what had just happened. Gaia had left the compound with Clio at dawn and it had taken them most of the next five hours to reach the outer edge of Darwin. They had flown non-stop and at full speed. She did not know the faerie that accompanied them and Clio did not introduce her. She was a drab looking creature with dull rust coloured wings. She did not speak the entire journey and as they drew closer to the city they had to slow down to accommodate the faerie's weariness.

'We will have time to rest once the task is complete. We will head back tomorrow at a slower pace,' Clio had informed them both.

'You are to wait here,' she said directing Gaia to a shady tree.

Clio and the rusty faerie continued on toward the city and were soon out of sight.

Half an hour later, Clio returned, alone.

'We will rest here in the branches,' she said choosing a hollow filled with decaying leaves for her bed.

Gaia propped herself in a sitting position and half-dozed. She could sleep lightly when she needed to and awaken instantly if her super-tuned senses told her there was danger. She had been born to be a guard.

They had rested for less than an hour when Clio woke with a start. Gaia was fully awake in an instant.

'What is wrong your majesty?'

'Lucy is escaping!'

Gaia saw the ring on Clio's finger glowing; Clio was communicating with someone back at the compound. There was nothing Gaia could do from here, but thankfully, Clio was powerless too. Renee had a chance; it would take Clio and Gaia hours to get home.

'Come with me, quickly,' Clio ordered, and Gaia was surprised to find them heading toward the city. They should be heading in the opposite direction if they were heading home. Were they going to get the other faerie first?

They flew until they reached a park in the centre of Darwin. Amongst a grove of trees was a boulder, it had a bronze plaque commemorating a past event. Clio guided Gaia to the rear of the stone and they landed in the grass, still in their tiny faerie form.

At faerie height, there was a circle carved into the stone, no bigger than a plate in a children's tea set. The centre was carved with intricate intertwining patterns.

Clio grasped her hand.

'Do not let go of my hand or this spell will kill you.'

Gaia stared at her in astonishment. Clio did not usually perform spells, she had others to do them for her and she had never heard of her performing a dangerous one.

The word that Clio said was completely foreign to her, but the circle on the stone began to glow in a rusty colour. For a moment, Gaia thought she heard a faerie scream and then she was in a whirlpool of light and sound and colour and she was trying desperately not to vomit. She held Clio's hand so tightly she feared she would break her bones.

Then the madness stopped and she was standing in front of another stone in another place, this one glowing a midnight blue. And there was another screaming faerie somewhere. It was then that she realised that they were in the valley beyond the faerie compound. The glow had dimmed and Renee and Lucy had darted past them and the chase had begun.

Somehow, Clio had created her own portals. Not with living trees but with stones. Gaia had a bad feeling about what had happened to the faeries that had accompanied them on their travels. There was a young girl missing from the compound; her mother was insane with worry. The girl had midnight blue wings. If what she was thinking was possible, it would be a truly evil magic. Clio must have tricked the faeries into it. Her anger surged and she stopped flying suddenly, her second in command almost flying into her.

'What now, Gaia?' he asked. 'There has been no sign of them for over an hour.'

'No. I can't see any sign that they came this way. We head back to the castle for further instructions.'

Ryan and the Thief

The prison guard, Trevor, watched as the gurney was wheeled towards the waiting ambulance. Bill was secured to it with a belt across his middle. His eyes were open, their whites bloodshot, and the left side of his face was slack. Drool was dribbling out of the side of the oxygen mask and running into his collar. His hands lay loosely on his lap and his fingers looked blue and lifeless.

He wasn't dead, but he might as well be.

There was no way he was going to recover from that. Not mentally anyway.

Trevor wandered over to the breakout area to call Johnny.

Tom and Constable Peale had been waiting at the sign in desk at the gaol for some time. That was unusual; police were usually fast-tracked to the interview rooms.

They were surprised when Mr Gordon, the police liaison officer for the gaol, appeared looking flustered.

'I am dreadfully sorry about the delay, could you come with me please?'

'Why do I get the feeling you are going to tell me something that I don't want to hear?' asked Tom.

The man did not respond but guided them through the check-in process and on to his office.

'Please, take a seat D.I. Hayes; Constable,' he said gesturing to two vacant chairs in front of his desk.

'I am afraid you won't be able to interview Bill Doyle today, maybe not for some time. There was an incident last night.'

'What kind of incident Mr Gordon?' asked Tom.

'Bill was found hanging in one of the interview rooms. He has been sent to Redfern hospital. There will be a full inquiry of course.'

Tom folded his arms and stared at Mr Gordon.

'When did this happen?'

'Sometime between the bed check at midnight and the cell check just before breakfast. When we discovered he was missing the gaol went into lockdown and we did a full search. It was some time before he was found. We haven't worked out how he got access to the interview rooms yet, the security footage appears to have been tampered with.'

'Someone on the inside again?' asked Tom.

'I think it is a bit too early to jump to that conclusion.'

Tom did not even try to hide his look of incredulity.

'Anyway,' Mr Gordon continued, 'the hospital is assessing his condition at the moment, so I'm afraid I can't say when he will be back with us. I can let you know when we have an update.'

'Don't bother, I'll talk to the hospital directly. Well, since Bill is not available, how about a chat with his cellmate. I assume you can arrange that?' Tom said.

The liaison officer scurried off to make the arrangements.

'Who do you think would have tried to kill Bill?' asked Peale.

'Who knows? A rival, his boss? Hell, the things he has been up to, if that became common knowledge the inmates would have been queueing to string him up. A lot of them don't like thugs who target youngsters.

'As soon as we get out of here, I want you to head over to the hospital and get a full update on Bill's condition.'

'Yes, sir.'

'I just hope he is going to be fit enough for trial,' he said angrily.

Twenty minutes later Tom and Peale were guided along the corridor to the interview rooms. The door to one of them was open, but it had police tape strung across it. Tom nodded to the forensic officer inside as he passed. It was one of George's off-siders, but Tom couldn't remember his name.

He only had a second to glance inside, but he noticed that the camera had been removed from the far wall and the metal bracket that would have supported it was bent at a strange angle.

Their guard escorted them into one of the rooms further down the hall. A man in prison greens was already seated, watched over by another guard.

'Would you two mind waiting outside please?' Tom had already got the run-down on the man they were about to interview and was confident that they were not in any danger; except from eavesdropping guards.

Once the guards had left the room, Tom and constable Peale sat down and turned on a recorder.

'I understand you are the cellmate of Mr Bill Doyle.'

'Yep.'

'And your name is?'

'Larry Muir.'

'Have you been his cellmate since he arrived at the gaol, Mr Muir?'

'Yep.'

'Did Mr Doyle talk to you much about his crimes?'

'No. He wouldn't, would he? I've heard some rumours about some of the shit he was up to outside, but he seemed okay and you can't trust rumours in a place like this — they can get you killed.'

'What sort of rumours had you heard?'

'Look. I'm due out next year. If the others find out I've been helping the cops, I'll get hammered. I just don't need the pain man. I just want to get home.'

'Where are you from?'

'Down south, near Wollongong.'

'How long you got to go?'

'Nine months.'

'What are you in for?' Tom didn't need to ask, he already knew, but he found prisoners a bit more compliant if they didn't think of you as Big Brother.

'Stealing cars.'

'First offence?'

'Nah. Second.'

'Well, the guards aren't in here so they won't tell any tales and we can make this off the record if you prefer. I am on a fact-finding mission, I don't need you to stand up in court for me.'

The inmate relaxed his posture.

'Okay, no tape and I'll talk, but there has to be something in it for me.'

'Well, I can't guarantee you anything, because I don't know what you have to tell me, but you must be due for a parole hearing soon?'

'Yeah. Two months.'

'I'm prepared to put in a good word for you at the hearing if you have something for us — but it has to be legit.'

'There's one other problem. One of the guards. If I talk, I could get the same treatment as Bill.'

'You've got a clean prison record. This close to the end of your sentence it wouldn't be unusual for you to get moved to one of the minimum-security prisons closer to home for the last stretch.'

'You can do that?'

'I think that can be arranged, especially since someone abducted your cellmate in the middle of the night; things like that can be a bit traumatic.'

'Okay. Deal.'

Tom nodded to Peale. Peale turned off the voice recorder.

'What can you tell us?' asked Tom.

'The night that Bill got strung up, a guard came and took him out of his cell. They thought I was asleep. The guard's name is Trevor. He was watching Bill like a hawk from the minute he got in here. He scares the shit out of me, so you can't do anything about him until I am out of here.'

'No problem.'

'Rumour was that Bill was part of a gang that was grabbing street kids and pimping them to paedos.'

'Rumour is right.'

'Fucking bastard. If I had known that was true I would have —'

'— done nothing because your release date is coming up and you are a reformed character,' said Tom finishing his sentence.

'No of course not but, you know what I mean, guys like that...'

'Well, it's lucky you didn't know before, so you were never faced with the temptation,' Tom said with a wry smile. 'He didn't happen to mention anything about his business, in particular where he was operating from.'

'Nah. He was pretty switched on, he never said anything about it.'

Bugger, thought Tom. They really needed to find the den.

'There was one thing he had been crowing about though,' Larry said; Tom raised his eyebrows. 'He had been bitching for weeks about how his lawyer had done a bunk on him and then one day he comes in pleased as punch. He said he was blackmailing an old schoolmate into paying for another lawyer, a bloody QC at that. He said he was going to be out of here before he knew it.'

'You don't happen to know the schoolmate's name?'

'Yeah, Philip — like the prince. Sounds like he is as posh as a prince too. Some upper crust architect or something, rolling in dough.'

'And Philip was definitely going to fund the lawyer?'

'Oh yeah. Bill had some major dirt on this guy, but he didn't say what. Sounds like he hated this guy's guts.'

'Did Bill have any other visitors that you knew of?'

'There was this one guy, I think his name was Ryan. They were like brothers, he said. He said his real brother was a complete arsehole, but Ryan, he could be depended on. He kept saying if he couldn't get out with a lawyer, Ryan would help him bust out. But then, most guys on their first stretch talk about busting out. Hey — you gotta dream.'

Gaia led her patrol back to the compound. They reached the faerie gateway; a hole in the trunk of an old tree and as they passed through it, the view of the forest on the other side of the tree morphed and changed into the streets of the faerie village. Gaia nodded to the entrance guards as they passed through the archway on the village side of the gate. She turned to her second in command.

'Allow the troops water and then assemble them back here in ten minutes.'

She left him bellowing orders and flew into the castle.

As she approached the great hall she heard the sound of breaking glass. She increased her speed and entered to find Clio hurling things at the wall, screaming in a bitter rage.

When she sensed Gaia, she turned to face her.

'Well? Did you get them?'

'No, your Majesty; there was no sign of them.'

'Incompetence! Absolute incompetence! Why are all my guards such imbeciles!'

She threw another glass at the wall.

Clio walked towards Gaia and Gaia braced herself for a blow. She was surprised when Clio placed a hand gently on her shoulder.

'Gaia, you are the only one I can trust. You are the only one who never fails me. Lucy is not the only prisoner that has escaped! The head of the prison guards has allowed the invisible monster to slip away as well. My insurance, my secret weapon, has gone!

'He has been dealt with,' she said gesturing dismissively towards the window, 'but now, we must find Lucy. She must be tracked down and in order to capture her, we must find the monster too,' Clio said and strode back towards her throne.

Gaia allowed her eyes to drift to the window for a moment and saw a figure slumped against the wall below the window. There was a bloody streak dribbling down the wall above it. The body had no head.

Gaia forced her eyes back to Clio and her mind back to the matter at hand.

'If the monster is invisible, how will we find it, your Majesty?'

'It was my spell that made it invisible and I can remove it. Assemble your soldiers and I will instruct them. Once we have the creature, Lucy will be easily captured, their fates are tied together. Lucy just doesn't know it yet.'

Ryan walked down to the Rose and Crown. He didn't usually go to the pub during his lunch break; he wasn't a big drinker. The smell of stale beer assailed his nostrils as he entered and he grimaced as he made his way over to one of the tables. Its wooden surface was pitted and scratched and when he put his hand on it he realised it was sticky with old beer. He scowled as he sat down and wiped his hand on his trousers.

He sat stiffly for the next twenty minutes, his arms folded across his chest, checking his watch compulsively. Tim Crace was late. He didn't know the thief very well, it was usually Bill who dealt with him, but the man had been adamant that they meet (in this cesspit of all places).

He looked toward the bar and saw Tim ordering a beer, his motorbike helmet on the bar beside him. At last! Ryan had better things to do with his lunch hour than talk to scum like him.

Tim walked over with his beer and his helmet and sat down opposite Ryan.

He offered no apology and got straight to the point.

'You need to talk to Johnny. The boys inside have told me that Bill has been sent off to hospital. Someone strung him up. From what they say, he isn't dead but he might as well be.'

'Where is he? Which hospital?' Ryan asked frantically.

'Redfern, but you won't get anything out of him.'

Ryan tried to compose himself; he knew something like this would happen. The thief rummaged in his bag and pulled out a folded newspaper and placed it on the table beside them.

'Bill said, if anything happens to him, I was to give you this,' he said in a low voice, placing his hand on the newspaper. 'There are some papers in here that he was using to blackmail some dude; it was about some woman who got murdered. I ain't no murderer and I ain't getting messed up in that shit.

'I wouldn't open it here if I were you. Bill owes me a grand for those and I figure since you are the proud new owner, you should cover it,' he took a swig of his beer. 'I figure Johnny did the number on Bill and he might come for me next. I am getting the hell out of here, so I could use that money right now.'

Ryan casually looked around the room and when he saw that no one was paying them any attention, he slipped his wallet out of his coat pocket and into his lap. He had been starting to stockpile cash over the last few weeks in case he needed to flee. He had already been to see Blint to order new passports for himself and Bill; they should be ready soon.

He slipped ten bright green hundred-dollar notes from his wallet and passed them under the table to Tim's waiting hand. Tim counted them by feel and slipped them into his bag. His eyes did not leave Ryan once.

'You won't see me again.'

Ryan nodded.

The thief finished his beer and left.

Ryan took the newspaper into the men's room and locked himself in a cubicle. He would have more privacy here than back at work. He might want to destroy these papers here and now, especially if it was going to implicate him in a murder.

Inside the newspaper was a large envelope and inside it was another envelope addressed to Philip Cole and a handwritten note. The note was a description of a woman's daily routine and appearance. She was described as heavily pregnant. One sentence stood out:

The baby has to go too.

Attached to it was a photograph of Rebecca Cole, Philip's wife. Ryan had met her once at a school reunion.

He opened the envelope addressed to Philip. A photocopy of the same document was inside and a typewritten note:

I have the original of this. I am sure the police would be very interested to see it. I also have a receipt for the twenty grand you paid the boys to do the job. Just in case you thought I was bluffing. Now get on with it.

So that's why the garage boys had done it. Perform the hit on the woman and then take the baby to on-sell for some extra cash. Only things hadn't gone as planned.

Ryan had known Philip for years — well, he thought he had. He knew the bastard was cold but, Jesus, this was icy — paying someone to murder your wife and unborn child.

But maybe the thief was wrong about Johnny; maybe it wasn't Johnny who attacked Bill. If Bill was blackmailing Philip, maybe Philip had paid someone to murder Bill in gaol.

He had to talk to Johnny. But the papers — he would keep those as his Get-Out-Of-Jail-Free card.

Clio guided Gaia and the soldiers to the Blue portal stone; although there were few humans living in this part of the Blue Mountains, they flew in miniature as a precaution. When they landed beside the stone, Clio turned to Gaia and said:

'To you, my trusted friend, I give the instructions for the stone portals but to no other. You must keep this secret until your death. Understand?'

'Yes, my Queen.'

'This stone is linked to all the other stones that I have created and you can travel between them in an instant, as we did when we returned from Darwin. You will open the portal and take the soldiers through, then you will spread the soldiers over the length and breadth of the city like a net. Once I have removed the invisibility spell, the creature will shine like a blue beacon for a moment and it will not be able to hide from you.

'Capture it and return swiftly.'

'Yes, your Majesty.'

Clio turned to face the stone.

'Inside the stone is a faerie mind, you must order it to open the portal. It will struggle against you, but you must be firm. A promise was made that must be kept. Lie to it or use force if you have to, but remind it that the promise must be kept. Probe the stone and find the mind.'

Gaia suspected what she would find when she reached the mind hidden in the stone and she was unsure if she would be able to control her grief. Gaia had known the missing girl. Poor Morrighan!

She closed her eyes and probed the stone with her mind; a single beam of concentration focused on the stone. She did not know if Clio had the ability to intercept her thoughts once they entered the stone, but keeping them focused would make it more difficult at least.

Morrighan, are you there?

Gaia?!

I am so sorry Morrighan! If I had known what she was going to do I would have stopped her.

Gaia, I can't move! It is so dark and cold. Please, get me out of here!
I'm so sorry Morrighan, I can't, at least, not yet. Clio is here. I have to make her trust me. I will help the rebels to overthrow her, and when I do I will find a way to set you free.

Gaia, there are others, sometimes I hear them screaming!

I will find them and free them all my darling, but I can't do it yet. I am so sorry Morrighan!

She heard Morrighan sobbing in her mind.

She could feel Clio pacing up and down beside her. Patience was never Clio's strong point.

'Threaten to destroy her with fire, lie to her and tell her you will set her free when the moon is full, do whatever it takes to make her obey!' Clio raged.

Please Morrighan, let us pass through to the Sydney stone. I will find a way, I promise!

The portal opened, a dark blue glow creating a tunnel of light. The sobbing continued and Gaia bit her tongue hard, tasting blood and forcing back tears. She turned to her soldiers and said in a loud voice:

'Hold hands. Do not let go until I give the order or you will send your fellow soldiers to their deaths.

Once the soldiers had made their faerie chain she grasped the hand of her second in command and led them into the portal. Most of the soldiers had confused faces, but some were grim in the understanding that this was faerie magick at its worst.

The light changed from blue to green as they passed through and when the green light died down on the stone at their destination, Gaia and her soldiers found themselves standing in the long grass among towering gravestones and tombs.

'You can let go now.'

Hands were released but slowly, each faerie hesitant to be the first.

They were in Rookwood Cemetery, on the western side of Sydney. Gaia had been here once before with Clio and a green-winged faerie called Nerida.

'We have a special mission to accomplish,' Gaia said to her second in command. 'Spread the soldiers to cover as much of the city as possible. On my command they are to watch for a bright blue glow. It will only appear for a few seconds. They are to remain in position and report to me directly via my ring if they see it. Let me know when they are in position.'

While the soldiers were mobilising, she flew as quickly as she could to old pepper. Andy and the others should be there if they had stuck to their plan.

'Old Pepper, can I come in?' she asked, placing her hands on the tree's knobbly bark.

'Of course, my dear, as long as you haven't brought that other riff-raff with you.'

'No. It's just me,' she said slipping into the knothole and dropping to the chamber floor.

'What are you doing here?' said Andy standing up in alarm.

'They aren't back yet?' asked Gaia, her voice as alarmed as his.

'No. And how can you be back from Darwin? Renee told me you left the signal!'

'I did, and we shouldn't be back. Clio has used dark magic to set up portals. As soon as she was informed of the escape we were able to travel from one portal to another — we were back in minutes!'

'Oh my god. How many of these does she have?'

'Dozens all over the country. I don't know where she discovered the dark magick to make these, but I know she has deceived and trapped faeries to make them. I don't know if I will be able to free them! I have a dreadful feeling that it is only their minds that are embedded in the stone, that their bodies have been destroyed!'

Andy sat down heavily.

'I always knew she was a monster but to do this to her own kind?'

'She will stop at nothing to get what she wants.'

'No. I dare say you're right.'

'Renee and Lucy got away from the compound and were hiding in a dumping ground filled with old iron machinery. Clio and I lost the trail. I am hoping they were able to slip back to Old Blue.'

Gaia suddenly tensed; listening.

'I have to go. I have just received word from my sergeant, the soldiers are almost in position. Renee has Lucy, but she also has another creature with her — one hidden by an invisibility spell. When my soldiers are in place, I will give the order and Clio will break the spell. If Renee and Lucy are not safely hidden when that happens the creature will glow and give away their location. I can only delay the command for so long or it will raise suspicion. Can you contact Renee?'

'If I do, and there are other faeries close by, I might give them away.'

'You will have to risk it. If they can get inside Old Blue they should be safe.'

Andy quickly made contact with Renee.

'They are almost there.'

'Tell them to get to Old Blue and stay there until I give the all clear.'

'Okay. Done. But please, take me through the doorway to Old Blue, I can't pass through by myself!'

Gaia held his arm and stepped through the portal.

'Andy!' Old Blue exclaimed.

'Renee will be here soon, Old Blue.'

'I'm sorry Andy, I have to go,' Gaia said. 'I will return as soon as I can.' Gaia flew quickly back through the tree portal to Old Pepper and on to re-join her troops.

Tom was in his office reading through the phone company records for Tim Crace's mobile phone. It was a listing of phone numbers for all calls to and from Tim's phone in the last three months. Constable Ivan Peale knocked on the edge of the open door.

'Yep,' Tom said, looking up.

'The hospital just got back to me about Doyle, Sir.'

'Come on in and shut the door.'

Peale closed the door behind him and took a seat in front of the desk.

'He's still alive, but the lack of oxygen to his brain has given him severe brain damage. After they cut him down he had a stroke; he's paralysed down one side. They are ninety-nine percent sure the brain damage is permanent. There is no way he will be fit to stand trial.'

Tom sighed and ran his hands through his hair.

'Shit, shit, shit,' he said, leaning back in his chair.

'What now, Sir?' asked Peale.

'Well, the case against Bill can't go any further, not unless he has a miraculous recovery, but we still haven't found his captives and there are all the other gang members to clean up as well, including the Stonefish. So, we keep going.'

'What do you want me to do next?'

'Go and get a warrant to search Tim Crace's place. I've been trawling through his phone records and a few minutes ago I found a phone number I recognised. It's the main switchboard number for the nursing home where Bill worked. Tim Crace called someone there yesterday. Looks like we have another rotten apple in that barrel.'

'Any way of finding out who he spoke to?'

'That will depend on how modern the phone system is over there. If they don't have automated records, the receptionist might be able to remember. It was only yesterday. But I'd put my money on Dr Ryan Porter.'

'I'm on it. I'll go there first and then head over to the court to get the warrant.'

'Perfect.'

Sky Blue Wings

Renee flew through the knothole and collapsed onto the floor inside Old Blue.

'Hello, what is this? I sense three not two!' exclaimed Old Blue.

'I have her, Andy!' Renee put her hands on the floor to allow Lucy to step off and then increased Lucy's size to match her own.

'Lucy! My you have grown!' exclaimed the old tree.

'I can see you!' Andy exclaimed, 'How did you break Clio's cloaking spell?'

'It must have been tied to the ring! We got rid of it.'

'Dad?' Lucy asked.

'Lucy! My Lucy!' said Andy, his eyes filling with tears.

'The Queen told me you were dead, that she killed you!' Lucy said.

'No, my darling, lies — all lies,' he said holding out his arms.

She moved forward slowly as if not quite believing and then allowed herself to be wrapped up in his hug.

Renee sat on a bench and wiped the tears from her eyes.

'Who else is with you, Renee?' Old Blue asked.

'I am afraid I don't know. Clio has hidden her from everyone and she isn't wearing one of Clio's rings, so I can't work out where the spell is based.'

Renee reached inside her bag and she felt a pressure on her finger.

'Do you want me to increase your size?'

There was a single tap on her finger.

Renee helped her out of the bag and onto the floor. She increased her size, but it was pure guesswork to decide when to stop.

'Are you about the right size?' she asked.

There was another tap on her arm.

'Are you able to break the spell Old Blue?'

'No. I'm afraid not. This isn't tree magic.'

'No need,' Andy said, breaking away from his daughter. 'Clio is going to break the spell soon. She wants to flush you out, Renee, and there is going to be quite a glow when she breaks it. Old Blue, can you block the entrance for a while, just to be safe?'

'Yes, Andy, and I will close the portal to Old Pepper for a while too. That should contain it.'

The gateway to Old Pepper wobbled as Old Blue spoke to the other tree, 'Yes, Old Pepper, just for a while. Thanks.' The wavering surface of the portal went still and then closed; the surface changing to wood.

They waited, holding their breath.

'When was she going to break the spell?' asked Renee.

'Gaia said as soon as she had her troops in position she was to give the word to Clio and then Clio was going to —'

The tree was suddenly filled with a blinding blue light. They all covered their eyes with their hands and turned away from the fairy who was emitting it.

'Blimey,' exclaimed Andy, 'she wasn't kidding about it being bright!'

'Nancy!' Old Blue cried, overjoyed.

'What?' said Andy, spinning around to face the fairy, squinting his eyes to try and see through the glare.

The light dimmed and a fairy stood in front of them. She was thin and haggard and her arms were badly burnt. Her pale hair was long and lank and her eyes were sunken; in a startling contrast, her wings glowed a bright sky blue.

Andy was staring, his mouth open.

'Nancy?'

'Aye, Andy. Clio has a lot to answer for.'

Lucy was staring at Nancy in disbelief.

'No. I saw Clio kill you!' Lucy cried.

'No, my darling, you saw Clio wave her sword and you saw a shower of sparks. She hid me with a concealment spell. The sword never touched me.'

'And you've been in the dungeon the whole time and I have been feeding you ...' Lucy said horrified.

'She is a wicked, wicked faerie, my love. None of this was your fault.'

'All of this was my fault! I was the one who ran off, I was the one who got sucked in by her!'

'All of that is over, Lucy,' said Andy. 'It's all water under the bridge. I never thought we would all be together again, safe. We're all safe!' said Andy moving to embrace his wife, tears flowing down his face.

They sobbed into each other's shoulders. Lucy stood watching them, her face blank.

Renee sat on the ledge and thanked whatever gods were out there that she had decided to bring the unknown fairy with them. After a while, Andy stirred.

'Nancy,' Andy said, 'do you need to sit down?'

'Yes, I think that would be best,' she said. She was very frail.

Andy guided her to a ledge, careful not to touch the terrible burns on both her wrists.

Nancy turned to Lucy.

'Oh Lucy, I am so sorry. I never meant to scare you, please forgive me.'

Lucy was watching her in silence, her arms wrapped around herself. She opened her mouth to speak, but no words came out.

She shook her head; an act of bewilderment.

'How could I not sense you?' she finally managed to say, 'My own mother?' Tears were welling in her eyes.

'It's not your fault darling…'

'I thought you were a monster — I threw food at you one day!' Lucy was crying now.

'No one could sense me but Clio. She has the power to break bonds; to sicken and destroy. They are the only abilities she has and she has honed them well. You are free of her now and I will make sure that she can never get her hands on you ever again.'

Nancy held out her arms to the fairy woman-child. Lucy hesitated for just a moment and then rushed forward to hug her.

Tom said goodbye to Constable Peale and placed the phone back on its cradle. Peale had just confirmed that the call Tim Crace had made to the nursing home had been to Dr Ryan Porter. It looked like Tim Crace and Dr Porter were a part of Bill's gang of scum bags. Was Philip Cole a part of it too, Tom wondered? And if so, was he also involved in his own wife's murder? If Philip had a mistress, perhaps Rebecca was in the way…

Tom was able to obtain the student lists for Camperdown High School for the whole of the nineteen eighties. William (or Bill) had been a popular name at the time and there were several at the school during Philip's time. But there was no Bill Doyle.

Another lie? Philip was looking shakier by the minute.

He was just about to give up when he saw another name that he recognised. Ryan Porter. This just got better and better.

He needed to talk to Renee.

He needed to tell her about Bill, to let her know that Bill would probably never go to trial. He also needed to know if she knew Ryan Porter or any of her husband's old school friends. Perhaps Bill's gang went all the way back to his teenage years and the death of the old homeless man.

He drove over to her house and stood on the verandah for five minutes waiting for someone to answer his knock. There were a wooden table and two chairs out the front and he sat down to ponder his next move, hoping that Renee and Andy had just ducked out for a few minutes.

Doctor Ryan Porter — he didn't know much about him. Gardiner had started looking into his history, but she hadn't given Tom an update yet. He would chase that as soon as he got back to the office. When Gardiner and Peale had interviewed him the first time, he had played it very cool, understating his involvement with Bill and describing the relationship as work colleagues only. Now Ryan was linked to Bill, Tim Crace and Philip Cole.

Time to apply some pressure, thought Tom.

He wandered back to his car and drove over to the nursing home.

The day was not going well for Tom. Ryan Porter had taken the day off work, so he left the receptionist his business card and a message for Dr Porter to contact him. Then he drove to Ryan's house, but Ryan was not there either. He gave up in disgust and went back to the office, hoping that Peale was having better luck in getting the warrant for Tim Crace's place.

An hour later, armed and kitted out with bulletproof vests in case things turned ugly, they headed over to Tim Crace's apartment. Two additional uniforms had been commandeered to assist.

It was just after midday; the thief was a night owl so there was a good chance he was home and still asleep. They found his motorbike in the carport, chained and padlocked; so far, so good.

'Okay, everyone. Cracker Crace is a complete unknown. We are going to take this very cautiously. Gardiner and Peale, I want you two to come into the flat with me in case there is trouble. Peale, bring the battering ram. Burke, I want you down here in the car and ready to move if he runs,' Burke nodded and climbed back into the car. 'Smith, I am going to position you on the stairwell, one floor down from the apartment, covering the front door.'

'Roger,' said Smith.

'Okay, let's move.'

Tom led the way up the stairs. The building was silent except for their footfalls. Once they reached the second floor he gestured to the point where he wanted Smith to stand guard. Smith took position and Tom, Peale and Gardiner continued up the stairs.

He pointed to Peale and Gardiner in turn, motioning for them to take up positions on either side of the door, guns drawn. He pulled the warrant and his police badge from his pocket and knocked on the door three times, hard then moved to one side of the door out of harm's way.

'Mr Crace, open up. This is the Police, we have a warrant.'

There was no sound. He waited thirty seconds before banging again, harder, louder. Still nothing. Staying to one side of the door he reached forward and tried the door handle. It was locked as expected.

He moved behind Peale pocketed his badge and the warrant and drew his gun.

'Okay, use the ram,' he said to Peale.

Peale holstered his gun and moved forward with the battering ram and Tom and Gardiner moved in to cover him. Peale positioned himself in front of the door and swung the heavy steel ram. The first blow made the windows in the stairwell rattle, the second sheared the locks off the door. He stepped to one side and Tom pushed the door fully open. He made his way into the apartment, his gun ready. Gardiner followed Tom and Peale waited just inside the door, his gun ready in case anyone tried to make a break for it.

The short hall led into a combined lounge-dining room and an adjoining kitchen. Tom ducked low and peered behind the kitchen counter before giving Gardiner the thumbs up. There were two doors leading off the lounge and they moved quietly to the first. Gardiner opened the door and Tom entered quickly gun held in front of him. The bed was empty. Tom quickly scanned the room and the cupboards. It was all clear. They moved to the next door.

If he wasn't in here, then he wasn't home. If he was in here, then he was not being co-operative. He glanced at Gardiner, she was nervous, good, she recognised the situation as well as he did. He held up three fingers and tapped the third with his other hand. She nodded. One, two, he mouthed, holding up one and then two fingers, when he raised the third finger she pushed the door open and he ducked down and through. Just inside the bathroom he stopped and lowered his weapon.

Gardiner followed him in.

Sprawled in the bathtub was the recently deceased Tim Crace. His head was slumped awkwardly onto his shoulder. There were deep cuts running down both cheeks and he was missing two fingers. The small round hole in his forehead was hardly bleeding at all, Tom knew the back of his head would not be so neat. The plug was in the bath and blood had pooled around the dead man's feet. It was still bright red but was starting to congeal.

'Alright, Gardiner. I think the killer is long gone. Go and tell the others to set up an exclusion zone for forensics; no one in or out of the building until I say. Then do a door knock and tell anyone that answers to stay inside. I'll call George.'

Once he was sure she had gone he swore loudly.

Sydney, Australia twenty-two years ago

It was night. He could feel the bandages pressed tightly over his skin. There were machines making strange noises and there was terrible pain.

He could hear a hushed conversation at the door.

'He's not going to make it, is he, doctor?' It was his grandmother.

'No. I don't think so. Most of the burns — they are third degree and they cover more than half of his body. I think his heart will give out soon.'

'Has anyone told him about his parents?'

'No. That must be kept from him for now. He isn't strong enough.'

The woman started to sob quietly.

Consciousness slipped away.

It was dark. He didn't know how long he had been asleep. Grandma was sleeping in a chair next to the bed.

There was a strange blue light.

All the other lights were red and green. When they flashed there were beeps and pings.

This blue light was silent.

He could feel a plastic tube up his nose. It felt like a huge booger.

His face wasn't hurting so bad now and the bandages had been removed. The skin didn't feel like it was going to split anymore.

His arms and his stomach were still bound tightly in compression bandages and they felt awful; so hot, so sore. He was about to start crying again when the little blue light came closer.

It was floating.

It landed on the bed next to him.

He felt sleepy again and even though he really wanted to see what it was, he couldn't keep his eyes open. He struggled hard against the urge to sleep; it would be like falling asleep at a quarter to twelve and missing the feast. But it was no good.

He slept.

Twenty-two years later

Tom woke from his dream and, for a moment, he was surprised to find himself in his own bed. The dream from his childhood had been so vivid that it stayed with him and he found no more rest that night.

Doctor Ryan Porter

The phone rang in Johnny's office and he picked it up immediately.

'Yes?' he said into the receiver.

'Blint here. Got news — 'bout Ryan.'

'Go on.'

'He came and got the passports he asked for, the ones with the new names. Told me he didn't need the one for Bill anymore, but I said I didn't want the fucken thing. I made him pay for both.'

'Email me the details now.'

'Will do.'

Johnny hung up the phone and unlocked the screen on his computer. Within a minute the email from Blint had arrived.

He picked up the phone again.

'Sergeant Palmer,' said the voice on the other end of the line.

'It's me. I have a job for you,' said Johnny.

'Go ahead.'

'Airline trace. Forwarding you the details now.' Johnny forwarded the email from Blint to an email address stored in his contacts list.

'This is Ryan's new ID. I want to know the second this guy books a flight anywhere. Here or overseas.'

'Got the email. No problem,' said Sergeant Palmer.

'Good.'

Next, he rang a mobile phone number.

After a few short rings the phone was answered with, 'Yep.'

'Got an update on Ryan for me?' asked Johnny.

'He has been behaving himself. Nothing but work and home since he met Tim Crace at the pub. Oh, and a visit to Blint — Blint said he would call you about that.'

'He has. All Good.'

He ended the call and rang another number.

'Hello, this is Doctor Porter.'

'Doctor Porter, it's Johnny Black. I need you to come and see me right away.'

'No problem, sir, I can be there in ten.'

'I look forward to it.'

Johnny's office was in a luxurious office block with views out over Double Bay. It was only a ten-minute walk to the nursing home, but Johnny rarely walked anywhere; he preferred to travel in style in his Ferrari. Ryan, being the kind of doctor who practised what he preached, preferred to walk everywhere. Johnny wasn't sure if he even owned a car.

Fifteen minutes later, Johnny's secretary showed Ryan into his office.

'Thought it was time for a little catch-up,' said Johnny smiling and offering him a seat on the other side of the desk.

'Sure,' said Ryan sitting down. Johnny thought he looked a little wary. Not surprising really; Ryan wasn't stupid and it was very unusual for Johnny to invite anyone to his office.

'A little bird told me that you had a meeting with Tim Crace the other day.'

'Yes. Bill owes him money. I sorted it.'

'Anything else?'

'Yes. He told me that Bill has been attacked in gaol — someone tried to kill him.'

'Yes. I heard about that. Very sad. But well, you can't work in this industry and not make a few enemies. And for some reason, inmates aren't too keen on child pimps.'

Ryan was staring at him and chewing his lip; Johnny could see the sweat forming on his brow.

'And?' Johnny asked. 'Something else?'

'Tim said you ordered the attack.'

Johnny sighed and steepled his fingers in front of him.

'People talk, Ryan. You can't believe everything you hear. You don't want to cross me, Ryan, especially not over a silly rumour. You've seen what happens when people cross me. It may not happen straight away, but I will catch up with you eventually. Just look at dear old mum. Twenty years wasn't enough to save her.'

'What?' asked Ryan, confused.

Johnny threw a file across the table to him.

Ryan opened it cautiously. It was a DNA report.

'Strange twist of fate isn't it that the old bum you drag in off the street happens to be my mum, hey?'

Ryan stared at the report and then at Johnny.

'You asked me to kill your own mother!' the shock and outrage were clear on Ryan's face.

'Yep. You always said the old crone reminded you of her, didn't you? Was that why you chose her?' Johnny laughed.

Ryan sat and stared down at the file in front of him. Silent.

Ryan walked into the hospital, his white coat and doctors ID declaring him to be a legitimate visitor to the wards. He had always been able to move around any of the hospitals in the area without challenge. Each one had a slightly different pass colour and format, but their forger, Blint, knew them all and had made him an entire set. More than once, Ryan had visited a business rival in hospital and gently finished them off.

This time he had come to see Bill. He was in a secure ward with other sick prisoners. There was a hospital security guard seated at the end of the hall and the prisoners that were considered particularly dangerous also had a police guard positioned outside their door. Bill did not. That was not a good sign.

He entered the room and walked over to the bed. Bill was asleep or unconscious. He was not strapped or chained to the bed so he was not deemed to be a flight risk.

Bill's charts were hanging from the end of the bed, Ryan picked them up and flicked through the pages slowly taking in the details; interpreting the medical meaning behind the comments. There were tears in his eyes as he placed the chart back on the rail at the base of the bed with a dull metallic thud.

'He's really fucked you over hasn't he, Bill? Your own fucking brother.

'But then, he fucks everyone, doesn't he?

'There are only two people in this world that I care about, Bill. You and your mum. Now Johnny has practically killed you and made me kill your mum…

'Oh god Bill, I am so sorry. I didn't know it was her…

'Johnny knew! He knew!'

Ryan shook his head, trying to hold back the tears.

'Is this Karma Bill. Are we getting what we deserve?

'Is this our punishment for killing your dad? For killing all those others? Why did we keep going Bill, why didn't we just flee after we killed your old man? Why did we go along with Johnny and his plans? We both knew what he was capable of, why were we stupid enough to think he would be loyal to us?

'If I stay, at some point Johnny will kill me. I can't do this stuff anymore. I signed up because you needed my help, but I don't owe Johnny anything and I am not going to die for him.

'I'm off Bill. Sorry, but I won't be able to come and see you again. I am going to disappear. I know that Johnny will come after me, but if he is in gaol it will be harder for him to get me. I am going to send everything I know to the police. I hope you are okay with that. I would never betray you, Bill — you are my blood brother and I love you. But the only way I can bring Johnny down is by bringing it all down. I've looked at your charts, Bill. You aren't going to recover from this, you are as good as dead. Please forgive me.'

He bent down and kissed Bill on the forehead.

Ryan had his plane ticket to Paris, France booked in his new name, now there was one last thing he had to do.

He bundled the papers together, everything that the thief, Tim Crace, had given him, plus photos, working notes, names and a map of the lower parts of the nursing home. There was enough there to bring down the whole fucking lot.

It was a large parcel and it was too important to risk it getting lost. He caught the bus from his home to the centre of Sydney and walked into the office of a courier company. He used his own name as the sender. It was probably the last thing he would ever use it for; after this, he was Ryan Porter no more. He carefully wrote out the name and address of the police officer who had been trying to contact him.

They assured him it would be delivered the same day. It was the best he could do without raising suspicion.

He caught another bus to the airport. He had a small satchel on his shoulder and six thousand US dollars in his wallet. At the current exchange rate, that should be less than ten thousand Australian dollars. That was the maximum he was allowed to carry out of the country. The last thing he wanted was to fall foul of immigration and have his cover blown.

He and Bill had set up a slush fund in Switzerland. Once he was in Paris he would be safe. He would hire a car and go and get the cash and then he could go anywhere in the world that took his fancy. He just had to get safely out of Australia.

He was waiting in the airline queue to check in to his flight when the uniformed policeman tapped him on the shoulder and showed him his police ID.

'I am Sergeant Palmer of the New South Wales Police Force. Doctor Ryan Porter, you are under arrest, you are not obliged to say or do anything unless you wish to do so, but whatever you say or do may be used in evidence. Do you understand?'

Ryan nodded dumbly.

The policeman was a big guy. There was no way he was going to be able to overpower him and escape. The policeman pulled out his handcuffs and Ryan allowed his hands to be secured in front of him without a fuss. The policeman guided him out of the airport.

How had they found him? He had told no-one of his plans. He had used a public phone to book his airline ticket, and that was in his new, false name.

Didn't coppers usually work in pairs?

He ducked his head as he was pushed into the back seat of a marked police car. There was a Perspex panel between him and the front seats and he had expected to see the policeman's partner sitting in the front passenger seat but it was empty.

Sergeant Palmer slid into the driver's seat and they drove out of the airport carpark and out of the city.

Something wasn't right. They were going the wrong way. He was about to try and reach for the door handle when he realised that there wasn't one. He was trapped.

'Where are we going?'

'You have an appointment.'

'With who?'

'Your worst nightmare.'

Ryan began to bang on the glass, his handcuffs restricting his efforts. Sergeant Palmer laughed.

'Settle petal, if you're lucky, he'll just give you something to think about. A gentle reminder to pull your head in. Maybe one less toe,' the policeman smiled a cruel smile.

Half an hour later, the policeman turned onto a dirt track. Further down the road was an old farm shed, its doors open; they drove in. The policeman climbed out and opened the back door of the car, his gun pointed at Ryan's head.

'Don't mess about, or your brains will be everywhere. Got it?'

'Yeah.'

Ryan wriggled his way out of the car and the policeman pushed him toward a door at the rear of the shed. It was a small room, an old farm workshop, kitted out with all sorts of old tools for mending farm machinery and repairing fences. Johnny was sitting at a battered table inside.

'Take a seat, Ryan,' Johnny said pointing to the chair opposite him.

The policeman forced Ryan into the chair and then stood to guard the door.

'Did you really think that Blint was going to give you a nice new identity and not tell me? What the fuck were you thinking?'

'I want out.'

'Yes. I can see that. But I haven't finished with you yet. There are things to do.'

'You killed Bill.'

'Well, not me personally but, yes, I did.'

'How could you do that? How could you kill your own brother? And your mother?'

'Hey don't forget who started this. Bill was the one who started the whole familicide thing. You were there when he killed dear old dad.'

'He was saving your life!'

'Bull shit. He was playing the big man and went too far, as always. No subtlety.'

'I don't care. I'm out. I have had enough. I never signed up for this crap.'

'Oh yes, you did Ryan. You have had your share of the cream and you are in it up to your neck.'

'I have insurance. I was worried you might try to stop me from leaving. If my contact doesn't hear from me before 3 pm tomorrow he is going to post a parcel to the police. Let me go now and I will contact him and you will never see me again.'

'As tempting as that offer is, I think I have a better way,' Johnny nodded to the policeman.

Sergeant Palmer reached for the bolt cutters hanging on the wall.

Ryan wasn't a strong man and he wasn't hardened against pain. Twenty minutes of torture left him screaming for it to end.

'There is no contact. There is no phone number. I posted the papers to the police myself this morning. It's done. You are finished.'

Ryan began to laugh hysterically. He couldn't help himself. He had just signed his own death warrant and he no longer cared.

'You destroyed everything and now, I have destroyed you!' Ryan continued through his laughter.

Johnny looked at him in disgust.

'You stupid fuck. Right. I'm over this. We have work to do Palmer and fast. Give me your gun.'

Palmer handed him his pistol.

Johnny pointed it at Ryan and shot him in the head. Blood splattered on the wall behind him and he slumped forward in his seat.

Johnny handed the gun back to the policeman and then called a number on his mobile. When it answered, he didn't hold back.

'Where the fuck have you been? You were supposed to be following Ryan,' Johnny yelled.

There was a muffled reply.

'What? You can't even catch a fucking bus?'

The voice on the other end continued.

'And you didn't think to tell me that straight away? Which courier?' Johnny was red in the face, his anger flaring in his eyes as he listened.

'I'll deal with you later,' he said and hung up.

'Get to the courier on Elizabeth Street. See if you can intercept the parcel. Who would he have sent it to?'

'Detective Inspector Tom Hayes is the one that has been grilling Bill.'

'Right. Try to intercept the parcel at the courier — if that doesn't work, kill Hayes before anyone else sees it.'

'That is a big ask — killing a fellow copper.'

'Don't worry. I will make it worth your while.'

'Alright, but it better be good,' the policeman said and left.

Johnny looked at Ryan's body sitting slumped in the chair and decided to work out some of his anger.

Kraken Awakes

Bill lay in the hospital bed, his mouth slack, his eyes open but unseeing. The nurse took his pulse and temperature and checked the drip. She recorded her findings on his chart and replaced it on the end of his bed with a metallic clunk.

Her shoes squeaked on the linoleum as she walked to the door and dimmed the lights. She stopped to chat with the guard on duty in the hallway and then two of them wandered down to the coffee machine deep in conversation. They knew that Bill would not be going anywhere.

The night was mild and the window was ajar, letting in the autumn breeze. Out of the darkness, a swarm of golden lights appeared, a surging ball of brilliance hovering outside the window. One by one the lights slipped inside and moved over to the bed to float above Bill's face. Two of them dropped onto his cheeks and slipped into the corner of his eyes. The rest moved away and formed a tight group in the centre of the room.

Bill's eyes went from dull and unfocused to awake but confused. His head moved from side to side on his pillow as he took in his surroundings. When he saw the ball of lights hovering at the foot of the bed he froze.

Something was speaking to him. Something was telling him to get up. He felt a strange warmth in his arm and looked at the filigree scar on his wrist. It was glowing. He had to go. He didn't know where; he just had to go. Something was wrong with his head. Everything felt strange.

He pulled the sheets back and slowly moved his legs off the side of the bed. His left leg did not want to move. He pulled it across the sheets to lie next to his right leg. He tried to get up, but something was tugging on his hand. He looked down and saw the cannula protruding from the back of it. There was a plastic tube leading out of it; the other end connected to a drip on a stand. The stand was wobbling, threatening to fall onto the bed. He tugged the tube free from his hand, it dropped onto the bed and a pool of wetness started to spread across the sheets.

Something was calling him.

He managed to stand although his left leg threatened to collapse under him. One of the golden lights slipped away from the glowing ball and dived into the cannula in his hand. His arm lit up as the tiny light moved up inside his arm and across his chest cavity before it dived down into the wobbling leg. His leg stopped shaking. He placed his weight on it and shuffled forward. It was still weak but it was functional. He moved forward with his right leg and dragged the left one behind him. The floor was cold under his bare feet.

He did not know where he was going, he just knew that he had to go. The lights moved in front of him and he followed. He wasn't sure if he was awake or dreaming; his head felt fuzzy.

The lights stopped at the door and then darted across the hall to the door to the fire escape. He followed them and opened the door. They slipped inside and he followed them down the stairs, limping from one stair to the next, dragging his left leg behind him. Two flights and he was at the bottom. There was a fire door and he knew that an alarm would go off if he opened it. He was stuck. The lights surrounded the door. Something told him to open the door and he complied. The alarm did not go off. Once he was through the door, the lights slid around the door frame to join him and he pulled the door shut. They re-grouped into their surging mass and beckoned him onward.

It was colder out here. A sudden thought intruded — he had to save his mother. No, his mother was dead. No, he had to save his mother's soul. He had to stop Johnny. Johnny was going to put her body with their father, trap her with him forever. For a moment he wavered, drawn in a different direction, and the lights surrounded him, their intensity pulsing, their flight sporadic and frantic. He was confused, what did they want?

Then his scar spoke to him in images. He had to go to the old tree, the lights were taking him there. Everything would be okay once he got to the old tree.

They guided him up one road and down another, through an alleyway and into a park. The grass was long and unkempt. In the centre stood a huge dark shape. Part of his mind rebelled; he did not want to go any closer. The dark shape loomed like a sinister alien creature.

It is Old Kraken, the old tree, go to the old tree, the lights told him.

He had no control, his legs dragged him closer to the monstrous dark shape. There were dozens of suckers drooping from the branches down into the earth like serpents frozen in time.

He stood at the base of the tree and stared into the dark canopy, entranced. A huge limb twisted around behind him and scooped him up into the air, knocking the wind from his lungs and ripping the hospital tag from his wrist. The branch twisted toward the enormous trunk and as he looked down he could see that the centre of the tree was a gaping chasm that seemed to go down into eternal blackness. He screamed as the branch twisted even further and pushed him down into the void.

The branch returned to its normal position, the silver amulets and trinkets strung along its length tinkling for a moment and then the night was silent.

When Bill awoke he was lying in a room made of wood. He felt alert; his mind was no longer a foggy mess. He stretched his legs but only one moved in response. It was as if his left leg belonged to someone else and it had been tacked onto his body for appearances only. He tried again and was able to move it a little. Eventually, he gave up and dragged it into position with his hands so he could sit up.

'I have given you back your mind,' a voice said to him from nowhere. 'You have one chance to redeem your miserable life. Fail and you will die. If it were my choice alone, I would kill you now, slowly, painfully and with great pleasure. Just as you killed Babayaga. But she gave me instructions before her death and I promised I would fulfil them.'

Bill sat silent. His renewed and frightened mind threw up the memory of his last time with Ryan. He had not comprehended Ryan's words at the time but now they were clear. Was Ryan right? Was this karma?

'See the spoon on the floor?' the ancient voice asked.

Bill scanned the floor around him and stopped when he saw the silver spoon sitting a few feet away. The filigree handle was unmistakable.

'Pick it up.'

Bill wavered. He did not want to touch it.

'Pick it up or I will kill you now!'

Bill stretched out his hand and took the spoon gingerly, expecting it to burn him. It was cold. He turned it over and saw the engraving on the back. It was the spoon from the photos that the policeman had shown him.

'How?' Bill asked, confused.

Old Kraken ignored his question.

'I am sending you back in time, twenty years before you first met Babayaga — before you got your scar, before you were even born. You have two tasks to accomplish and you will have twenty years to prepare yourself.

'The first task…you must kill a fairy named Clio. You will find her at the address and date engraved on the spoon. She has red wings. There will be another faerie with her, her wings are pink, do as you like with her, I do not care if she lives or dies. Take iron with you; it will sap their strength and then you will be able to kill Clio.

'Second… you must contact your younger self. You must stop him from becoming a murderer. You have twenty years to work out how to do that before your future is set in stone. It must be done before your younger self meets Babayaga or there will be no return.

'If you fail, you will die at your own hand. If you succeed, Babayaga will not die and you will have another chance at life — a chance to save your soul and maybe even a chance to save your mother. Babayaga gave me the power to do this once and once only. If you fail there is nothing I can do. I suggest you do not fail.'

Bill stood, numb and disbelieving. Before him, the wooden wall became a door and as it opened there was a brilliant flash of light.

'The door will open soon,' Bill muttered to himself, remembering Babayaga's curse.

When the light receded, the hollow in the tree was empty.

Bill rolled over, there was something hard and knobbly underneath him and it was poking into his back. He came fully awake and realised he was lying on a lumpy tree root. He was under a tree in a park and there was an empty wine bottle beside him. He picked it up and drank the last of it. "Ben Ean," the label said. That couldn't be right. That brand hadn't existed for years. His head was funny and not just from the wine. He couldn't think properly. There was something he was supposed to do, but he couldn't remember what it was. He turned suddenly, feeling a presence, and found the old witch looking at him from the other side of the tree. Babayaga.

'Fuck off, you demented old cow!' he yelled in her direction. He tried to stand but stumbled. He looked down to realise that one of his legs was not cooperating. A cold breeze rushed past him and when he looked back to where she had been, Babayaga was gone.

He twisted his head from side to side, trying to locate her. She had done something to him once, something bad, but he couldn't remember what.

Well, fuck her. He had been having some awesome dreams lately about cutting her to pieces. He chuckled as he wandered over to the public toilet. Man, he needed to piss, must be the grog and the cold weather. God, he hated winter. He would get another bottle to warm him up later; he still had some money somewhere. He pulled some notes from his pocket. Flimsy paper stuff. Where had all the plastic notes gone? They were much sturdier than these old things and survived a wet night in the open much better. People just looked at him funny when he said he missed the plastic money. Well, fuck them all! They were the crazy ones, not him. He zipped up his pants and wandered off to find a bottle shop.

Bill sat and watched the people walk by. They were all wearing op shop clothes. Bell-bottomed trousers and turtle-necked sweaters in awful combinations of green and brown and orange. Not a mobile phone to be seen anywhere. He had lost his somewhere; he felt lost without it. He was going to call Ryan and then realised it was gone. Ryan would know what to do.

He wandered over to Ryan's flat instead. He wasn't there; neither was the flat. Where it should have been there was a grocery shop and a milk bar. A milk bar! He hadn't seen an actual working milk bar since he was a kid. Something was really wrong. The world was all backwards. Sometimes he thought he must be in hell.

He remembered someone telling him that he needed to do something. That it might even save his soul. Well, maybe this was hell. How did you get out of hell? Maybe he needed to be good? He couldn't remember the last time he had done something good; maybe he'd better try.

The youngsters all sought Bill out when they ended up on the street. Word was that he could find you a warm place to sleep and good easy pickings — food, booze, anything you needed. He was a bit weird though. He must have been a big Sci-Fi fan once 'cause he was always spouting shit about futuristic things — but he spoke like they really existed! Like phones you could carry with you anywhere, small enough to fit in your pocket — with no cord! But he was harmless. It was funny to hear him talk of stuff like that and, anyway, more than one kid had survived a freezing cold winter thanks to his help.

He wasn't sure how much time had passed, but he felt stiff and sore today in spite of the warm sunshine on his back. This time he turned to find her watching him from the bench across the park. Her usual spot on sunny summer days. Bill wondered if her name really was Babayaga. He had read the Russian fairy tale when he was a kid. Something about a little hut on chicken legs and an old witch who lived in it called Babayaga. Sometimes she was evil and forbidding and at other times she was helpful. A complete nutjob; but powerful.

He couldn't help but notice that his thoughts were clearer today. He wondered what day it was. Babayaga was still watching him. She was very old, he knew that; older than should be possible. Was she really a witch? She must be. He was certain that he had killed her, and yet, here she was. He nodded in her direction; a small acknowledgement of respect. She gave him the smallest nod in return.

He wished he could remember what it was he had to do. He slipped his hand into his pocket to reach for the filthy handkerchief he kept there and his fingers landed on the spoon. He pulled it out and turned it over in his hands. He was getting old now and his eyesight wasn't what it used to be, but he knew the engraving on the spoon by heart.

What date was it today? Kraken had said he was sending him back in time. Or was that just a dream? He walked over to the newsstand set up at the entrance to the park. He squinted at the date on the top of the nearest paper. Yes, he had gone back in time. He vaguely wondered how old he was now. How did it work if you went back in time?

'If you aren't buying, piss off. You stink!' the man behind the stand said to him.

He wandered away; he couldn't afford trouble.

Today was the day of the spoon. He just couldn't remember what it was that he had to do.

Another year, another winter. The arthritis in his old bones was flaring up worse than ever. The gang had lit a fire in a bin over at the park. He had got hold of some rum, if he shared it around, they might let him get nice and close to the fire.

Bill dragged his leg behind him as he made his way towards the yellow glow. He sensed her before he saw her. Babayaga emerged from the shadows and started to walk beside him. She had never done that before.

'I'm sorry,' he said. I remember what I did to you. I'm sorry...'

'Perhaps there is a heaven and a hell, Mr Denny, perhaps not,' she said, her accent heavy. 'Perhaps you have lived your purgatory, perhaps not. Fate will have its way. Goodbye, Mr Denny.'

He felt the breeze swirl past him and knew that she was no longer beside him. He did not even bother to turn his head. He made his way up to the fire and shared his bottle around. When the young runaway with the baby appeared, he moved aside to let her warm herself and her child. He had not seen the young man approach, so he was taken by surprise by the sudden shove to his chest.

'You fucking loser, get out of my way,' the young man snarled at him.

Bill overbalanced; he tried desperately to move his palsied leg to steady himself, but it was no use to him and he toppled to the ground. The girl with the baby moved away, pulling her child close to her; fear in her eyes.

The young man's friends moved in close; Bill was surrounded by a group of young thugs. Bill's eyes locked onto those of the young man.

'You?!' Bill cried. 'It can't be time yet? God please, not now, I'm not ready. Please, Bill, don't do this!' old Bill muttered from the ground, his paralysed face making his words slurred. His eyes were bright with fear.

'How the fuck do you know my name you piece of shit! What good are you for anything, you parasite? Pathetic. You're not a man, you're a worm!' the young Bill screamed at him; his cronies laughed, ready to join in when the kicking started.

'You can change this,' old Bill said, choking and coughing. He clutched his chest. 'It doesn't have to be like this Bill, there is still time!' he spluttered, reaching out to grab young Bill's ankle.

'Don't touch me you filthy hobo!' young Bill spat at him and shook his ankle free of his grasp, then he placed a well-aimed kick at old Bill's face.

Bill rolled onto his back and lay still.

Old Kraken waited and he was afraid. He sat outside of time watching its flow. There was a convulsion in time as Bill landed in the past; it rippled forward disturbing everything in its wake. He could not see all the details, only glimpses here and there and the impact on the flow of time itself. The ripple spread and caused other impacts, each spreading and causing new ripples in history. Old Kraken saw the night of fire — the burning of the house — and watched as the pink and red lights disappeared into the darkness unmolested.

The flow faded into a hazy blur, but one point in time stood out, the time of the scar, like a milestone in the gloom. He saw the wave hit its surface and the details were revealed to him. He saw Young Bill goad and shove Old Bill. He saw Old Bill collapse clutching his heart and Kraken's own heart leapt as he saw Babayaga appear from the shadows. He felt the scream in his mind as Babayaga branded Young Bill with the white-hot fork she held in her hand. And he saw Old Bill die. Old Bill had failed; neither task had been fulfilled.

The ripple in time faded and dissipated and a surge of faerie energy hit him bodily; Babayaga's energy. With it came the truth that she had kept hidden from him.

No...

No.

No!

'Babayaga!'

'Babayaga!' the old tree screamed again with a wooden voice.

The night creatures clamoured to hide from the disturbance and the birds of the day awoke in a fright and screeched as they rose from their perches in the trees around him.

The world did not change. Old Bill had failed. There was a Babayaga shaped hole in his existence. And he knew that Babayaga had lied to him.

He howled into the night; a primeval scream.

Lights went on in the houses surrounding the park. People with torches emerged, banding together for comfort, scanning the streets to find the source of the terrible noise.

Kraken disregarded them all and fell into his own leaden grief.

Just before dawn, Kraken roused himself.

Old Bill was dead. He could take some comfort from that small revenge.

But Clio still lived.

And that could not be endured.

A year ago, Babayaga had woken him from his tree slumber. She had given him a purpose and had made him *feel* again. She had given him a quest. But she had always known that Bill would fail.

The wily old bitch.

She had sacrificed herself so that he, Kraken, would have the power he needed to complete her quest — and Kraken had promised to complete it if Bill failed. She had started this chain of events twenty years ago when she branded Bill with her magical fork. In doing so, she had stored a magical reserve within Bill, ready to be released when the time was right.

Tonight, the circle of time had been closed by the death of Bill. Babayaga's spell had been completed, releasing the power she had stored inside Bill; releasing it now that Kraken was strong enough to receive it.

That power was swirling inside him now; trying to find a way to enter the core of his being. Finally, he understood. He submitted to Babayaga's will, allowing her power to pour into his soul, pulling it free from its wooden cage.

It had been a hundred years since Kraken, in his despair, had chosen to become a dryad. At the time he had thought that he would never want to leave the tree again. If Babayaga hadn't given him her power he would have been trapped as a tree forever. But now... now he had a purpose.

He pulled his shape together, taking resources from the living plant to supplement his own and he pushed his arm out of the wood and into the first rays of the morning sun.

The light shone on the smooth wooden skin of his arm and he pushed harder, breaking free of the tree. He stood in the fresh air — a nightmarish puppet. His head, chest and groin were covered in rough bark; a parody of hair. He stood and blinked at the sun with reborn eyes. He turned to the tree and patted it, relieved that it had not been harmed.

He spoke to the tree in its own language and the tree offered him a cluster of leaves. He fused them together to form a loin cloth — aware of his nakedness in spite of all the years he had spent as a tree. Satisfied, he moved off to explore the modern world.

A Wooden Casanova

Tom was furious.

He wasn't one to yell and scream in public, instead it simmered under the surface until he was ready to let it emerge. Running, swimming, working out in the police gym, these were where he found release.

Ten minutes ago, the constable stationed at the hospital had called; Bill was gone. The nurse doing her morning rounds had found his bed empty. Constable Peale had gone over with a team to search the grounds. There was no CCTV footage available and the constable guarding his room had not seen Bill leave or seen anyone else enter the room. The hospital was investigating the possibility that Bill was faking his injuries. Tom had every airport in the country on alert and had set up triggers at the bank should he try to access any of his accounts.

He entered the gym and tried to ignore the hushed conversation between two plainclothes officers when they saw him take up position in front of the punching bag and start to strap his hands. The pair retrieved their towels and quickly left the room. When he had the place to himself he didn't hold back his punches or his language.

Twenty minutes later, sweating and exhausted he sat down on one of the weight benches and removed his boxing gloves. His gym singlet was soaked and he wiped a hand across his forehead, brushing away the wet hair. As he slowly unwound the bindings from his hands he concentrated on slowing his breathing.

He saw a face peer cautiously around the corner and sighed.

'It's okay, Gardiner, I promise I won't bite. What's up?'

Constable Gardiner entered the gym tentatively. She's been forewarned, thought Tom, grimacing. It wasn't a reputation he wanted.

'Constable Peale called back, Sir. There was a witness who saw Bill leave the hospital grounds on foot. They said he was dragging his foot a bit but making good progress.'

'Shit. Tell Peale to keep looking and we'll get over there as soon as we can. I need a shower first.'

As the day grew brighter, more and more people appeared on the streets. It became harder for Old Kraken to move around without being seen. Everywhere he went, dogs barked, for although he could camouflage himself from human eyes with relative ease, these yappy animals could sense him and their alarm could not be silenced by a friendly word. He was too alien to them; they would not be appeased. They drew attention to him, causing observant humans to see shadow and movement that would otherwise be overlooked.

He was tired. His new legs felt strange to him and the exercise was weakening him. He scuttled back to the safety of his beloved fig tree and rested in the shadow of its towering branches. The outside world was daunting, but he would take his time, feeling his way until he was ready to leave the tree for good. He stroked the old tree and the tree allowed him to push his way back through its bark into the safety of its wooden interior.

Half an hour later Tom and Gardiner were at the hospital trying to get some answers from the medical team. Two of the doctors were arguing with each other. One insisted that Bill was too mentally and physically impaired to have escaped alone and another was sure that he was faking his injuries. It appeared to be an old animosity rekindled by the current situation.

It was going nowhere. Tom left them to it and phoned Peale.

'Where are you?'

'Three blocks over heading toward the city. I have another witness that I am talking to.'

'Be right with you.'

Tom and Gardiner walked back to their car and drove toward the search party. They found Peale standing in front of a house chatting with a couple of women over the front fence.

'He seems to be heading toward the city so I've got three uniforms spreading out asking anyone they happen on if they have seen him. Not much so far, but Ros and Alice, saw him last night.'

'Thought he was drunk,' the one called Ros said. 'Then I saw the hospital PJs and thought he must have wandered off. I sang out to him, but he ignored me. I tried to ring the hospital, but they put me on hold and, well, I had better things to do.'

'You hung up?'

'Yeah, the hubby was hollering and the dinner was gonna burn so I just didn't have time for that.'

'What time was this?'

'Bout nine?'

'Thanks, if you remember anything else, can you give me a call, please?' Tom said handing her his card; she nodded. Tom and the two constables walked over to the police car and leaned against it.

'He's got 12 hours on us and he was making good time, even with a gammy leg,' said Tom.

'Yeah, both witnesses so far have said he was getting along pretty quickly,' said Peale.

'I sent a patrol to drive past his old flat before we left the office, in case his brain is working on autopilot. The flat has been packed up and locked up tight. The big guns were going to try to seize it under proceeds of crime laws if he was convicted. No idea what happens to it now if the doctors say he's too mentally incapacitated to stand trial,' said Tom.

'Do you think he really is though?' asked Gardiner. 'I mean, he has made a pretty good getaway on his own for someone who is supposed to be all but brain dead.'

'We'll have to wait and see when we find him.'

'But he won't be able to get into his old flat?' asked Peale.

'No. The locks have been changed,' said Tom, tapping his fingers absent-mindedly on the car. 'Did he own any other properties?' he asked Gardiner.

'The garage was the only other property we were able to trace back to him,' she replied.

'I can't see any reason he would go there, but since we don't have anything else at the moment, we might as well do a drive by. Then I think we will pay a visit to the nursing home to see if our old mate Ryan has heard from him.' He turned to Peale, 'Peale, can you keep the search team moving street by street toward the city. Call me if you get any other leads.'

'Yes, Sir.'

Tom and Gardiner climbed into the car and headed to the old garage where the three mechanics had met their maker.

They parked down the road from the old butcher-shop-cum-garage and made their way slowly toward it on foot. The other businesses in the area were open and there were cars and utes parked along the road, tradesmen and customers were coming and going. The garage, by contrast, was shut up tight and there was rubbish accumulating in its forecourt. They tried the front door and found it locked. The roller door was also locked. The laneway down the side was empty as was the parking area at the rear of the building.

The back door banged on its hinges in the breeze. Tom glanced at Gardiner and they both pulled out their weapons.

Gardiner moved to one side of the door and caught the door on its outward motion, holding it fully open. Tom moved low and fast into the room, gun stretched out in front of him in both hands.

'Woooahh shit, man! Be cool, be cool!'

Tom heard Gardiner enter the room behind him. There was a man in grimy clothes sitting on the cement floor, hands in the air, a look of terror on his face.

'What are you doing here?' Tom asked, lowering his gun.

'Dry, warm, quiet,' said the homeless man, slowly lowering his hands. 'Nobody comes near this place, man, it's cursed!'

Tom held out his police ID. Gardiner didn't bother since she was in uniform.

'Anyone else been around here lately. We're looking for a guy in hospital pyjamas.'

'Nah man. Well, not that I've seen. I was pretty out of it last night, though.'

'Okay. Mind if we have a look around?'

'Sure. Be my guest.'

Tom and Gardiner walked into the main garage area. The three stains were still visible on the concrete floor.

'You were there, weren't you, Sir. When they found them.'

'Yeah.'

'Is it true that all that was left of them were three piles of ashes…'

'And three pairs of shoes. Yeah.'

'Do forensics have any ideas...'

'No. That one is never going to get put to bed.'

Tom shuddered. Knowing how it had happened didn't make him feel any better about it. It was a grim reminder that no matter how trustworthy Renee appeared to be, she was still dangerous.

The place was empty.

Another dead end.

Tom and Gardiner approached the receptionist at the nursing home where Bill had worked. She appeared flustered. Finally, she turned to them and asked, 'Can I help you?'

Tom showed her his police ID.

'I have been trying to get in touch with Doctor Ryan Porter. I left him a message, but he hasn't called back. Is he available today?'

'I'm afraid no one knows where he is. He was supposed to be on the early shift this morning, but he hasn't shown up and we can't contact him.'

'Do you have a next of kin recorded for him?'

She turned to her computer terminal and pulled up his record.

'It hasn't been updated in a while, he had Bill Doyle listed, so I suppose that isn't much use to you?'

'No. Interesting though. Are there any other staff members that he is close to? A girlfriend?'

'Not that I know of, I'm afraid. Do you think he is okay? He hasn't been caught up in all the horrible things Bill was doing, has he?'

'Is it unusual for him to miss a shift?' Tom asked, ignoring the question.

'He never has before. Always punctual and polite.'

'Let me know if he turns up,' Tom said, passing her his business card. 'I'll get someone to call past his house.'

Gardiner's radio burst into life.

'Gardiner, you there?' it was Peale.

'Receiving, over,' replied Constable Gardiner moving away from the desk.

'We've had another sighting and some weird happenings, you might want to get over here.'

'Give us your position, I think we are finished here,' she said turning to Tom for verification. He nodded in agreement and they headed back out to the car.

An hour later they had witness statements from three people who had seen Bill stumbling along their street and another two who had heard an unholy din around one in the morning and had gone out to investigate. They both described a terrible scream of incredible volume that had woken them. The noise had continued for a couple of minutes — they pointed in the direction of the overgrown park. The pair had done their reconnaissance by torchlight and found nothing and no one. Neither of them had reported it.

Tom and the constables searched the park and the surrounding streets but found no sign and no further witnesses. It was growing dark.

'Peale, tell the search team to pack it in. You two might as well go and get some sleep. We'll go over it again in the morning. I think Bill has made a clean break,' Tom sighed and rubbed his eyes.

He sat on the bonnet of his unmarked police car and watched the two constables climb into their patrol car and drive away.

He gazed absently toward the park and the old Moreton Bay fig tree that dominated it. It was a dark expansive thing. He couldn't help feeling it was malevolent. A hundred years ago the young fig seed would have been deposited onto a smaller tree by a bird. There it would have grown, fed by leaf litter until it was strong enough to drill into its host and begin to feed off it. Next, the long tendrils, the roots, would have been lowered to the ground, surrounding and strangling the host, but not too fast, it had to keep the host alive long enough to form its own self-supporting structure. Eventually, the host tree would be completely assimilated into itself.

What on earth made him think of that? he wondered, shivering. The night was getting colder and darker and as much as the tree creeped him out, he found a strange compulsion to see if he could find any trace of the original tree tangled in the mass of roots and suckers. He pulled a torch out of the glove box and walked slowly toward it. The moon had just risen and its light was glinting off the necklaces and amulets that had been hung off the branches. Most of them were pagan or satanic symbols. He had seen them earlier in the day when they passed this area during their search. Perhaps it was those rather than the tree itself that was giving him the jitters.

He circled the tree, shining his torch along the twisted roots. The shadows moved strangely over the uneven surface giving the impression of movement. He felt compelled to look back over his shoulder, constantly feeling an invisible presence there.

The whole place felt wrong. He suddenly regretted his desire to approach the tree and decided it was time to go. He turned around and found a large branch behind him. He was certain it had not been there before. There was a circle of pale blue plastic dangling from a broken twig. He slipped it off the branch. It was a patient ID band from the hospital. *Bill Doyle* was printed on a slip of white paper attached to the front.

Tom took a deep breath. His sixth sense was screaming at him to get the hell out of there, but he wasn't going to give in to it, he had to look for any other signs of Bill. He had already searched around the base of the tree, now he cast his eyes up to the higher branches, looking at each of the trinkets in turn.

There was a branch within reach and wrapped around it was a golden chain. The chain threaded its way through a pendant made of two loops of gold linked together. He had seen it before, in a photo. On his desk. There was no mistaking it — it had belonged to Rebecca Cole.

He reached up to retrieve it, but before he could grasp it the branch moved away. Suddenly he found his feet lifted from the ground — a branch as thick as his leg was wrapped around his waist.

'This necklace isn't for the likes of you, little man,' a voice growled at him and he realised instantly that the voice was not audible — it was travelling through his body to his head via the branch wrapped around his waist. The tree was speaking to him.

He gasped and looked at the trunk in front of him; its surface was vibrating. Two of the oldest eyes he had ever seen appeared in the bark and looked him over. Another branch snaked out and slipped the hospital band out of his hand.

'Shall I eat you like I ate this Bill Denny?' the tree asked him in a heavily accented voice, waving the hospital ID near Tom's face. The voice was rough and masculine and the eyes were hard and cold.

'Denny? You mean you ate Bill Doyle?'

'Well — not literally — but it amounts to the same thing — he is dead.'

'Why?'

'Because he killed Babayaga.'

'You knew Babayaga?'

'Everyone knew Babayaga.'

He was trapped. Tom could feel that he was close to panic and the deep growling voice and the barely hidden malice were not helping. The tree had the upper hand and he wasn't sure how he was going to get away from it in one piece. First faeries, now talking trees, what the fuck was going on? The branch was tight around his waist and the gnarled surface was digging into his flesh.

'Will you let me go, please?' Tom asked, trying to keep his voice level.

'No, I think not. I am enjoying this conversation. It's not every day I get to wrap my arms around a handsome policeman,' the tree purred and chuckled, his old eyes twinkling with mischief. 'Besides, I can sense that you are a special one. What makes you so special I wonder? — I can smell that you have been touched by fairies not once but twice!'

Tom's unease increased exponentially.

'What did you do to Bill?' asked Tom.

'Don't you worry your pretty head about Bill, there are much more important things to worry about than him,' the tree said passing the hospital ID back to Tom. 'Where he has gone he won't be troubling us again. Besides the night is young, you are young and I have been a lonely old tree for far too long. I see now that it is time for me to come alive again.'

Tom felt a branch stroke his hair and knew that he had to end this, right now.

'I'm sorry, but I'm just not interested in starting a romance with a tree right now…'

'But I'm not just a tree…'

'Well, not with a magical male creature then.'

'I have been told that sometimes humans call men who desire other men "fairies"? Is that true?'

'Well yes, but …'

'So, you're trying to tell me that you are not a fairy?'

'Well yes…'

'How deliciously ironic!' the tree rumbled with glee. 'You would not believe how strong the temptation is to pull you inside myself and keep you as my plaything, my captive — I can do that you know,' the menace was back again. 'I hate humans almost as much as I hate the faeries in this country… But Babayaga would not want that.' The tree grew quiet again and his old eyes looked off into the distance.

'She held you in high esteem,' the tree continued, 'I would even go so far as to say she trusted you,' he said, looking directly at Tom. 'I do not have the gift of sight, but she told me that you would play a part in what is yet to come. So, I am afraid, I must forgo my pleasure this time.' The voice became petulant, 'Might I suggest that you keep your distance in future — you remind me too much of my lost love for your own good.'

Tom felt the branches release him and he stepped away quickly. A single twig connected with his arm and he heard the tree say:

'Tell Rebecca that I have her necklace. She must come to me if she wants it back — and believe me, she is going to want it back. Tell her this from me, from Kraken. She will be afraid to come but she must, the future depends on it. The old man — the one who helps her — he will not want her to come. He is an overprotective fool. He lost one daughter because of his need to control, will he lose another do you think?'

'How did you know Babayaga?' Tom asked.

'And now you have made me sad. Go away little man and tell Rebecca she must come.' The branches pulled right away from Tom and he got a distinct impression that the tree was sulking.

He moved quickly away from the tree and jogged back to the car. He had wanted to walk calmly away, but he was too rattled; at least he wasn't sprinting.

He climbed into the car and locked all the doors. He stared over at the old tree and tried to convince himself that it had all been an illusion, that he was just overtired from overwork. But he felt the hospital band in his hand and knew that he was not losing his mind. For some reason, he had been entrusted with the knowledge that fae creatures really exist.

Tom entered his house and went straight to the kitchen. He was shaking as he poured himself a large scotch. He downed half of it in one go, then he stood staring absently at the kitchen table. Eventually, his mind let go of his fear and he began to notice the day-to-day objects around him. He noticed the dents and scratches on the surface of the wooden kitchen table. This had been his grandparents' house, his grandparents' table. He had spent hours sitting here drawing when he was a boy...

'Oh Tom, these pictures are so beautiful. You'll be an artist when you grow up I think...

...but, your grandfather will be home soon. He's worried about you. This fairy thing, he thinks it's not good for you darling,' she said holding up the picture of a fairy drawn with exquisite detail.

There were several others on the table, each as beautiful as the first.

'She made me well, grandma,' the young Tom said.

The old woman looked at him with worried eyes.

'Well, when you want to talk about her, you come and talk to me. But don't talk to your grandfather, okay? He doesn't understand.

'I think we will put these somewhere safe, I'm afraid he would destroy them if he saw them. I know — we will put them in this folder and tuck them up in the roof space with the old books. They'll be safe there.'

His grandfather had passed away while Tom was a police cadet; his grandmother a few years later. Tom had returned to the house and made it his home.

He had forgotten about the roof space; he wondered if his grandparents had ever cleaned it out.

He retrieved a torch and the step ladder and positioned it in the hallway under the access cover for the roof. He climbed up the ladder and pushed the hatch up into the roof.

He climbed higher until his head and shoulders were inside the roof space; it was hot and stuffy. The torchlight revealed several cardboard boxes balanced on the beams within reach of the manhole. The rest of the roof space was empty except for the garlands of cobwebs decorating the roof trusses. He pulled out the boxes one at a time and deposited them in the kitchen. Each one emitted a cloud of dust as it connected with the floor.

Once he had them all down he started to go through them; disturbing a few daddy-long-legs spiders in the process. Books, books, books, folders, photos, clothes.

Most of it was rubbish, but he found a few photos of his parents and grandparents that he put to one side. Then he found what he was looking for. A large plastic folder with his name written on the front in a childish hand.

He had expected to find several childish drawings inside, but his talent had shown itself younger than he remembered. They were beautiful.

Some were delicate line drawings, others were colourful pastels; each one was of the same subject. A faerie with sky blue wings and the face of an angel.

Sydney, Australia twenty-two years ago

'Come on, Tom, it's time to go home.'

'But I don't have a home anymore.'

'You're coming home with me, poppet. You are going to come and live with grampy and me. We're going to look after you now. Come and get your clothes on, grampy's waiting in the car.'

His clothes were neatly laid out on the bed. His grandma went to the door — to give him some privacy he suspected — after all he hardly knew her. He had only met her once before the fire.

He could hear his grandma and one of the doctors talking just outside the door.

'I have never seen burns heal as fast as that, there is no scaring at all, except for that bit on his back,' he heard the doctor say.

'Why is his back different?' his grandma said.

'We don't know. Perhaps the burns were just a little bit deeper there? Maybe the skin wasn't as healthy to start with? Who knows. However it happened — it is an absolute miracle in my opinion. Never seen anything like it in all my years on the burns ward.'

'He keeps talking about a fairy visiting him in the night,' his grandmother said in a lowered voice, but the hospital was so quiet that Tom could still hear her. 'My husband is worried that Tom is losing his mind.'

'I don't think there is anything to worry about, in times of stress the mind can create all sorts of fantasies as a coping mechanism. Once he has settled into his new life, I think you'll find that he will forget all about it. Just give him some time.'

There was a mirror over the sink in the corner of the room. He pulled off his pyjama top and turned so he could see his shoulder in the reflection. The skin was raw, red and puckered. He felt like he had been in the hospital forever but this doctor was saying he had healed fast. So why was his back different? He should feel grateful that all the pain in his face and chest was gone, that the skin there was back to normal, but all he could think about was this horrible mess on his back. It still hurt and it looked awful.

Why hadn't the faerie healed this bit too?

A Pocket-Sized Faerie

They were all exhausted — physically and emotionally. Renee lay on one of the ledges, resting. On another Andy and Lucy lay on either side of Nancy; the reunited family were talking quietly amongst themselves. They were all safe inside Old Blue for the time being.

Renee looked at her watch. It had been an hour since the spell on Nancy had been broken. Gaia's troops would still be scouring Sydney looking for them. It would not be safe to make their way home for some time yet.

'Old Blue,' she said quietly, not wanting to disturb the others, 'Can any of the other fairies, any of Clio's fairies, sense you?'

'I don't know, Renee. Gaia could, but I am sure one of her parents was a tree faerie. Maybe some of the others are the same.'

'You aren't in any danger, are you?'

'I don't think so. Even if they could sense that I am different, I don't think they would know why. So little faerie lore has been passed down since Clio took over and started the faerie war.'

There was a murmuring sound that travelled through the floor of the room.

'Excuse me. Old Pepper is calling me,' Old Blue said, and for a moment there was murmuring to and fro; a vibration through the wood.

The doorway between Old Blue and Old Pepper reverted from solid wood back to a rippling mirror and Gaia stepped through.

'Thank you, Old Pepper, Old Blue,' Gaia said.

'My pleasure,' Old Blue replied.

Gaia turned to Renee. 'The search is still on. Clio is angry that breaking of the spell did not expose you. Is the creature with you?'

Gaia turned to look at Andy and Lucy and caught sight of Nancy.

'You?!' Gaia exclaimed in surprise. 'You are the creature!'

'Yes. Bit of an anti-climax isn't it,' said Nancy weakly.

'Why? Why did she hide you like that, make you out to be a monster when you are just a faerie?'

'I was supposed to be dead. I can only presume she didn't want the rebels to try and free me. Andy and I had been causing her a few headaches.'

Gaia sat down and looked at Nancy, at her burnt arms and thin face. 'I am sorry. If I had realised, I would have tried to free you. Has the iron disabled you?'

'For the moment, yes, but I will recover.'

'Are we safe here, Gaia?' Renee asked.

'For now. The troops are spread out all over Sydney looking for you. I will regather them soon and we will head back to the compound empty-handed. Then you will be able to slip away through Old Pepper. I have been careful not to stray too close to Old Blue or Old Pepper when there are other faeries are about. Clio knows nothing of tree magic. The old ones were wise enough to keep those secrets from her.'

Andy stirred, 'Well she has learnt something from someone — the worst kind of magic,' said Andy looking over to Renee. 'Clio has been making portals all over the country and Gaia thinks she has been killing faeries to do it, trapping their spirits inside the stones.'

'The blue runestone!' Renee exclaimed. 'You and Clio appeared suddenly next to a rune stone in a flash of blue light!'

'Yes,' Gaia said. 'She was a young faerie called Morrighan, I knew her. How Clio managed to trick her into this, I don't know, but I think she is trapped in the stone forever,' Gaia said.

Renee shivered, it was horrible. If Clio was capable of this, what would she do if she got control of the country...

'She has set up portals all over the country,' Gaia said. 'At least a dozen faeries have been entombed alive. This is what she has been doing on our travels. This is the secret she refused to tell me. All the faeries that accompanied us — she wasn't using them as spies, she was turning them into portals!' Gaia said appalled and distressed.

'The general,' Nancy said weakly. 'The general has taught her how to do these things.'

'Who is the General?' asked Andy.

'Her old mentor. He died many years ago, before we came to Australia. Some of the refugees told me about him. He knew a lot of bad magic, but he kept most of it to himself; it was his wild card.'

'Yes,' said Gaia. 'When the faerie war first started, we thought that Clio was his puppet, that it was he who killed her brother and put her on the throne, but then we discovered that she was much worse than him, that she had killed her brother with her own hands.'

'What do you think Clio will do next? Why is she creating all these portals?' asked Renee.

'I think it is the start of her invasion plan. She is setting up a means to attack multiple fronts, but how she plans to attack, I don't know. Even if we were the most powerful faeries on earth, three hundred would not be enough to overpower the entire country, let alone the old world too.'

'She wants to take over the UK as well?!' Andy exclaimed.

'Yes. She sees it as our spiritual homeland. She thinks all of Australia and the United Kingdom should come under faerie rule — her rule.'

'Do you think she has the power to do it?' asked Renee.

'I used to think that she was mad, that there was no way she could achieve such a thing. Now I am not so sure. The thing that puzzles me though, is why now? The General has been dead for over fifty years, why put his knowledge into play now? She could have started this years ago.'

'Do you have any idea when she plans to attack?'

'No. I don't think she is ready yet but, every day, she seems more sure of herself. She has not mentioned any more travel. I think she has finished creating her portals, but how many more of us will die to execute her plans — who can tell?'

Gaia held up her hand for a moment, and they heard the familiar buzz of a thought conversation. Gaia's ring softly glowed.

'My second in command has just reported back. They are moving further west. It is time for me to go. Wait another hour before you leave. Clio has given her home guard separate orders. I suspect they will stay in the city tonight so you will have to be careful to avoid them. Keep an eye out for a faerie with purple wings, she is called Odette,' Lucy gasped at the mention of the name. 'She is absolutely ruthless,' Gaia continued, 'and has a grudge against Lucy to make things worse.'

'Was she the one who got caught in the metal trap when you tried to rescue Lucy?' Renee asked Andy.

'Yes.'

'She still has scars on her arms from the burns and she has never let me forget it,' Lucy said. Andy gave her a hug.

'We will be well away from them very soon, my blossom. Once Nancy is fit to travel we are going to move away from Sydney. Where we are going, we will all be safe,' Andy said.

Renee thought that Lucy looked confused and not entirely happy about this and Renee saw her open her mouth, about to protest, when Gaia said suddenly:

'I have to go. Clio is looking for me.' She slipped back through the doorway and into Old Pepper.

'Old Blue. Are you able to disguise Andy, Lucy and Nancy with the same tree spell you put on me?'

'Nancy and Lucy, yes, but not Andy. It only works on faeries.'

'That should be good enough. They won't be able to sense any faeries nearby and if the three of you hide in my bag the only one they might catch sight of is me. If I change into a Christmas beetle that should throw them off.'

'It could work,' Andy agreed. 'Now we just need to wait for the troops to leave.'

Old Blue performed the charm on Nancy and Lucy and then they waited. They sat quietly for the next hour and then gave their thanks and bade farewell to Old Blue. They pushed through the arched doorway into Old Pepper.

''Bout time you lot showed up,' Old Pepper said in a huff. 'Old Blue boy is hogging your attention way too much these days!'

They felt obliged to stay with the gnarly old tree for a while to placate her injured feelings, but it was probably for the best anyway. The longer they waited the greater the chance that Clio's home guard had moved on to another part of the city.

Two hours later and they were ready to go.

'I think we had better make a move, Old Pepper. Thank you so much for sheltering us.'

'Anytime. I feel absolutely sprightly!' She was revelling in the fairy contact; the magic awakening her from her decades-old stupor.

'Renee, once we are safe at home, are you willing to try to heal Nancy? We can't risk weakening you until we are all safe,' said Andy.

'Of course, Andy. I will do what I can.'

'Then let's move. Any sign of trouble out there, Old Pepper?'

'No. Nothing nearby but, take care, I can only sense a few hundred metres,' she replied.

Renee shrank Andy, Nancy and Lucy and slipped them into the pocket of her satchel. Nancy was placed in the sling, and the other two secured themselves as best they could. Renee slipped the satchel over her neck and then shrank herself as well. She changed into her Christmas beetle impersonation; her brown opalescent shell shining green and pink in the warm glow from the tree.

Renee held the handle of the bag with her pincers to make sure it wouldn't slide off her smooth shell and flew up to the exit, the knothole to the outside world.

It was dark. The flying foxes were hovering over the loquat tree planted a short distance away. Now and then a half-eaten fruit would drop to the ground with a wet thud.

She did not want to go directly back to the house. First, she needed to make sure that none of Clio's guards were following her. She flew toward the centre of town, not really aware of where she was going, her senses alert checking for any sign of the guards. She stopped on the window sill of an office building and looked around. A moment later she felt something. There was a fairy somewhere nearby. She could sense it.

There is a faerie somewhere close, Andy thought to her via her filigree ring.

A purple light flitted around the corner of the building two floors below her and continued down the street.

She's gone, she thought to Andy.

But then the fairy stopped and turned around. She darted about the building, obviously searching for something.

Somehow the fairy had sensed her. The thought talk!

How? Andy started, but Renee shushed him.

The fairy was close now but was still too low to see them so Renee the Christmas beetle waddled along the window sill, carefully avoiding the spider's web that stretched across one side of the window. A large St Andrew's Cross spider was positioned in its web, just above the ornate cross pattern it had woven in its centre. Its striped abdomen stood out against the night sky as it guarded its cache of flies and beetles. The purple fairy would not want to fly too close to that, Renee thought, as she ducked under an anchoring strand of spider silk and positioned herself behind the web. The spider drew closer to investigate but she was safely out of reach.

A purple flash of light announced Odette's arrival and the spider sat completely still, watching and waiting. The fairy started when she saw the spider and moved back from the web. She cast a glance over the beetles and flies ensnared in its sticky strands, but when the spider started to move toward her she quickly flew further up the building.

Renee waited, barely breathing. She could feel the fairy energy moving further and further away from them until she could no longer sense it. At what distance could she sense a fairy she wondered? That was something she would have to test in future.

When she was sure that they were safe, she started to crawl along the sill and out from behind the web. The spider walked along its web, following her progress, and then suddenly, it broke into an eight-legged run, out-pacing her clumsy beetle legs and launching itself on to the sill in front of her; a strand of web acting as a safety line from its abdomen back to its web.

They stood facing each other, the spider's pincers twitching, its large black eyes fixed on her. For a moment she panicked, she couldn't think straight. She had never been particularly worried about spiders, but she had never encountered one the same size as her before!

The spider began a slow advance, in a terror, Renee turned back into a fairy and pushed her glow to maximum. The spider stumbled backwards, using four of its legs to shield its many eyes from the blinding light. In the flurry of movement, it slipped and dropped off the edge of the sill. It swung back and forth, dangling from its web by its safety line.

It would not take the spider long to climb back up, so Renee slipped past the web, dimming her glow as she did and took off into the night. She hoped the flare of light had not been seen by Odette or any of the other guards.

She sensed the fairies before she saw them, they were coming from behind and closing in fast. She could see their glow reflected in the windows of the buildings as she flew past and could see that they were gaining on her. She flew up to the top of a building and then wove down and around the stainless-steel ducting and piping that covered the roof. It didn't bother them at all and they kept on coming. Then she saw a large metal shed, the kind that contained electrical or plumbing meters for large buildings. It was painted, but in some places, the grey paint was flaking and orange rust marks dripped down its surface. Rusty iron. She took her chance and slipped inside a small air vent on its side. She hovered just inside the vent and peered out. Renee hoped there was enough exposed iron to keep them at bay.

The purple-winged fairy hovered in front of the box but kept her distance, ten feet at least.

'You can't stay in there forever,' Odette yelled out.

A group of fairies appeared behind Odette and she turned and gestured to them. Renee saw the other fairies fan out and suspected that they had surrounded the shed she was hiding in.

Renee surveyed her surroundings. One side of the shed had a bench running from one wall to the other. There was enough room for a person to stand inside the shed in front of it. The bottom of the bench had two cupboards locked with padlocks. The top of the bench had a large control panel mounted onto it. The panel appeared to be some kind of electrical control board; dials and knobs covered its surface.

There was no way she was going to be able to fly out of here, she was cornered, but she might be able to slip inside the building if there was a hole for the electrical cabling. On one edge of the control panel a screw was missing; the hole providing an entry point into the cavity behind it. She increased her glow and leaned over the edge of the hole to peer inside. A mass of cables streamed from the back of the panel and disappeared down into the darkness.

It was her best bet. She made herself a little smaller and slipped into the hole, fluttering over to the nearest cable. She followed it down to the floor of the cavity. Several cables were bound together with cable ties into a single cord and it disappeared into the mouth of a plastic tube set into the floor of the cupboard.

The cables did not fill the tube entirely, there was room for her to fly into the tube, but it was claustrophobic, and the thrumming of electricity along the wires made her feel distinctly uncomfortable. If there was a short in a wire anywhere, she could end up fried.

Andy. I think we are far enough away from the others that they won't hear us. Are you all okay in there?

Yes. It's been a bit bumpy, but we are fine. Where are we? he asked.

I am inside a pipe filled with electrical wires. I'm going to follow them into the building and then try to slip out somehow. There are at least six fairies up on the roof and Odette is one of them.

Be careful Renee. If she catches us, we are in deep trouble.

I know.

She moved forward, keeping as far away from the wires as she could. Sometimes the pipe ran horizontally and she could walk alongside the wires, but at other times the pipe would turn a corner and drop vertically and she would have to fly. Sometimes when the pipe made a turn around a corner the wires would block the way forward and she would have to stop and climb over them to find room to move.

She followed the wires until she emerged from the end of the pipe and found herself inside another dark cavity. She increased her glow and saw that there were bricks on all sides except in front of her where she could see the back of another electrical panel. The main collection of wires separated into smaller groups and these smaller groups headed in different directions to join connections on the back of the panel. She flew up to inspect it. The wires were soldered to various metal connections. There were no gaps large enough for her to slip through. She had never made herself smaller than she was now and she did not want to try; the smaller she was, the harder it was for her to keep her bearings. Things that would normally appear close faded into oblivion if you got too small.

She flew back to where the pipe emerged from the brick wall, hoping to find a gap, and noticed that there was a set of wires did not lead to the electrical panel but instead snaked off to the left and into a roughly cut hole in the bricks. She was able to climb through this hole and into another cavity. One side of this cavity was brick and the other was plasterboard. She was in the wall cavity of a room. She followed the wires further into the building and when another group of wires separated from the group she followed them up the wall to where they emerged from the plasterboard into the back of a white object.

There was light shining into the object through a grill at the front. She moved forward and peered between the bars.

There was a room. The light was on, as far as she could see there was no one inside, but at this size, the distance faded out before she could see the far wall. She decided to take a chance and slipped through the grill and landed on a table. She increased her size to normal fairy size to allow her eyes to see the whole room properly. It *was* empty. She was relieved and exhausted. Looking up, she could see that she had entered the room through an air conditioner.

There was a bookcase to her left and she noticed books that she had seen somewhere before. She turned and saw a computer and a chair, a coat rack and a window. It was all familiar.

There was a sudden thump at the window and she saw a yellow light hovering outside, watching her. In an instant, a purple light had joined it. She had forgotten to dim her light when she entered the room and made herself bigger. They had found her.

She wanted to cry. She was exhausted. All that effort for nothing. She collapsed onto the table.

A large shadow moved past her and before she could focus on it, it had moved over to the window. The yellow and purple fairies disappeared into the darkness. The man at the window pulled the blinds closed and turned around.

Tom!

He moved over to the table and bent down to look at her.

'You look like you have been through the wringer. I take it those two weren't friends of yours.'

She shook her head, too tired to assume human size.

'Need a lift home?'

Oh God, yes! She nodded furiously.

He held out a hand and she stepped onto it. From there she flew up into his shirt pocket and dimmed her glow, flopping down into the soft warmth.

He peered into his pocket, surprised.

'Okaaaayyyy... Let's get moving then,' he said, grabbing his coat from the stand.

He searched the skies above as he drove out of the basement garage, but he saw no more of the faerie lights.

Ten minutes later with no further sign of the rogue faeries, Tom drove past Andy's house and pulled over and parked a short distance from Andy's house. He sat for a few minutes to see if there was any movement, but it was all clear.

'You still okay in there? I don't think we were followed,' he said looking down into his pocket.

She nodded.

'There are some things I need to tell you, can I come in for a while?'

He saw her nod so he opened the car door and crossed the road. Once they were at the door she slipped out of his pocket. The leadlight window above the door was propped open an inch and he watched her as she flew through it. A moment later the door was opened and she stood before him as Renee Roswald.

'Come in, please,' she said to him with very tired eyes.

He wondered what was going on now. Had the queen of the faeries been making trouble already?

He made his way down the hall to the kitchen.

'Grab a seat, I'll be with you in just a moment,' she said and disappeared into one of the rooms.

A few minutes later she entered the kitchen and put the kettle on.

'I didn't expect to see you in the office so late,' she said to him.

'I didn't expect to see you in my office at all,' he said with a laugh. 'Have you been keeping tabs on me?'

'No. Well, not recently,' she admitted. 'Months ago — we had to check you out before we approached you about Bill. I'm not entirely sure how I ended up in your office tonight — it was a case of any port in a storm. Would you like tea?'

He nodded, accepting her change of subject, and felt strangely pleased that she had chosen his office as a refuge even if she wasn't ready to admit it.

'I have been trying to get in touch with you and Andy for the last two days. Things have been crazy.'

'Yes. Same with us. We have been running around all over the place. Thank you for hiding me from those fairies. They were two of Clio's henchmen.' She put a cup of tea in front of him and slumped into a chair opposite him with her own.

She drank deeply.

'Sorry to lay this on you now but, the sooner you know, the better,' said Tom.

Andy came into the room.

'How is she?' Renee asked Andy.

'Sleeping. So is Lucy. They're okay,' he turned to Tom. Thanks for the lift home. We were in quite a bind.'

'Pardon?' Tom asked, his eyebrows raised.

'I was in Renee's bag,' said Andy.

'You were in...' Tom's mind slipped back to the image of the faerie in his hand. Yes, she had been carrying a bag. 'You know what, I am not even gonna go there right now. Some crazy things have been happening that you need to know about.'

Andy made himself a cup of tea and joined them at the table while Tom told them all about the attack on Bill and his subsequent escape from the hospital.

'So, Bill was faking it?' asked Andy.

'No. I don't think so. Things got a lot stranger after that though. We were searching the streets around the hospital looking for him and I found this tangled in the branches of an old fig tree,' he said and placed the hospital wristband on the table.

Andy looked at him curiously. 'When you say, an old fig tree, you don't mean the old Moreton Bay fig tree in the overgrown park —'

'—down near the warehouses. Yes,' said Tom.

'Old Kraken,' said Renee.

'Yes. He said that was his name,' said Tom, feeling slightly relieved that they already knew about the tree.

'He spoke to you?' asked Andy.

'Yes.' For a moment a wave of embarrassment passed over him and he felt his face redden. He had no desire to tell them how he had been propositioned by a tree, so he decided to tell them a cut down version of the night's events.

'He told me that he had taken Bill. At first, he pretended that he had eaten him, then later, he said that he had sent him somewhere where he would not bother anyone again; that Bill was as good as dead. He said he had done it because Bill had killed Babayaga.'

'Kraken knew Babayaga?' exclaimed Andy.

'He said everyone knew Babayaga. He told me to tell Rebecca to come and see him. He has your necklace, Renee — the one with the loops twisted around a chain.'

'My necklace! I have been looking for it everywhere. How on earth did Kraken end up with it? Do you think he took it from Bill? That Bill took it when they…'

'I don't know. Do you remember if you were wearing it the day they took you?'

'I don't know. I definitely didn't have it when I woke up as a fairy, but I don't remember if I was wearing it when I went to the cafe that morning or not,' said Renee.

'Don't go anywhere near him, Renee. Old Kraken is dangerous. I don't know what game he is playing, but it is his game and it has nothing to do with us. We have our own issues to deal with,' Andy said firmly.

'Dad?' a voice echoed down the hall into the kitchen.

'Excuse me,' Andy said and made his way up the hall towards the voice.

Once Andy was out of hearing range, Tom continued. 'Old Kraken said that Andy would react that way. He said that if you wanted your necklace back, you had better come and talk to him. He indicated that you were definitely going to want it back.'

'He didn't say why?'

'He said the future depended on it.'

'And he knew it was my necklace somehow.'

'Yes.'

'I think that I will have to go and see him. But I won't tell Andy until afterwards.'

'Do you want me to come with you?' he asked, his concern for Renee overshadowing his fear of the monstrous tree for a moment.

'That might be a good idea but better if you keep your distance, in case I need rescuing.'

'Yes,' he said, glad there was a reason for him to stay away from the tree's groping branches. He suspected his relief was a little too clear on his face when she said:

'Did he scare you?'

'Scared the bejesus out of me,' he admitted.

'Yeah. He did that to me too,' she said.

'I have to tell you. We are getting nowhere fast with finding Bill's den. We found the thief, but he was dead before we could question him. We have one more lead we are following up, but we keep hitting dead ends.'

'I might be able to spend some time scouting around a bit. The project that Andy and I were working on is pretty much over now. But I may not be in Sydney for much longer. Clio's troops are getting pushy. We might have to go into hiding.'

'Is she about to start her war?'

'I don't think she's ready yet, but she is definitely planning something. She is secretly killing some of her own people in the process.'

'Will there be enough of you to fight her?'

'I don't know. I just don't know...'

Renee saw Tom out, lingering at the door until he had disappeared from sight and then she walked down the hall to Andy's room. Nancy was tucked into his bed, Lucy nestled beside her, asleep, and Andy was sitting on a chair beside the bed.

She knocked gently on the door frame and Andy waved her in.

'How are they doing,' she whispered to Andy.

'They are both exhausted. Nancy is weak, very weak. I am afraid for her.'

'What can I do? Do you want me to work on her burns?'

'I don't know that you will be able to do much there. Iron burns are often permanent. Flakes of iron embed themselves in the skin and prevent the magic from healing. In her case, the iron was on her wrists for so long…' his face crumpled and she pulled him into a hug.

'There was nothing you could do about this Andy. Stop kidding yourself that there was. None of us knew she was alive, not even Lucy. Clio was wise to keep her hidden. If you knew she was alive you would have killed yourself before you gave up.'

'Stop. You know that is absolute bullshit and so do I. I knew Lucy was alive, Christ, she begged me to save her. What does that say about me as a father? She was begging for help and I gave up. I gave up on her Renee. How will I ever live with myself?'

'You didn't give up. If you had, they wouldn't be here now. How could you have done anything for them? You didn't even know if she was alive. You couldn't talk to the trees without fairy help, you certainly couldn't travel through them and there weren't any other fairies about volunteering to rush to your aid were there?'

He sat quietly mulling over her words.

'As soon as you had the means, you got on with it. If you had given up entirely you would never have helped me in the first place,' she continued. 'You would have given me a wide berth.'

He sighed and gave a single reluctant nod.

'Now. Let me have a look at her wrists and see if there is anything I can do. It looks like we are safe for the moment. I think if the others had followed us home they would have made their move by now.'

'Yes. I think we would have sensed them if they had got close enough to see where we were going. Tom turned up just when we needed him.'

'Yes. I think it has been a beneficial relationship so far,' she said and reached for Nancy's hand, ignoring the knowing smile that was playing on Andy's lips.

When she concentrated hard she found she could see the tiny flecks of iron embedded in Nancy's skin. Each one was a pinprick of poison spreading its influence into the rest of Nancy's body. She decided to leave the burns alone for the time being and concentrate on drawing each sliver of iron out of her skin instead.

In the same way that she had drawn the bullet out of Tom's rib cage, she focused on a sliver of iron and pulled it free. It wiggled through Nancy's skin making a tiny channel; a fresh, but tiny, wound.

'Could you get me a bowl please, Andy,' she said, holding the tiny iron shard in her hand.

While he was gone she found another shard. It was close to where the first one had been so instead of creating a new exit wound she slid the shard sideways until it entered the channel cut by the first one and guided it out the same way. Once she had removed as many pieces as she could she would heal the wounds created by drawing them out.

Nancy did not flinch or wake during the process. She dropped the tiny slivers into the bowl that Andy held out to her and continued with her work. Two hours later she had removed almost a hundred of them. She paused and stretched.

'Don't overdo it. You must be just about spent by now,' said Andy.

'I'll close up these wounds and leave it at that for tonight I think,' she replied. 'I can have another go tomorrow.'

He nodded and watched her as she gently sealed the tiny sores created by the removal of the splinters.

At last, she stood up and stretched her aching spine.

'Come on. Nightcap and then bed,' he said.

She followed him out to the kitchen.

It was early the next day, just after dawn when Renee was awoken by a knock at the front door. Knowing how exhausted the others were, she hurried into her dressing gown and down the hall, checking her appearance in the mirror as she passed it to make sure she was in her human disguise.

She peered through the spy hole and saw a very worried looking Bruce rocking back and forward from one foot to the other. She opened the door immediately.

'Bruce! Come on in,' she whispered.

'My god, I've been so worried,' he said in a low voice as he entered, quietly closing the door behind him. 'There have been faeries buzzing all over the place like a swarm of bees. Are you and Andy alright? Did you get Lucy?'

She put the kettle on and sat down with him at the table.

'We got her, and we are both fine, but we had quite a job getting away. Tom ended up getting us to safety.'

'Tom! How on earth did he end up involved?'

'I flew into a building to escape them and ended up in his office. He took us down to his car and out of the building. The fairies were none the wiser. He thought he was just rescuing me, but when we got back here he spoke to Andy, so he knows that Andy was in my bag, but not the others.'

'Others? You mean Lucy and Gaia?'

'Umm. No. Lucy and Nancy.'

Bruce stared at her.

'Nancy is alive?' he said quietly.

'Yes, she's in a bad way. I have been treating her. I think she will be okay eventually.'

Andy wandered out into the kitchen, his hair sticking up at odd angles.

'Bruce! We have had a phenomenal win! Nancy is alive! We got her too!'

Bruce stood up and threw himself into Andy's bear hug. Renee could see his face over Andy's shoulder and she could not help but notice that it looked troubled; she would almost say devastated. He hitched a smile onto his face as Andy pulled back to face him.

'Come, come! She is awake, she wants to see you,' Andy said, putting a guiding hand on his shoulder.

The two men disappeared up the hall and she heard a weak voice call in excitement:

'Goodness me! Here is my Nancy Boy!'

She could imagine the tears as she heard the laughter of old friends united, but there was something else here too. Bruce had recovered well from his surprise, but she wondered why he wasn't entirely glad to have Nancy back.

Over breakfast, Andy and Renee updated Bruce on the events of the last couple of days. He had been fretting the whole time they were away and Renee felt guilty that she hadn't thought to contact him as soon as they were safe. Andy had been too absorbed by Lucy and Nancy to think of it, but *she* should have.

Renee took a tray of breakfast down to Nancy and propped her up in bed to eat. She left Lucy to tend to her. Renee wondered how the dynamic would play out now that Andy had his real family back together, and she wondered if Bruce was having the same misgivings.

She sat back down with her boys to discuss the future. They could not stay here long. Clio would not give up on Lucy easily, her food talents were too valuable. The fairies could not sense Renee, Lucy or Nancy due to the concealment charm that old Blue had placed on them, but there was nothing to stop them being seen if they left the house. Renee was able to disguise herself as a beetle to avoid detection, but Lucy would have to stay a prisoner in her own home until Nancy was well enough to travel. Andy was worried about how Lucy would take this.

'She has always been a wilful one,' Andy said.

'Yes,' agreed Bruce. 'She wasn't too keen on staying hidden before this mess happened, we can only hope she has learnt her lesson.'

Lucy entered the kitchen and placed the tea tray beside the sink. She poured herself a glass of water and joined them at the table.

She was only a few years younger than Renee and she was very pretty. Clio's spell had broken overnight and her wings had returned; they were a pale lavender colour with silvery veins running through them. They sparkled in the light. Her hair was the same pale blonde colour as her mother's.

She turned to Renee, 'Who was the man you were with last night, the one who drove us back here?' she asked, her eyebrow raised.

'Tom Hayes, he's a policeman,' Renee responded, a little surprised that this was the subject of their first real conversation.

'He's very handsome. Is he your boyfriend?' she asked in a voice that was trying hard to appear disinterested. Renee saw Bruce roll his eyes and Andy's face clouded.

'No,' Renee said, not pleased with where this was going.

'Stay away from Tom, Lucy,' said Andy, 'We have enough problems to deal with at the moment.'

'Relax dad, I was just asking,' she said.

Renee wasn't sure if she imagined it or not, but the look that Lucy flashed her seemed like a challenge. It was over before Renee could be sure. Lucy turned back to her father and laughed.

'Anyway, dad, policemen aren't really my kind!'

Lucy had been captured right on the brink of puberty and had been enslaved ever since. Renee wondered how much interaction she had had with the other fairies. Although she was in her twenties, her behaviour, so far, had been more like that of a petulant teen.

'Until we have made it to the safe house, you are going to have to stay hidden Lucy. And by that, I mean in the house. If anyone comes to call other than Bruce, you will have to make yourself scarce. If word gets out that there are other people staying here, it could lead to disaster.'

'Why did you free me from Clio if you are just going to cage me up here?' she said, irritated.

'It's not for long. As soon as your mother is well enough to travel we will be off,' Andy said.

'Off to where?'

'I can't tell you that yet. Not until everything is settled. It's safer that way.'

Renee wondered how Lucy would feel about leaving the city for a small country town now that she was finally free from Clio's compound. She had the impression that Lucy was not going to make life easy for any of them.

Kraken and the Necklace

Later that morning, Renee worked on removing more of the iron splinters from Nancy's wrists. Andy had to usher Lucy out of the room as she was distracting Renee from the task.

'I don't see why you won't let me try,' Lucy said in a huff. 'I am sure I would do a better job than her and I am her daughter after all!'

'Out, Lucy, Renee knows what she is doing and has done plenty of healing before; you haven't. Come on and I will get us some lunch.'

'I am sorry about Lucy,' Nancy said in a weak voice once Lucy was out of hearing. 'She means well, but I suspect she is a little jealous of your relationship with Andy.'

'Yes, I suppose your right.'

'She found Andy's watch yesterday, the one you gave him.'

'Oh. That wouldn't have helped...' Renee had given the watch to Andy as a thank you present and had engraved the back with a message: *To Papa Andy, Love Renee.*

'Well, I hope she gets over this sibling rivalry thing soon because we have much more important things to worry about,' said Renee.

'I'm afraid jealousy is a common trait in faeries.'

Renee glanced up, but Nancy's face was unreadable. Renee sighed inwardly and said nothing.

She managed to get the last of the iron shards out of Nancy's wrists; preventing the iron poisoning from spreading any further.

'They really don't affect you at all do they?' Nancy asked, looking at the sliver of iron in Renee's hand.

'No.'

'I don't know how that's possible. Andy doesn't either. Neither of us have ever encountered a faerie that was immune to iron.'

'Has he told you about how I became a fairy?'

'Yes. And none of that makes any sense either.'

'Great,' she said despondently. 'I was hoping you might be able to give me some answers.'

'Sorry. I can't. It is beyond my knowledge.'

Nancy seemed to be healing faster now that the iron was out of her system and Renee went to tell Andy the good news.

'Her own body is starting to respond to the injuries now the iron is gone. Hopefully, she will be fit to travel in a few days.'

'Thank you, Renee,' he said taking her hand. 'For everything. I know things have been a bit of a challenge the last few days...'

'It's fine Andy. We have all been stressed. You helped me when I needed you, it's only fair...'

Andy nodded.

'I am going to go to Old Pepper now, Andy. I have to talk to Gaia. I need to find out what Clio is up to and if the home guard is still patrolling the city. Don't wait up okay, it might take a while to get in touch with her.'

'Be careful,' he said, like clockwork.

'I will; don't worry,' came her standard response, but she had a flash of guilt. She was going to go and see Tom and Old Kraken as well.

She flew in beetle form to avoid detection and did not change back to a fairy until she was safe inside the tree. Old Pepper was pleased to see her as always. Gaia was quick to arrive when Old Pepper sent out the call and Renee suspected that Gaia had been waiting somewhere close in expectation.

'The others are safe?' Gaia asked.

'Yes, all safe. Nancy is healing, we will be able to move her out of the city soon.'

'Good. I fear that Clio will make her move soon. She seems jubilant.'

'Any ideas where she will strike first?'

'None, I'm afraid. She is keeping her plans very close to her chest, but that is not the only reason I am here. Kraken has been calling out to you.'

'You heard him?'

'Yes. He has been calling for the last day. I don't think any of the other faeries have heard it, but I am worried that if one of them has dormant tree-faerie powers and they get too close to him, they will. You must go to him now, before they do. You must make him quiet. Most of the home guard has returned to Clio, but Odette is still around.'

'Thank you. I'll go now.'

She changed back to a beetle and slipped off into the surrounding suburbs. She had told Tom that she would take him with her, but time was short; she couldn't afford the time it would take to reach him and bring him back with her. She would have to go alone and hope for the best. If something went wrong, at least Gaia knew where she was.

She flew straight to the old park nestled near the warehouses. The grass was long and untidy and there were empty beer cans and rubbish hidden in its depths. Even though the day was warm and bright, the canopy of the tree was thick and dark, casting the branches and roots below it into shadow. In spite of this, the silver amulets glittered on the branches as if lit from within. She could hear the low rumbling call coming from the heart of the tree.

She landed in the grass a few feet from the shadows. The long grass would provide adequate cover from any passing fairies so she shed her beetle disguise. She revealed her fairy form as it had been the day that she was transformed. She was Rebecca Cole again but only a couple of inches tall and she had green fairy wings and shining green opaline eyes.

The call stopped. He knew she was there. A long branch bent toward her and a small twig connected to her shoulder.

'You are Rebecca Cole,' the tree said, its words entering her mind via the twig on her shoulder. It was a statement, not a question.

'I was, yes.'

'Yes. We all have stages of existence.'

'Tom told me you have my necklace.'

'Yes, the beautiful man with the blue eyes.' Another branch moved out of the shadows for a moment, a golden chain shone in the light, and then the branch disappeared into the shadows once more.

'You can't have it yet,' the tree rumbled. 'Once Clio is defeated — then you can have it.'

'Why not now?'

'Because it is the way it has to be. Fate.'

'I don't believe in fate.'

'Believe whatever you like — I cannot give you the necklace until Clio is overthrown.'

'How did you get it?'

'My sister gave it to me.'

Your sister? Who is your sister?'

'She was called Babayaga.'

'Babayaga! How can she be your sister?'

'Because she was a faerie, just like you and I, and the survival of both faerie and humankind will depend on you defeating Clio,' he said. 'The call to arms will come soon. You will have to defeat her or you will see the whole world burn.'

'You tried to hurt me when I was a child,' she said, 'why did you do that if I was destined to save the world?'

'Tree, faerie, human; we all make mistakes. I hated all humans and faeries then, except for my beloved, Babayaga. I did not know who you were and Babayaga had not yet told me what was coming. If you had been a weaker child... disaster. For that, I am truly sorry.'

He did sound sorry, but she didn't trust herself to be a good judge of his character. He had tried to harm her in the past, but even before that incident, she had felt wary of him. Just as she instinctively felt that she could trust Andy and Tom, she felt that she could *not* trust Old Kraken.

'If what you say is true — what do I do? How do I defeat Clio?'

'I cannot tell you, because I do not know. Babayaga could not tell me everything. She could not see everything. All I know is that you must find a way to defeat her. You can't run from Clio, and you can't hide forever. She will find you. She will hunt down the old man and his wife and child and make an example of them.

'Old Blue, you and I will all have roles to play. Soon, you must be my messenger, my lobbyist. You must convince Old Blue that I am sorry; that I beg his forgiveness. He will be suspicious of me, I wronged him once out of stupidity; I hated the whole world. This is important. He and I must cooperate to re-open the doorway between us, then we can communicate, then we can unite for the good of all.

'The policeman, Tom, will also be needed. Babayaga told me that it will all become clear soon — and you will need to help each other to succeed. Go to Tom and tell him to think about what I said to him. Tell him that Doctor Ryan Porter is not as innocent as he pretends to be. Help Tom to free those who were enslaved by Bill. It was what Babayaga wanted. Go now, the tide is about to turn.'

Sergeant Reg Palmer was in deep shit. He had gone straight from Johnny to the courier to try and intercept Ryan's parcel, but he had been too late. The courier company told him that it had already been delivered to the police station. His only hope was that Tom had been busy with something else and hadn't opened it yet.

He put the siren on and charged through the traffic towards the Surrey Hills office. When he was a couple of blocks from the office he turned off the siren, not wanting to alert those inside.

If Tom hadn't opened it yet, he could claim he had a tip-off about it — anthrax or a bomb inside. Then he could get the parcel taken out of the office and "lose" it somewhere. There would be lots of red tape to deal with, but he was an old pro at that sort of thing.

He mounted the stairs two at a time then stopped to catch his breath for a minute before pushing the door open and emerging from the stairwell.

Tom and his two constables were standing in the open office area around a large table, papers spread all over it, a large yellow envelope visible on the edge of the desk. Palmer strode casually past on his way to the kitchenette and glanced down. Dr Ryan Porter was written in large clear letters in the sender's address box on the back of the envelope. In the short time it took him to walk past, he saw photos of the dungeons and inmates spread out on the table. Tom and the team were in a hurry, scanning the enormous pile of documents, desperately trying to sort the wheat from the chafe.

Palmer didn't miss a step as he walked past, turning into the men's lavatory and closing the door behind him. If it had just been Hayes, he might have been able to lure him out of the building. Three of them; not a chance.

He hit a quick dial number on his phone and waited for an answer, checking that each of the cubicles was empty as he waited for the call to connect.

As soon as he heard the familiar voice on the other end, he said:

'The bird has landed, it's time to go.'

'How long?'

'Half an hour — absolute tops.'

The phone clicked and went dead.

Palmer opened the back of his mobile phone and pulled out the SIM card. He crushed it under his heel then swept up the shards in a piece of toilet paper and flushed it down the toilet.

The three police officers sorted through the papers, there was enough here to put several people away for a long time, Ryan Porter included, but that was not their focus at the moment. The photos of the prisoners had sent them all into overdrive.

Tom replaced the phone receiver and turned to Peale and Gardiner.

'Ryan didn't show for work today, so Peale, grab a backup officer and get over to his place. Break the door down if you have to. Arrest him if he is there; the super has given the go ahead.

'Gardiner, get over to the airport. I've sent two officers over there now, but I doubt he will be flying under his own name, so they might need you to spot him. I've put alerts on all major airports, but unless there is a small miracle, I think we are going to be too late.'

The two officers disappeared and Tom returned to his main task. He was hoping that somewhere in all this paperwork was the location of the cells. There were receipts, company details, dossiers on clients — that was a gold mine in itself — but nothing to indicate a location so far.

The covering letter was signed by Ryan Porter. It was a confession of just about everything. Murder, abduction, sexual slavery, you name it, he said he had done it. It smelled off. Why would you confess to all this without handing yourself in; without plea bargaining? What good would it do him? Unless of course, he was clearing his conscience because he was about to commit suicide. Or was it revenge? Not against Bill; he was gone. But one other name kept appearing over and over again. Johnny Black. He had heard that name somewhere before and he was sure it was in relation to the investigation into Bill Doyle.

He took the sheaf of papers into his office and logged onto his computer. He keyed in a search and as he waited for it to return the data he wondered about Bill Doyle. Bill's name had appeared in the documents several times as well. Ryan obviously knew that his mate Bill was too far gone to be impacted by his confession.

Something was nagging him. Something someone had said about Bill. He couldn't put his finger on it. He re-read Ryan's confession. Ryan said that Johnny Black was the ringleader of this murderous enterprise.

His search for Johnny Black came back with results. He scrolled through them looking for something relevant. Johnny Black — owner of a prestigious nursing home in Double Bay.

Ryan, Johnny and Bill all linked to the same nursing home.

There was a pile of papers that had not been examined yet, he riffled through them searching for anything about the nursing home.

A blueprint; the ground floor layout of the nursing home. Attached to the back was another floor plan, this one was a much older document, its edges were yellowing. It was a plan for the older part of the building that had once been a convent and was dated 1880. There was no certification stamp on it, so he guessed that it had been drafted for the benefit of the builders rather than to meet planning requirements. It included a large basement.

'Holy shit!' Tom exclaimed. They had searched the nursing home when Bill had been arrested. There was no basement, just a small boiler room.

The old drawing showed a staircase leading down to the basement, but this did not exist on the newer plans. There was a key taped to the old plan.

A green light flew in through the door and landed on the floor and before he could say anything, Renee stood before him.

'Kraken said that Doctor Ryan Porter is involved with Bill,' she said. 'I know him. He was a friend of Philip's — he works at a posh nursing home in Double Bay!'

'Ryan Porter has just sent me the plans to the nursing home, it has a hidden basement, and I suspect that the Stonefish owns the place! We need to get over there now and check it out. Can you sneak me in? Carry me like you did with Andy?'

'Of course. But I'll need to shrink you, can you cope with that?'

'Shrink me. Does that hurt?'

'No. But it feels a bit strange.'

'What if something happens to you? Am I stuck tiny forever?'

'Well, unless you can find another fairy to make you big again, yes. But don't worry. Andy can help if anything happens to me.'

'Alright. I'll risk it. Hang on! You went and saw Kraken?'

'Yeah, I'm sorry, I didn't have time to come and get you. He was calling to me. If any of the rogue fairies had heard him...'

He felt slightly mollified by that, but he couldn't help feeling a little disappointed that he hadn't been there to back her up. He felt that he was in her debt already and that made him a little uncomfortable.

She showed him the pocket in her satchel and explained how to use the sling chair and seat belt. He suspected that if he was ever going to get seasick, this was going to be the time, but he agreed anyway.

He picked up the floor plan and the key and closed his eyes as she shrank him to the size of a chess piece. She gently picked him up and placed him in her bag. He coped well with that, but what she failed to mention was the fact that she was then going to shrink herself even further (with the bag on her shoulder) which meant he would get proportionately smaller again.

By the time she was ready to fly, he figured he must have been close to microscopic. His field of vision was minuscule. At least it was unlikely that he would get seasick; there was nothing to see. Outside the satchel's plastic window, the entire vista was a single nondescript colour. He had been effectively blinded.

He hardly felt the motion as she lifted off the ground and flew out the vent and into the afternoon sky.

Renee arrived at the nursing home to find the fire alarms blaring. Smoke was drifting into the sky from one of the out-buildings and the police and firefighters were already on the scene. Patients were being wheeled out in their beds and the scene was a strange mixture of calm and chaos.

Renee landed in a tree a short way from the commotion and took Tom out of her bag. She increased his size to match her own. They were beetle sized; completely unnoticeable.

'Fire. It had to be fucking fire,' Tom said staring at the scene in front of him.

'Where do we go from here?' asked Renee.

'They've locked down the building, there is no way we are going to get to the basement in time if we go through the front door, not even with my badge. I am betting the bastard is trying to destroy the evidence. He's probably set the basement alight. The question is, has he killed the occupants or left them to burn?'

'We have to go in.'

'Yes. We do.' Tom shook himself and Renee suspected he was gritting his teeth. He obviously wasn't a big fan of fire.

'Can you fly us inside and get us into this staff room, that's where the stairs should be,' he said pointing to the floor plan he pulled from his pocket.

'Yep. Hold on to me,' she said and slipped her arm around his waist. As soon as he had his arm around her shoulders, she lifted him off the branch and flew towards the main entrance.

The front doors were propped open and Tom and Renee were so small that they slipped through unseen. The fire seemed to be contained to an area at the back of the building, but the smoke was getting thicker. The alarms were going off everywhere and some of the patients were visibly distressed by the noise and smoke; the staff were trying to calm them as they rushed them out of the building.

At first, she stayed close to the ceiling to avoid the gurneys and chairs being wheeled out of the building, but as they got closer to the staff room the smoke got thicker and she had to scoot along the floor instead. The emergency lighting had been activated and she noticed that the alarms had been turned off in this part of the building. She suspected the firefighters had turned them off so they could hear the cries of the stranded.

They reached the staff room and noticed that the main seat of the fire was further up the hall. Perhaps it wasn't the Stonefish's doing after all but a standard kitchen fire. She flew against the door but found it locked.

'We need to be smaller,' she said to Tom and shrunk them both so they could slip under the door.

Once they were on the other side, she returned them to human size.

Tom wobbled a little.

'Are you okay?'

'Yeah, just a bit dizzy from the change in perspective. Do you ever get motion sickness from all that shrinking and growing?'

'Not any more,' she said, smiling, 'but I've had a bit of time to get used to it.'

The only thing in the room was a huge old wardrobe with a mirror on the door. He pulled the handle and found it locked. He pulled the key off the floor plan and was relieved when the door opened.

It was empty. He tapped on the back of the wardrobe; it sounded hollow. He ran his fingers over the surface but could not find any locks or handles.

He took a step backwards and kicked hard. The back of the cupboard shattered and he was able to pull the pieces aside to reveal a dark staircase.

He grabbed a chair to prop the cupboard door open.

'Just making sure we can get out again,' he said.

She nodded and they both descended the stairs.

The hallway at the bottom had a cement floor. The painted walls were mostly white but the paint was flaking, revealing mottled patches of green and grey paint from previous years. There were a few dim lights along the ceiling encased in wire covers. There was no smoke down here yet, but alarms could be heard in the distance.

Renee looked around nervously.

'It feels like an old insane asylum,' she whispered.

'It's an old building, maybe it was an asylum once,' he replied quietly.

They walked slowly to the first doorway and Tom gestured for her to stay back while he took a cautious look into the room. He relaxed and waved her onward. She looked into the empty room, as they passed; it was a kitchenette and lounge area.

Further down the hall, there was a large door reaching almost to the ceiling, similar to those found between wards in hospitals. There was a low murmuring coming from the other side. Tom opened the door as quietly as he could but the hinges gave a terrible squeal. There was a sudden cacophony of yelling and banging. The hall continued on the other side of the door and there were heavy metal doors on both sides.

Each door had a metal viewing hatch and Tom approached the first door and opened the hatch. Renee moved beside him and looked in to see a small cell with a cement floor. A girl was sitting in the corner hugging her knees. She looked up with eyes that were more dead than alive.

'We're going to get you out of here,' Tom said and held his badge up to the opening.

She stared at them but did not seem to see them.

They heard a crash ahead of them as a door slammed shut. A man emerged from a doorway six feet from them with a petrol can in his hand. He looked up and stopped in his tracks when he saw Tom. He dropped the petrol can and pulled a gun from the belt of his pants.

'Don't move,' he said. 'How the fuck did you get in here?'

Renee moved out from behind Tom's shoulder and the man's gun swivelled toward her, his eyebrows jumping and his mouth dropping in shock as he caught sight of her glowing wings.

'What the fuck?' he said, his gun lowering a fraction. Tom took advantage of the distraction; he stepped forward and swung his hand down hard onto the man's gun hand, knocking the revolver flying. It skittered across the floor behind Renee, but before Tom could regain his balance the man kicked the petrol can hard. The rusty can split open showering petrol everywhere. Tom instinctively ducked to one side but still received a spray of petrol in his eyes as the tin bounced off his shoulder. One side of his coat and shirt were doused in it and so were the floor and walls.

Tom desperately wiped his eyes, blinded, and the man pulled a lighter from his pocket, igniting the flame and dropping it into the puddle at Tom's feet. A sheet of orange flames shot up in front of them and Tom's shirt and coat burst into flames. The man turned and ran.

Tom threw himself away from the fire and dropped to the ground; rolling from side to side to try to extinguish the flames. Renee scanned the walls, but there were no fire extinguishers, so she dropped down beside Tom and lay across him to smother the flames. She felt the fire enter her body and understood that it was a part of her. Old Blue had told her she was part fire fairy, but she hadn't really believed it until now.

The fire was spreading up the walls in front of them, but she had to help Tom first. She touched Tom's burning clothes and pulled the flames inside herself, not really knowing how she did it. Once the flames on Tom were extinguished she helped him up. His coat was smoking and she helped him to pull it off. He was groaning in pain. His shirt was smouldering, but his shoulder holster was preventing him from getting it off. They struggled to disentangle him and were finally able to remove the holster and the shirt.

'God, I hate fucking fire,' he swore loudly over the roar of the flames.

He was shaking and panting. The skin on the left side of his chest and shoulder was red and blistered. Feeling a little self-conscious, she quickly placed her hands over the burns and drew out all of the heat; the blisters retreated. She didn't have time to heal him completely, but she had stopped it from getting any worse and had taken away the pain. She checked his back, but there were no fresh injuries, just a large scar on his shoulder that had obviously been there a long time.

There was no sign of the arsonist and the fire was spreading down the hall. The inmates' cries intensified and so did the banging.

'Go after him! I can put out the fire and release the prisoners,' Renee yelled over the roar of the flames.

He turned to her as if to argue, but she held up her hands and the fire began to retreat from them. He nodded once and bent down to retrieve his gun from the discarded holster. He picked up the man's fallen gun and held it out to her, but she would not take it, so he tucked it into the back of his trousers and began his pursuit.

Tom ran down the hall jumping over the spot fires that dotted the floor. The smoke caught in his lungs and he knew he wouldn't have his usual stamina in these conditions. The burns on his chest were making his skin feel tight, but whatever Renee had done had taken away the pain for now.

He turned the corner into a long hallway and saw the man emerging from a room at the far end. He had more petrol cans. The man saw Tom and ran across the hall into another room, slamming the door behind him. Tom sprinted after him and slid to a halt in front of the door. He tugged hard on the handle but it was locked. Tom banged on the wooden door and realised it was hollow; designed to deter entry, not to fortify against it. The plaque on the outside indicated that it was the boiler room.

The man had been disarmed, but he still could be waiting for him on the other side of the door with some sort of makeshift club. Tom didn't fancy having his head caved in, but the man had petrol and this was the boiler room; this could get bad really quickly.

He stepped back and aimed a hard kick at the door shattering the thin timber veneer and exposing the soft corrugated core. He ducked back behind the wall, waiting to see if there would be a response. Nothing.

He moved forward and kicked again and this time his foot broke right through the door. He pulled his foot free and ducked down to slip his arm through the hole. He fumbled for the latch, released it and flung the door open. He peered into the gloom with his gun raised. There was a glow coming from the furnace on the other side of the room and a mass of shadowy pipes and cables, but he could not see any sign of the man. He slid his hand along the wall and found the light switch, but it was useless; the firemen had probably cut the power. He moved cautiously into the room, peering around the doorway and aiming his gun into the darker shadows as he moved forward. The man could be hiding anywhere.

A door opened to one side and Tom spun around toward the noise. A fireman in bright yellow protective clothing and breathing apparatus came to a sudden stop in front of him and slowly raised his hands. Tom lowered his gun and flipped his wallet out of his back pocket to show his police badge. The fireman relaxed.

'Were you chasing a man in a suit?' the fireman said, his voice muffled by the mask. 'He just barrelled past me,' he said pointing back the way he had come, 'but you won't find him out there now — the smoke is too thick, you won't make it without one of these,' he said tapping on his face mask.

'Shit,' said Tom.

'The fire is under control, but we need to get everyone out or they are going to die of smoke inhalation. Is there anyone else here?'

'Yeah. We are going to need some help. There are a lot of people in really bad shape down this way, but it wasn't from the fire.'

The fireman took out his radio and called for assistance as Tom led him back through the broken door towards Renee and the cells.

She knew fire; it was a part of her. She watched the fire spreading along the ceiling and then burning down the walls to the floor. The passage was completely blocked now. With a gesture of her hands, she pushed the fire back against one wall and then by cupping and rotating her hands one at a time she began to fold the edges of the fire inward, drawing it into a ball like a baker working dough. Next, she moved her hand as if she were spinning a globe of the world and the ball of fire responded, turning wildly and drawing all the other spot fires into itself. It increased in size and she could feel it consuming the air. The superheat of the flaming monster was drawing the skin on her face tight. When all the fire was contained, she clapped her hands together and the fire collapsed into itself, smothering its core and depriving itself of oxygen. The thick black smoke was sucked into the vacuum and the inferno died with a sizzling sigh.

The fire was out, but the walls and floor were charred black and gave off incredible heat. She was about to open the nearest cell door when she realised she was still in fairy form. She changed her appearance to her standard human disguise. Her clothes were covered in soot and so was her face and hair.

Each door had three metal bolts holding it shut. She opened the first door and helped the girl into the blackened hallway. Some of the occupants were in chains and she wasted precious time looking for the keys. Eventually, she found them hanging in the last room, a small office. She found herself fumbling, desperate to help them all as quickly as she could, her hands were shaking and she kept dropping the keys. She gently coaxed the shattered people out of their cells and into the hall.

There they stood in a silent huddle. They were in varying states of distress, both physical and mental, but all were strangely quiet. There was no excitement about their new freedom.

A fireman in yellow appeared and when he saw the huddle of emaciated people he lifted his visor and stared.

'What the hell has been going on here?' he asked.

'Help me get them free,' Renee said, unaware of the tears that were flowing down her face leaving clean lines in the soot.

Tom appeared and suddenly the place was filled with people in yellow protective clothing. He walked over to her and looked at her tear stained face.

'Are you alright?' he asked.

'No.'

He held out his uninjured arm and she moved forward into a one-armed hug. She slipped her arms around his waist, careful to avoid his burns, and rested her forehead on his shoulder. She breathed deeply for a minute, composing herself. She had to keep it together; if she became a blathering mess with all these firemen around she could end up in real trouble.

A paramedic arrived and started to triage the victims who had been freed; firemen were still releasing others from their cells.

After a minute, she whispered to Tom:

'I have to go. I can't be here. There will be too many questions.'

He looked around, no one was paying them any attention, everyone was absorbed in their work.

'Now, while they're busy. It will take them a while to realise you are gone,' he said quietly.

He took her hand and led her into an empty cell.

She looked up into his incredible blue eyes and then her attention was dragged to the terrible burns on his chest and shoulder.

'I'll find you and heal those burns as soon as I can,' she said, touching his upper arm just below the burn.

'Don't worry. I'll be fine; it's not the first time and, with my luck, it probably won't be the last,' he said with a wry smile. 'Thank you. I couldn't have done this without you.'

Before she could reply, there were footsteps outside the door. She squeezed his hand once and then quickly regained her fairy form and shrank. She was flying out the door before the fireman entered the room.

Clio Returns

Between healing Nancy and helping Tom, Renee's energy reserves were almost drained. She was bone tired.

She was halfway home when she heard the call. It was Old Pepper. For a moment she thought about pretending she hadn't heard the summons, but she knew that Old Pepper wouldn't be calling her unless it was important. She turned around and headed for the Botanical Gardens.

It was late in the afternoon and the shadows were beginning to lengthen. Andy would be wondering where she was, but she needed to see what Old Pepper wanted first.

Renee flitted onto a branch and slid down into the knothole at its base. Gaia was there waiting for her.

'What has happened?' asked Renee.

'I could ask you the same!' Gaia said, looking her up and down.

Renee looked at her clothes, they had been blackened by the fire.

'Long story. I'll tell you another time,' she said to Gaia.

'Clio has sent me to find you. She wants to talk to you on neutral ground.'

'Another request to join her?' asked Renee.

'I would l guess so, and if it is, this will be your last chance. If you refuse she may order me to kill you. I have to appear loyal to her; I will do as she says. If I attempt to strike you, you must fight me off as if your life depended on it — no pulling punches — you must do everything you can to defend yourself or it will not look genuine.'

'Understood. When does she want to meet?'

'Now.'

'Now? Oh my god, I am dead on my feet.'

'I am sorry, but it has to be now. She told me that if you refuse to come she will track you down and kill you and Lucy and Nancy.'

Renee nodded. It had to be done.

'I need to tell Andy. He will be worrying where I am as it is.'

Gaia nodded and Renee established a thought connection with Andy with her filigree ring.

Andy?

Renee, where are you? His response was immediate.

With Old Pepper, she was calling me, Gaia is here with a message from Clio. I have to go and parley with her. I have a lot to tell you, but it will have to wait for now.

Oh God, Renee. Where are you meeting her — not at the compound?

No, Gaia said neutral ground, but she didn't say where.

Don't bet on it being neutral. If she is picking the place then there will be a reason for it. Have you thought about how you will get away from her if she attacks?

I have a couple of ideas up my sleeve.

I am not stupid enough to tell you not to go. Andy said. *If you feel you must then, you must. If you can, call me if you need help. Between Bruce, Lucy and I, we should be able to figure something out.*

Thanks, Andy.

Good luck.

She broke the connection and turned to Gaia.

'Okay. It's now or never, I suppose.'

'Come with me.'

Renee followed Gaia to the Rookwood Cemetery. The gravestones were casting long shadows as the sun hung above the tops of the hills. They landed in the grass between two gravestones. In front of them was a small stone with a swirling pattern cut into its surface.

'Take my hand and do not let go, no matter what happens.'

Renee nodded and took her hand. She watched as Gaia concentrated on the stone. A moment later the stone glowed a bright green and Gaia led her forward into the dazzling light. She could hear screaming, but it sounded distant. Renee trembled at the thought of the trapped fairies.

The light changed colour and then began to fade. They were standing at the base of a tall pine tree in another cemetery. This one was much smaller than Rookwood and was surrounded by a low green hedge. There was an old stone church to their right. Gaia released her hand.

'Where are we?' Renee asked.

'This is St John's church in Canberra. Another of her portals. I need to take you to another place, over the hill,' she said pointing to the east.

Gaia took the lead heading away from the sinking sun. Renee saw the Australian War Memorial with its large tarnished copper dome to her left as they flew out of the cemetery and over Anzac Parade with its red gravel centre. They passed a suburb filled with neat houses and playing fields, then flew over the airport. Gaia led her towards a large pine plantation and they flew down into the trees and started to fly along a winding dirt road. Finally, they landed in a clearing, dominated by a cement plinth in the shape of an aircraft wing.

The place was deserted. They landed and assumed human size.

'What is this place?' Renee asked looking around.

A flash of red in the trees caught her eye and she turned to see Clio emerging from the trees, her glow burning a brilliant red. Her glow receded as she walked towards them. She was wearing the same black, long-sleeved tunic and red armour that Renee had seen in the vision that Andy had shown her. The red wasps decorating the tunic at the cuffs and the hem were glowing a vicious red.

'Do you like my battle attire? Beware the red wasp — my sting brings death,' she said with a smile. Several of the red embroidered wasps on the hem of her tunic transformed into living, metallic insects. They flew into the air and circled Renee slowly as if waiting for the command to attack. Renee held her breath and tried to keep calm. Clio had not called her here to execute her, at least not yet, she reasoned.

Clio held out her hand and the wasps flew back to her and landed on her palm in formation, like miniature warplanes. Renee cast her eyes quickly toward Gaia and could see that she was surprised too. What other new tricks had Clio learnt?

'Welcome to my inspiration,' Clio said, casting her hands wide. 'For a while, I was stupid enough to think that this place was my undoing, but then I realised it was my salvation.

'This is the Air Disaster Memorial. Never heard of it? No, I am not surprised; humans seem to pay very little attention to history, which is why they will always repeat their mistakes.'

She released the wasps and they re-joined her dress, melting back into the fabric to become harmless decorations once more.

'Come, let me give you a history lesson,' she said. Clio nodded to Gaia and Gaia remained where she was, alert and on guard. Clio guided Renee over to a large boulder with a brown plaque attached to it.

'On the 13th of August 1940, right as the Second World War was intensifying, three Australian cabinet ministers and the Chief of the General Staff all boarded a plane together in Melbourne to fly to Canberra for a meeting. They never made it. This is the place that their plane crashed.

'In one fell swoop the General in charge of the Army and the ministers of Army, Aviation and Science were all killed. I am sure you can imagine the damage that did the Australian war effort? At the time, it was a terrible blow to me too. You see my own, dear, General Drake was also killed in the crash. For a long time, I did not know how it had happened, but now I do. You see, he brought the plane down. It was just the first step in his plan to put me in my rightful place as ruler of this country, but something went terribly wrong and he went down with the plane. For many years I have misunderstood — but now I see clearly. When I am Queen this site shall be my holy of holies and I shall reclaim the trees here as my own. This shall be the site of my palace. I know the way forward; Drake's sacrifice will not be forgotten.'

Clio was glowing with her fervour, her eyes wild with excitement or madness; Renee was not sure which.

'So now, you have a choice to make. A simple choice really. Join me or die. Either way, I will reclaim the cornucopia faerie and kill her mother just as I did her father —'

Renee flinched, she resisted the urge to look at Gaia. If Clio had found out that Andy was still alive then Gaia was in grave danger.

'— Yes, I have realised who the old man was,' Clio continued. 'I should have killed him years ago when I took his wife and daughter. But I have learnt my lesson, in a time of war there is no place for mercy.'

Renee inwardly breathed a sigh of relief. Clio doesn't know. Renee clasped her hands together and carefully inched her fire ring from her finger.

'You killed Andy. You have enslaved and tortured his wife and daughter for a decade. How could you imagine that I would ever join you?'

'Then your life is forfeit,' Clio said, her red sword suddenly in her hands 'And I will kill you myself.'

Before she could swing the sword, Renee had conjured a shield of flame and pushed forward, forcing Clio to retreat.

'Seize her!' Clio screamed at Gaia and Gaia advanced with her hands raised.

Renee called to the pine trees at the edge of the clearing and a multitude of roots swarmed into action, surrounding Gaia and engulfing her in a wooden cage. Gaia pounded against the roots in vain.

Renee let the flame shield drop and fled into the trees, making herself smaller in mid-flight so she could dodge between them at break-neck speed.

She heard the wasps before she saw them; their wings created a metallic buzzing. Could they smell her? she wondered.

She knew that Clio could not sense her, only see her, but what were these metal creatures capable of? She flew up above the noise into the top branches of a pine tree hoping to escape them. As she flew higher she saw blobs of orange coloured pine resin dripping down the trunk of the trees. They smelled strongly of pine. There was a crevice in one of the branches and beside it was a large resin globule. She slipped into the crevice; if the wasps *could* smell her, they would have trouble over the scent of the pine.

Renee listened hard. She heard the wasps pass below her and continue on away from the tree she was hiding in. She remained still, waiting. Then she felt a presence. Clio was slowly following the wasps; she could feel her approaching. Clio continued on, past the tree she was hiding in, but a moment later, she stopped.

Renee carefully peered over the edge of the branch. Clio was standing in the pine needles, human size, twenty metres from the base of the tree. Clio stood dead still, not making a sound. For the next ten minutes, the only sounds were the wind wuthering through the treetops and the creak of tree branches rubbing against each other. Then Renee heard the wasps return.

Clio gathered them on her hand and appeared to be conversing with them. They slipped from her hand and re-joined her dress.

'My wasps have lost your scent,' Clio shouted into the trees. But they aren't stupid. They know where the scent faded out. They know you are around here somewhere.

'So now, you will have to deal with me!'

Clio swept a regal hand toward the sky and Renee felt an intense pressure surround her heart. She gasped; Clio was stopping her heart. Renee thumped herself on the chest, willing it to restart, but nothing happened. She could feel her heart getting heavier and colder, turning into a solid lump of ice in her chest. She would pass out if she didn't do something soon. She placed her hand over her chest and was relieved to discover that she could look inside her own body. Her heart was surrounded by a layer of ice and it was getting thicker by the second. Renee forced a fine stream of heat out of her fingers and into her own chest, thawing the cold hand around her heart and causing it to retreat. Below her, Clio gasped.

'No! This can't be!' Clio exclaimed.

Renee felt Clio's spell strengthen, the cold coming harder and faster and Renee struggled to block it with her heat spell. Renee knew she would not be able to keep up the fight for long, her heart was frostbitten and silent. Clio battled to push the cold deeper into Renee's chest, but Renee's barricade of heat held her back. With Renee's last ounce of strength, she called to the tree roots and they slid behind Clio, unobserved right up until the moment they engulfed her.

Clio screamed with rage as the wooden cage surrounded her and her ice spell wavered and failed. Quickly, Renee melted the last of the ice encasing her heart and forced the injured organ to beat again. She repaired the worst of the frostbite and then fled back the way she had come, a stumbling flight back towards Gaia.

Gaia had managed to unwind several of the roots; a combination of brute strength and dormant tree power forcing them into submission. She would be free soon.

'I have to go, are you able to get out?'

'Yes. Where is Clio?'

'I have trapped her the same way. She is in that direction.'

'Don't worry, as soon as I am free, I will go to her and break her out. Run, in case she manages to free herself before I get there. I will tell her I did not see you. Go!'

Renee took off into the air and flew toward Sydney. There was no Old Blue or Old Pepper here to shorten her journey. She would have to rest soon and heal her damaged heart or she would not make it home at all. Clio's portals gave Clio a decided advantage; Renee would have to be careful that Clio wasn't waiting for her when she finally got back to Sydney.

Tom checked himself out of the hospital, he had too much work to do. They had bandaged him up and in spite of their protests, he had called Peale to come and get him.

He was still shirtless, but his chest and shoulder were swathed in bandages so he wasn't cold and he had spare clothes at work. Peale arrived in his marked police car and picked Tom up.

'Any sign of the arsonist?' Tom asked as they drove back to the office.

'No. The CCTV footage was useless. All it shows is swirling smoke. Gardiner is still interviewing people at the scene, but so far no one noticed a man in a suit slipping out of the building. Too much confusion.'

'Well, whoever he was, he was in it up to his neck and he was trying to destroy the evidence.'

'Yeah. The poor bastards.'

A squadron of ambulances had taken all the captives off for treatment. More had arrived to take the elderly nursing home residents to temporary accommodation. Gardiner had bullied Tom into going to the hospital for treatment and he had been loaded into an ambulance with a couple of elderly patients suffering from smoke inhalation.

The whole nursing home had been cordoned off. It was going to take weeks to assess it.

Peale parked the car and as they entered the police building, George from forensics fell into step beside them.

'Been in the wars again, I see,' George said looking Tom up and down, 'I've got something you might be interested in.'

Once they were in Tom's office with the door shut, Tom pulled a fresh shirt out of his cupboard and George continued:

'I have been running Bill's DNA through our database to see if I come up with any matches. Unsolved crimes. Haven't found anything on that yet, but I did get a match with a DNA request put in for analysis a couple of days ago. The request was suspiciously light on details and it hadn't been authorised. I finally tracked down which one of my minions was processing it and they confessed that it was requested by Sergeant Reg Palmer on the sly.'

'And?' Tom asked confused.

'The DNA request was to check for family ties between two samples. The pair turned out to be mother and son. But the interesting thing is, they were also related to Bill.

'Go on...'

'They were Bill's mother and Bill's brother.'

'Bill has a brother? None of the records show him having a brother.'

'No — and get this — his mother is known to police. Patricia Denny. She has a petty crime sheet as long as my arm, theft mostly and some domestic disturbances further back.'

'Denny. Why do I know that name?'

'No idea,' said George.

'What reason has Sergeant Palmer given for requesting it?'

'None on the request, I told you it was a bit dodgy. I haven't spoken to him — thought I'd better talk to you first.'

'Thanks George, keep this to yourself for now. I might have to keep an eye on Reg Palmer.'

'Oh, those other tests you wanted done — the spoon, the fork and the hair sample — it's going to be weeks before I can get you those results. I just don't have enough resources at the moment I'm afraid.'

'Okay. We've got plenty of other things to keep us busy at the moment, just let me know as soon as you have anything.'

George returned to his lab and Tom sat and looked at the photo of his parents on his desk. Until he knew more about the identity of the old homeless man and established the link between the old man's filigree spoon and Babayaga's filigree fork, that investigation would have to wait.

Finding the Stonefish and shutting down Bill's crime ring for good was the first priority. He mentally changed gear, pushing all thoughts of his parents to one side. He searched the police database for Bill's mother, Patricia Denny, and found a lengthy file spanning two decades. The later entries, all for petty theft, listed her home address as "no fixed address". He scrolled back to an earlier entry and found a police call out to a domestic disturbance between herself and her husband. Her two sons were listed as witnesses. William and John. William and John Denny.

Kraken had called him Bill Denny, not Bill Doyle! That was what had been nagging at the back of his mind for days!

They already knew that Philip Cole had gone to school with Ryan Porter and he claimed to have gone to school with Bill Doyle as well, but there had been no Bill Doyle enrolled at the school.

Tom searched the school records again and sure enough, William and John Denny both appeared. Both had been at the school when Ryan Porter and Philip Cole had attended.

Tom leaned back in his chair. So, William Denny becomes Bill Doyle and who did John Denny become? Tom was putting his money on Johnny Black.

Renee could not go any further. She saw the lights of a city before her and the welcome sign confirmed that she had reached Goulburn. She needed to rest. Gaia and Clio would be free of the tree cages by now and had probably already returned to Sydney via the portal at the church. It was unlikely they would be anywhere near here.

She flew over the outskirts of the city looking for a place to rest. She needed to do something about her heart before it gave up completely.

She approached a hill dominated by a large old building. Broken windows and missing roof tiles announced its emptiness; a large stone cross on the roof indicated its religious origins. A convent perhaps or an orphanage? It had all the signs of being abandoned and it was slowly decaying. She entered through a section of missing roof into a long hallway. The sun was below the horizon now and by the dim light, she could see that sections of the plaster walls had been kicked in. The plaster that remained had been covered in graffiti; a mix of obscenities, tags and satanic symbols.

She entered a room that had been left relatively untouched and landed on the top of an old cupboard out of sight of any passing vandals. She was safe for the moment.

Renee sat down and propped her back against the wall. She placed her hand over her chest, pushing her vision inside again. She watched her injured heart struggling to pump blood and was surprised that she had made it this far. Using her healing powers, she gently repaired the damaged muscle, feeling her body grow physically stronger with each beat but, at the same time, her magical energy grew weaker. She had never healed herself before and she guessed that it would be more draining on her than healing someone else. A patch-up job would have to do for now. Enough to get her safely home to Andy. Perhaps Lucy would be able to heal the rest of the damage for her.

Andy would be worried. She opened a thought connection.

Andy?

Renee, thank god, where are you.

Goulburn.

Goulburn?!

Yes. Clio took me to Canberra, I'm having a rest on the way home. I dare say she is back already, thanks to her portals, so be careful. I'm taking the long way home.

Did she attack?

Yes, but I'm okay. I am going to rest here for an hour or so and then make my way back. I need my strength up in case she has a trap waiting for me.

She will be expecting you to come in from the south, she probably has her troops waiting for you out the outskirts of Sydney, so don't come straight here. Head north to the Blue Mountains instead, then you can come back via Old Blue and Old Pepper. Hopefully, you will avoid her cronies completely.

Okay, Andy. I'm going to have a nap. I will see you in a few hours. Stay safe. Clio is definitely on the warpath.

She broke the connection and lay down. The top of the cupboard was hard and cold, but she was so tired she did not care.

Clio was not going to stop. Not ever. Andy was a fool if he really thought that they could all just slip away and live safely in Wattle Ridge. Once Clio started her war, nowhere would be safe. They couldn't just leave the battle to Gaia and the rebels. And what about Tom? She couldn't just abandon him to his fate, not after all he had done for them.

Andy deserved to have his family back together; he deserved some respite from all the pain of the last few years. But she knew she would not be able to go with them. She would do all she could to defeat Clio. She had to; no one else was going to be able to protect the people she cared about.

The sound of voices and footsteps disturbed Renee from her exhausted sleep. A bright light shone into the room and at first, she thought she had overslept and the sun was shining in her eyes. But then the light moved and she realised it was a torch. There were three people in the room examining the walls with torches. The smell of paint assailed her and she watched as the group drew amateurish tags on the walls in coloured spray paint. None of them were particularly talented and all of them were young; sixteen at most she guessed. They were passing a bottle of liquor around and making enough noise to wake the dead. Noisy, but not dangerous.

She checked her watch. She had slept for more than two hours. She changed into beetle form and slipped out the door. The hall was completely dark, but she could see the stars shining through the gap in the roof and made her way out through the hole and into the clear night sky.

She took Andy's advice and went home via Old Blue and Old Pepper, careful not to wake them as she passed through the portal. She arrived back at Andy's house and collapsed into a kitchen chair. Bruce was there, waiting for her.

'Andy's exhausted. I sent him off to bed. Tea?' he asked.

'Definitely.'

She watched Bruce moving around the kitchen and realised that his mind was not entirely on the job. He knew this place like the back of his hand but, tonight, he seemed absent-minded.

'What gives?' she asked.

He sighed.

'Now is as good a time as any I suppose,' he said. 'I need to sound you out on something.'

He placed their mugs on the table and by the changing expressions on his face and the fidgeting, she could tell that he was weighing up the right way to start.

Finally, he placed his mug down and looked her in the eyes.

'Clio isn't just after you is she, she wants Lucy and Nancy too.' It was a statement, not a question.

'Yes. She wants us dead or alive.'

'And she isn't going to stop if Nancy and Lucy disappear. She might let them be for a while but not forever.'

'Yes. I think that is a fair assessment.'

'So, to keep them safe, someone needs to deal with Clio,' said Bruce.

'Yes.'

'You're not going to Wattle Ridge. You've already decided. It's as plain as the nose on your face,' said Bruce. 'It was a nice dream, but it can't happen; at least not yet. And I'm not going either,' he said.

'I did wonder. You didn't seem particularly happy that Nancy was alive.'

'Ah, now don't get me wrong, I love Nancy and I am thrilled for Andy that she is alive, but it puts me in a terrible position. When Andy told me that Nancy was dead, I died inside too. The pair of us went on a massive bender. It didn't really stop until you showed up,' he paused and took another sip of his tea.

'You see, I loved Nancy. *Really* loved Nancy and I suspect she knew but was too kind to say anything. There was a time when I was really pissed off that she chose him over me, after all, I was the one with faerie blood. But then, Andy had known her for a lot longer than me. Andy introduced her to me. I knew straight away that she was a faerie, and she knew that I knew, so that conversation happened pretty early on. I think Andy was happy to have someone else to talk to about it all. Later when she chose him and they got engaged, well, I had a hard time, but I hid it well. We are mates and I love him like a brother, so I told myself to harden up and got on with it.

'When I thought Nancy was dead, it was as if a wall came down. I didn't have to pretend when I was around Andy and Nancy anymore. I felt like I could breathe again and be myself. Well now she's back and I have to put the walls back up. I can't do it anymore, Renee. Not all day every day; I can't go with them. I lose Andy if I stay but at least we will still be absent friends. If he found out…well, I couldn't see us staying friends, at least not close friends.'

'So, you want to stay and help Gaia and I battle Clio?'

'Yep. I'm old but I'm not useless. I probably have more faerie lore in my little finger than Andy has in his whole body. If I can't be with them, maybe I can do something to keep them safe. Let's beat this bitch together.'

'You're on.' The relief was incredible. She knew so little about fairy ways and she had been undecided on how to proceed but with Gaia's inside knowledge and Bruce's fairy lore and cunning, she felt like together, they had a chance.

The Winds of War

As soon as they finished sorting through the papers sent to them by Ryan Porter, Tom sent Peale and Gardiner to bring Philip Cole to the station for questioning.

An hour later, Gardiner knocked on his office door, 'He's in the interview room boss.'

'Thanks Gardiner,' Tom said, gathering his papers together.

Tom opened the door to the interview room and sat down in front of Philip.

'Am I under arrest?' Philip Cole was pale and nervous.

'Not yet,' said Tom. 'There are a few things we need to clear up.'

Tom slid a photo across the table, 'Do you know this man?'

'Yes. That's Ryan Porter. I went to school with him.'

'Is there anyone you didn't go to school with?' Tom asked. 'How long since you last had contact with Mr Porter?'

'Oh… years. There was a school reunion, probably five years ago — not since then.'

'You haven't been entirely honest with us have you, Mr Cole?' Tom's patience had been tested over the last few weeks and Philip had been a prime source of irritation.

'For example, you said you went to school with Bill Doyle. But it wasn't Bill Doyle was it — it was William Denny.'

'Well, yes, he did change his name at some point after he left school — I don't know why.'

'And his brother? Did you know him too?' asked Tom.

'Johnny? Well, a little bit I suppose, he was older than me.'

'And what name is he going by now?'

'Oh. Black, I think. Bill told me at some point, but I haven't seen him since school,' Philip said, flustered.

Tom slid another piece of paper across the table.

'This is a printout of Mr Ryan Porter's bank account. If you take a look at the figures highlighted in yellow, you will see that they are payments from your company, Mr Cole. Ten thousand dollars at a time, starting three weeks ago. That's a lot of money to send to someone that you haven't spoken to in years.'

Philip stared at the paper and said nothing.

'Now this,' Tom said pulling a sheet from the pile in front of him, 'this is really interesting. Our handwriting expert is looking over the original of this one as we speak and comparing it to the statement you made when you reported Rebecca missing last year.' Tom pushed a photocopy of a hand-written document over to Philip. Philip reached out to take it and then pulled his hand away as if it had been burnt.

'Let me show you the second page,' Tom said, sliding another page across the table. It was an A4 sized photo of Rebecca Cole. Philip turned away, refusing to look.

'Ah, but it gets even better,' Tom said turning back to the first page and pointing out a sentence, 'Here, this deserves particular attention...'

The baby has to go too.

Philip looked like he was going to be sick.

'We have been paying extra attention to your personal bank accounts and your business accounts in the last few days,' Tom said. 'We have the evidence that you paid for Rebecca's murder. You got a bad deal if you ask me, they were going to get plenty from the sale of the baby anyway.'

'That wasn't part of the deal! I didn't pay for that, I paid for them to kill her quick — her and the baby. Not this!'

'Well they didn't kill her quick, she died very slowly, over a number of hours in a pool of her own blood. And they didn't kill the baby either, at least not straight away. They let it die slowly, from neglect — it suffered for days. Your own son, Philip!'

'I didn't want any of this! None of this was supposed to happen!'

'So, tell me, what *was* supposed to happen,' Tom was calm on the outside, but the desire to reach over and thump the man in front of him was immense.

'Bill and his brother got into all sorts of shady stuff at school. I needed to get rid of Rebecca, but I couldn't divorce her — she would have taken half of everything *I* owned!'

The temptation to correct Philip was immense. Tom had seen their finances in minute detail. Rebecca had paid her share of the couple's joint expenses and was absolutely entitled to half the proceeds if they divorced. Instead, he bit his tongue, he needed Philip to continue his little rant.

'I knew that Bill and Johnny would know how to go about it. Bill told me to talk to Johnny and Johnny put me onto the guys at the garage. They were supposed to kill her quickly and get rid of her. They were supposed to get rid of the baby too. They moved too soon. I wasn't ready! The cafe was supposed to be my alibi!'

Tom sat back in his chair and crossed his arms over his chest, wincing and unfolding them again when he accidentally touched his burns.

'Was Ryan involved in all this? I notice *he* hasn't changed his name since school.'

'No. He was a good guy. He should never have got mixed up with those two. He could have been someone.'

'Been someone... Like *you*, you mean,' Tom said looking at him in disgust.

'I *was* someone! I *was* going places! All *she* had to do was abort the baby. If she had done as I said, then none of this would have happened!'

The morning sunshine dappled the hallway with a rainbow of colours as it passed through the stained-glass window above the front door. Renee stretched and went to see who was knocking.

She knew that danger would be on its way soon, but this morning was too beautiful to contemplate the evils of Clio's war plans. They were safe in this little cottage for now.

She peered through the peephole and opened the door immediately when she saw it was Tom on the threshold.

'Not too early, am I?' he asked.

'No. Andy and I have been up for a while.'

She let her human disguise slide off as she followed him down the hallway; stretching her wings and yawning. In the kitchen, Andy was busy preparing breakfast for Nancy and Lucy. They were both still tucked up in bed and Renee knew that Andy was enjoying himself playing nursemaid to them both.

'Morning, Tom,' Andy said as he turned the eggs in the frying pan.

'Morning, Andy. Thought I'd better come over and give you an update.'

'How are the captives?' asked Renee.

'Not good. They are getting the best medical help available, but it's going to take a very long time for them to regain any sort of normal life. We have been able to reunite a few of them with their families, but some of them are too traumatised to even talk yet.'

Andy shook his head, 'It is completely beyond me. I can't fathom how anyone could do that to someone. Did you catch the man — the arsonist?'

'Not yet, but I am pretty sure that he was Bill's brother, John Denny — also known as Johnny Black. He was well set up, so I suspect it will take us some time to flush him out. One good thing though — we have his DNA profile now and I think we have identified his mole on the police force. We're keeping a very close eye on Sargent Palmer. Hopefully, when things start to cool down a bit, Johnny will make the mistake of contacting him again.'

'You think Johnny is the Stonefish?' asked Renee.

'That's my bet,' Tom replied. 'We may not have caught him yet, but at least we have shut down his Sydney operations for good. I am just hoping that he hasn't spread further afield.'

Renee nodded, 'Well, I said I would get those burns sorted out for you, so — no time like the present — off with that coat.'

Tom looked like he was going to argue for a moment, but Andy shot him a don't-even-think-about-it look and he capitulated, allowing Renee to help him remove his coat.

Once his shoulder holster and shirt were off Renee gently unwound the bandages wrapped around his chest and shoulder. The burns were inflamed and weeping.

Renee pointed him to a chair and dragged another chair in front of him, sitting down to survey the damage. She placed her hands on his ribcage, carefully avoiding the lowest burns and closed her eyes, pushing her awareness along her hands and into his torso. She found the outer edge of the burn and slowly began to work her way through the layers of skin to the deepest part of the burn. From there she slowly healed the muscles and skin cells, moving outwards and upwards layer by layer.

'That isn't hurting too much is it?' she asked Tom as she worked.

'No. It feels kind of tingly.'

As she healed him she slid her hands higher up his body saving herself energy by being closer to the remaining injury. She desperately willed herself not to blush as her hands slid over his pectoral muscle but in vain. She held her head down hoping he wouldn't notice.

Within ten minutes the wounds were healed and she sat back and stretched her neck, composed again.

'Cuppa Tom?' Andy asked him.

'Yeah, thanks,' said Tom, reaching for his shirt.

'I can heal that one too if you want me too,' Renee said, gesturing to the older scar on his shoulder.

'Thanks, but no. I've grown accustomed to it. I think I would feel odd without it now,' he said, replacing his shirt.

'We found Ryan this morning. Or should I say, we found bits of him,' Tom said.

Renee winced, 'I met him once. It seems impossible that he would be tied up in all this, he seemed so nice. It was definitely him that sent you the parcel?'

'Yes, we have footage from the courier company. I'm guessing Johnny managed to snatch him on his way to the airport. I wouldn't have too much sympathy for him though, he confessed to some pretty horrible things in his letter, and even when he did confess, he didn't tell us how to find the prisoners,' Tom said. 'If we hadn't managed to put two and two together in time, they would have all burned.

'We did find something else in the papers he sent us...' Tom continued, 'Andy, would you mind giving me a few moments with Renee?'

'Sure,' he said and loaded the two breakfasts he had been preparing onto a tray.

Once Andy had left the room, Tom pulled some pages out of his coat and handed them to Renee.

'There was more to your death than just buying and selling babies,' he said quietly. 'These were in with the papers that Ryan sent us. Do you recognise the writing?'

'Yes. It's Philip's.' She struggled to comprehend the words in front of her. She turned the page and her own image stared up at her.

'Bill, Johnny and Ryan all went to school with your husband, Philip. You weren't a random target.'

She stared at him and then back at the words in front of her.

The baby has to go too.

'Why?' was all she could manage at first.

'He didn't want you to divorce him and he didn't want the baby.'

'He was never violent; how could he do this?'

'But he was emotionally abusive and controlling, wasn't he?'

'Well, yes, he was, but it took me a long time to realise that.'

'The most dangerous time for a woman in an abusive relationship — even one that hasn't been violent — is just before or just after they leave.'

'No. This isn't possible. You should have seen him. He was devastated.'

'I think Philip was devastated that things hadn't gone as planned, that he hadn't been able to set up a watertight alibi. We found evidence of the payments that Philip made to your murderers. We also found out that he has been having an affair with his secretary. He confessed to it all last night. I am afraid there is no doubt about it.'

Renee sat, stunned.

'Where is he?'

'He's at Concord Gaol.'

Renee felt numb. She wished that she could feel disbelief but, the truth was, as soon as Tom had suggested that Philip was devastated about his own situation rather than her murder, the final piece had clicked home. All those months ago when she had seen Philip sobbing, thinking that he was mourning her, she had been surprised. She could never have imagined Philip crying over her like that. It had felt wrong; like reality had been distorted. She supposed that some part of her had known all along that he had been behind it. He had never really loved her; he didn't know what love was. Everything had always been about him and she was just one of his possessions; tolerated or bullied as the mood took him.

'I know that if you wanted to, you could get to him in gaol and there would be nothing that I could do to stop you,' said Tom.

'Vengeance? No. I am not Bill and I am not Philip. I am not a murderer. I don't want to kill anyone. The mechanics at the garage — that was a mistake, I had *no idea* I could do that — and I have made damn sure that it will never happen again,' she said pointing to her ring.

'Is it a faerie ring?'

'Yes,' she replied and, as she said it, she realised that she trusted Tom completely. And she suspected that Andy did too.

'I noticed that Andy has two of those rings,' said Tom.

'Yes. I made one of them for him; his wife made the other,' said Renee.

'He's married to a faerie?' asked Tom, surprised.

'I shouldn't have told you that,' she said, realising too late that she was allowing her trust in Tom to override Andy's privacy.

'Don't worry. I won't tell anyone, who would believe me? It just explains a few things that's all.' He looked at her wings and she thought she could see longing in his face. 'The faeries at the window of my office, they glowed yellow and purple. Does the colour of your wings determine what colour you glow?'

'I think so. It has been that way with every fairy I have seen so far and there are lots of different colours. Andy told me that a fairy's wing colour is set at puberty by their surroundings. Before that, the wings are weak and transparent. I'm not sure how that relates to me though.'

Tom looked closely at the swirling patterns on her wings.

'The patterns look like lots of little Christmas beetles,' he said.

'Yes. I suppose they do,' she said, looking at her reflection in the shiny metal teapot on the table.

'There were lots of beetles in the warehouse where you were killed. And the green colour would be right too,' Tom continued.

'Yes...' she said, deep in thought.

'What is it like to fly?' Tom asked and she noticed that his eyes had lit up with wonder like a child. 'I mean when you carried me, that was pretty incredible, but to be able to flit around wherever you want — is it exhilarating? exhausting?'

Renee smiled, 'It is absolutely awesome. I cannot explain how good it is. All the crap that has happened, all the terrible things — I think flying is the one thing that has kept me sane. It doesn't compensate for my baby but things were so bad... if I hadn't been able to fly, I think I would have just given up; just lay down somewhere and died. Flying is absolute freedom.'

Tom smiled and looked into her eyes, 'When I was really little, two or three years old maybe, I have this strange memory of playing with a group of people. My parents were there too. It was someone's birthday party I think. But some of the people there had wings. When I was a kid I believed they were real faeries, but my grandparents told me there was no such thing as faeries, that they were just people dressed up as faeries. For a long time, I accepted that. But then I met you. And now, I don't think they were right. I think that I did meet faeries when I was a kid. And then when I spoke to Old Kraken he told me I had been touched by fairies twice...'

'Do you remember what the fairies looked like?' Renee asked, mystified.

'Not really. All I can remember is wings and bright colours. My grandfather didn't like the fact that I was so interested in faeries when I was a kid. He did some pretty awful things to try and shake me out of it. My grandmother was a bit more sympathetic — at least she kept my drawings — rather than burning them.'

'Do you still have them?' asked Renee.

'I inherited my grandmother's house when she died. The other day I remembered her hiding them in the roof cavity. They were still there.'

'I would love to see them sometime,' she said and then blushed when she realised that she had just asked to "come and see his etchings".

'Sure, any time,' he said smiling at her faux pas, 'Since you know where I work, I dare say you know where I live.'

Renee blushed even deeper and Tom laughed at her.

When she recovered a little, she remembered what she had been meaning to tell him. 'There is something else I haven't told you. When I got back from the fire at the nursing home. One of Clio's sentries contacted me and took me to speak to the queen. Clio told me to join her or die.'

'Why do I get the feeling that this is only going to get worse,' Tom said, his mirth evaporating.

'I'm afraid you're right. I can't tell you much because I don't know that much myself. But soon, very soon, I think, Clio is going to make a move. I think it is going to get very nasty very quickly.'

'A faerie war?'

'Yes.'

'Between faeries or against humans?'

'Both I think.'

'How can I help?'

'I need you to tell us if you hear of anything strange happening in Rookwood cemetery. She has made a gateway there, it links to her kingdom in the Blue Mountains. If they are coming to Sydney, they will come via the cemetery. She has set up portals all over the country — there is another in Canberra at St John's church in Reid.'

'What sort of strange are we talking about here?'

'The portal is a small stone with a rune engraved into it. It's in the grass near a headstone and, when a fairy passes through it, the stone glows bright green. Then there are fairy lights — they could be any colour or number or size. Also, I need to know if anything strange happens to the body of the murdered girl — the backpacker. I haven't told the others this yet, but when I was with Clio — she tried to freeze my heart.'

'Holy shit. So, she definitely killed the backpacker!'

'No doubt about it. But the other thing that scares me is the way she has been making these portals. She has been trapping fairies to create the portals and I am worried that she has trapped a fairy in the body of the backpacker.'

'Why would she do that?'

'I don't know. Maybe she wants to be able to enter the morgue for some reason? But if she has, I don't know if there is any way you can stop her. Even if the body was locked up, she would be able to shrink herself and get out of practically anything. I need to talk to Gaia again, she is our insider, and see if Clio has told her anything more about what is coming.'

'How many good faeries are there?'

'Well, apart from Gaia and I, there is a band of rebel fairies that have been hiding out for years, but I haven't made contact with them yet. Gaia knows them and will introduce us in time. Also, there are a lot of fairies in Clio's compound that despise her but don't have the power to overthrow her. I am hoping that Bruce and I can join up with the rebels and convince some of the others in the compound to join us as well.'

'What about Andy and his wife?'

'They have suffered too much already. They kept Clio at bay for years and I don't think they will have the strength to do any more. Clio is trying to kill Andy's wife, so they are going to go into hiding. We don't know what Clio's plans are yet, but Gaia took me to meet Clio at the Aircraft Disaster Memorial in Canberra. It has special significance to Clio. It commemorates the death of several important Australian military officials during the Second World War. Clio said one of her fairy generals was responsible for the crash and I suspect she will target the Australian military again. But how do we warn them? It would sound crazy,' said Renee.

'I don't know. But we have to do something.'

Epilogue

Nancy slowly drifted out of her doze. She could hear voices in the kitchen.

She was still very weak, but she was sick to death of lying in bed. She reached for the glass of water on the bedside table and found it empty.

Well, that gave her an excuse to stretch her legs. She sat up slowly and slid her legs out of the blankets and onto the floor, then she waited a while for the giddiness to pass. She pushed herself to her feet and held onto the headboard to balance. When she was ready she stepped slowly away from the bed. So far so good.

It was three shuffling steps to the bedroom door and another ten to the kitchen doorway. She was just about to enter the kitchen when she heard a voice that she didn't recognise. Friend or foe? she wondered.

The noise was coming from the other end of the kitchen, near the dining table. She cautiously peered around the door frame. Renee was in faerie form talking to a tall man dressed in a suit. She was helping him remove his coat. Nancy's eyes widened when she saw the shoulder holster strapped over his shirt. Police?

Andy was at the stove, unconcerned. Friend it would seem.

They had his shirt off now and Nancy could see bandages on his chest. Renee unwound them slowly and carefully revealing horrible red burns on his chest. The man turned his back to Nancy and sat down on one of the kitchen chairs and Renee pulled up a chair in front of him and began to work on the injury. Renee's boyfriend? Nancy wondered. She was certainly fussing over him, and why not? He was a fine-looking man. He was tall and lithe with toned muscles; he looked fit and healthy apart from his burns. He turned a little in his chair and she caught sight of a large scar on the back of his left shoulder.

She gasped.

She darted back behind the door, afraid that they had heard.

The talk continued as if nothing had happened, so she risked another look around the door. No, they hadn't heard her.

She looked at the scar again. It was old. She tried to see the man's face, but she could only see his profile now and again when he turned his head a little. Then he turned to put his shirt on.

No. It couldn't be.

She tried to guesstimate the man's age. It was about right.

'Cuppa Tom?' Andy asked him.

'Yeah, thanks,' the policeman replied.

Nancy steadied herself against the door frame for a moment and then hobbled quietly back to her room, her mind spinning.

'Oh my god! This changes everything.'

A QUICK QUESTION

Did you enjoy the book? Have you got a moment to spare?

If you could post a short review on the site where you bought the book I would really appreciate it. Reader reviews are really important for authors as they give our books credibility and exposure.

Thank you!

Rhonda Selg
Canberra, November 2018

ABOUT THE AUTHOR

Rhonda was raised in Bega, New South Wales; a small dairy town near the east coast of Australia. She spent most of her youth barefoot and tanned roaming the farms and beaches in the region and developing a love of plants, animals and nature itself. After school, she moved to Canberra to work and study and still lives there with her family and her pet chooks.

Rhonda is a member of the Australia Society of Authors and has worked as a technical writer for over ten years.

You can find out more about her upcoming books or subscribe to her mailing list at: https://www.rmselg.com.

Or why not visit her on Facebook at:
https://www.facebook.com/R.M.Selg/

or on Pinterest at: https://au.pinterest.com/rhondaselg/